Delinquent Daddy

by

Linda Kage

Delinquent Daddy

COPYRIGHT © 2010 by Linda Grotheer

Cover Art by *Angela Anderson*

The Wild Rose Press
PO Box 708
Adams Basin, NY 14410-0706
Visit us at www.thewildrosepress.com

Publishing History
First Champagne Rose Edition, 2010
Print ISBN 1-60154-850-8

Published in the United States of America

Dedication

For Doris Lee

Chapter One

Boston Kincaid needed a woman. Bad.

Even his secretary had about tempted him into falling for one of her seduction attempts this afternoon. Not that Crystal was homely looking or easily turned down. On a scale of one to ten, she rated a high eight, if not an outright nine with her long, shapely legs and high, proud breasts.

But it hadn't taken him long to realize she'd most likely slept her way into her current position. All those glowing references—given by men, of course—definitely hadn't come because of her filing abilities or correspondence skills.

Boston swore he'd keep his distance. But today, it had been hard...literally. He wanted sex. He wanted to feel some soft, giving skin, breathe in that intoxicating smell of woman, and lose himself between a pair of lush breasts and smooth, sleek thighs.

Sighing, he shifted in the suddenly cramped driver's seat of his Infiniti and glared out the window at the soggy rain coating the manicured lawn in front of the house where he'd parked.

"Stupid rain," he muttered.

If Boston wanted to be perfectly honest with himself—and in this situation, he did not—he'd admit it wasn't Crystal who had made him so horny. It was this god-awful drizzle running down his windshield, stirring up unwanted yet too-delicious-to-forget memories.

He closed his eyes and wished his passenger to hurry her sweet tush up so he wouldn't have to sit here, waiting—and remembering—any longer. But with his lids clamped tight, the constant tap, tap, tap of raindrops on the glass seemed to taunt him.

You'll never, never, never forget, they goaded.

His ears twitched and focused on the sprinkle outside, making his body tighten with the memory of the first time he'd ever made love in the rain. In his mind's eye, he saw long flowing hair, big brown eyes and sweet, curving lips that had always been able to send him to his knees. He'd never been with anyone so responsive or responded to someone so fully in his life.

The vision stirred as much as it aggravated. God, he hated the rain. This kind of slow, continuous spray always made him want sex. It made him want...Ellie.

"Ellie," his lips formed the name, though he refused to speak it aloud.

Letting out an irritated growl, he opened his eyes and ran a harassed hand through his hair. Great. He'd thought her name. To Boston, even *thinking* that name was a bad omen. He might as well go to a mirror and say Bloody Mary three times because now he was going to be plagued with haunting memories.

But, oh, what fine memories they were.

His seat grew even more uncomfortable. Boston arched his back and reached down to readjust, thinking how easy it'd be to relieve himself off that single memory alone.

He snapped his hand from his crotch, humiliated with his moronic thoughts. Just because he'd had the best sex of his life a decade ago with some old flame in the drizzly-ass rain didn't mean he had to make a complete fool of himself every time the clouds turned gray.

The porch light to the house came on and Boston straightened, guiltily wiping a bead of sweat from his brow. He watched the front door open. A ladybug umbrella appeared first before it lifted to shield the woman under it from the damp evening.

Boston sucked in an audible breath. The vision that dodged puddles on her sidewalk as she hurried toward his Infiniti blew Crystal's nine totally out of the water. Olivia Banks was a straight eleven. Petite, curvy, and soft in all the right places.

He knew too. He'd seen her naked once. Purely by accident, but it wasn't the kind of thing he was likely to forget, especially in his current frame of mind. Yet a night with Olivia was not meant to be. She belonged to his best friend...his best friend who also happened to be his first cousin, business partner, and ultimate pain in the ass.

So, what was this goddess of womanly delights doing, spending the evening with Boston Kincaid? Actually, it was all because of his pain-in-the-ass first cousin, business partner, best friend. Cameron was out of town on a business trip, and when he'd called an hour before with his request, Boston had only managed to wing up his eyebrows in surprise.

"Excuse me? Did you just ask me to spend the evening *alone* with your gorgeous wife?" Boston gave a quick, ornery grin. "Well, sure thing, buddy. No problem."

"You guys won't be alone, smartass," Cam growled through the phone. "I already know you're headed to your brother's for supper. I just want you to take her along for company. She misses me bad this time."

Boston snorted. "No, she doesn't. She loves it when you're gone. Then she can finally spend time—*alone*—with me."

It had to be one of Boston's favorite pastimes to needle his cousin about his gorgeous wife. Cam had never been so prickly or possessive before. It'd been sickening and a little heartrending to watch his best friend take the plunge into marriage. Sometimes Boston couldn't help but be a tad jealous when he saw a grinning, satisfied Cameron stroll into work each morning...especially when he knew exactly what his friend was getting every night.

"In your dreams," Cameron scoffed, "I mean, go ahead and try your best to steal her, but..." He let out a self-satisfied sigh. "You won't succeed. I fear I've ruined her for every other man out there."

Boston chuckled as he hung up. In the back of his mind, though, the little green bug of envy nipped at him, and his antsy, twitchy need for sex doubled.

Olivia opened the passenger side door, and a cool, damp breeze entered with her.

Entertained by watching her try to close the umbrella and shut the door at the same time, Boston grinned. He genuinely liked Olivia. Not only was she fun to hang out with, but she loved his best friend to distraction and had pulled Cameron from the depths of depression a year ago, probably saving his life. Boston would be forever grateful she'd come into his cousin's world.

"Hey, beautiful," he said and leaned toward her for a kiss.

Obliging, Olivia pressed her cold, wet mouth to his and pulled away grinning. "What's Shannon cooking tonight?" she asked, more concerned with eating than smooching on him.

Instead of answering, Boston continued to lean toward her. "I've got an idea. Let's skip supper at Monty and Shannon's and run off to Tahiti together instead."

"But I'm starving," Olivia said, fluttering her lashes in a begging manner.

Boston cocked his most devastating grin. "I'll stop by a drive-through on the way."

She smiled and stroked his face. "Tempting. But maybe next time. Shannon really is getting better

Boston tore the note from Olivia's hand.

Dear Mr. Montgomery Kincaid,

My name is Cassidy Trenton. I am nine years and ten months old. I am looking for my dad. My mom is Ellie Trenton. She will not tell me his name, but she met him in college. She said he was the son of an astronaut and named after a state capital. I read about you in the magazine. You married the famous model Shannon March. They said you went to the same college my mom went to. They said your dad was a real-life astronaut. You are named after the capital of Alabama. Are you my dad? Please come meet me.

Sincerely,

Cassie Trenton

Frozen with horror, Boston could only gape. The blood congealed in his veins.

Yes, he'd done it now. He'd thought Ellie's name, and look what atrocity had emerged.

Dear God. She'd even dubbed the baby Cassie—the very name he'd chosen.

His stomach churned.

This was wrong. All wrong. It wasn't possible. That baby was *dead.*

He clearly remembered Ellie saying, *"There is no baby. The baby's gone."*

"Umm...guys?" came Olivia's voice from beside him. A moment later, Monty tore the letter from his grasp.

Boston lifted his face.

His brother's jaw sagged. "Holy Shit, Boston," he said, glancing down at the child's scrawl. "This letter was meant for *you.*"

Boston shook his head briefly to deny it. "No," he rasped. "It can't be. Ellie...she told me she had a miscarriage."

with this whole cooking thing."

Ever since she'd been married to Boston's brother, his sister-in-law, Shannon, had enrolled in cooking class after cooking class as a hobby. She was currently learning all things Thai.

Boston sighed. "You're shattering my ego here, darling. I'm not supposed to be thrown over for a home-cooked meal."

"Aww," Olivia cooed and kissed his cheek in a motherly gesture. "Don't worry. I still love you."

Finally returning to his side of the car, he laughed and rolled his eyes. "I'm guessing you've already talked to Cam," he said, transforming from playful to all business. He was better with business anyway.

"He told me he talked Spellman up to eight percent," she chirped and patted his arm with congratulations. "That's amazing. I'm impressed. But honestly, you guys earned it. You've both put a lot of hours into this deal."

"Yeah," Boston agreed as he shifted the car into gear and started them toward Independence, Missouri where his brother lived.

He ignored the ghostly reflection he swore he saw of Ellie's face shimmering in his driver's side window and settled into a comfortable conversation with his passenger throughout the rest of the trip.

Boston was actually grateful Cameron had asked him to bring her along. Not only did he have someone to talk to on the forty-five-minute trek to his brother's, but he wouldn't feel like such a third wheel once he reached his destination.

His younger brother, Monty, had been married to Shannon for five months now, and a person had to believe they were stuck in the honeymoon stage. Boston always wanted to squirm when he was around them because they cuddled nonstop. And if those two were going to be their usual lovey-dovey-make-me-pukey selves, then he wouldn't feel quite like the odd man out with Olivia at his side...even if she was just a cousin.

She'd become one of the closest friends he had. So it wouldn't feel too weird pretending she was his other half for the evening. Still, his stomach tightened into knots as they pulled to the curb in front of Monty's place. Yes, it was time for another distinct reminder he was totally and utterly alone. He'd rather just go home and *be* alone.

Tangy smells of an Oriental meal wafted their way as Olivia and Boston strolled up the walk toward the opened front door. The welcome sounds of family floated out to greet them.

"I want to see it again," Shannon said as Boston opened the screen door to let Olivia precede him inside.

"I still can't believe it," Montgomery Kincaid uttered in a hollow voice as he handed a sheet of folded stationary to his wife. "Every time I read it—"

"Hey, guys," Olivia called as Boston stepped inside behind her. "What's going on?"

"You won't believe this," Shannon said, popping to her feet and hurrying their way. "Monty got a letter today from a nine-year-old girl in Lawrence, asking if he's her father."

"Ohmigod, seriously?" Olivia turned wide eyes to Boston's brother.

Monty immediately shook his head and lifted both hands in surrender. "I'm not," he was quick to declare.

"I want to read it." Olivia snatched the letter from Shannon.

Boston nudged his brother with his elbow and wiggled his eyebrows. "You sure it's not your kid?"

In response, Monty flipped him the bird and called him a dirty name.

Too curious to stay away, Boston grinned and

strolled forward to peek over Olivia's shoulder. Seeing the youthful handwriting made his skin prickle. As he read the salutation, a strange buzz filled his ears. His smile dropped flat.

"Wow," Olivia murmured, scanning the page. "I bet you had a cow when you first read this," she said to Shannon.

"*Her*?" Montgomery yelped in outrage. "What about me? The thing was addressed to me, remember."

He glanced at Boston and shook his head miserably. But Boston was too busy frowning at the note to pay him any notice.

Monty turned back to Olivia. "I don't even know this woman she says her mom is. I never met a—" He paused and cocked his head thoughtfully to the side, deep in thought. "Now, wait a second. Maybe I *do* know her."

"What?" his wife croaked.

He snapped his fingers. "Yeah. We had a class together in college. Calculus. Her hair was long and dark, and she always sat in the front row next to this bald lesbian."

Shannon went sheet white. "*Montgomery*," she whispered.

"Whoa. Hey. I never *slept* with her," he swore. "Never even talked to her, I don't think. I just remember my friend Alex asked her out once. She turned him down. Said she was already seeing someone."

"I wonder who she was seeing," Olivia murmured. "I bet *he's* the father."

Three feet away from them, Boston tore the note from Olivia's hand.

"Boston! What—"

But he didn't pay attention to the way she broke her words off, and he totally ignored how she studied him with a scrutinizing squint of the eyes. The dizzy spell that almost dropped him to his knees made his vision blur. He blinked repeatedly until he could focus on the words again. But no matter how many times he examined them, they continued to read the same.

Dear Mr. Montgomery Kincaid,

My name is Cassidy Trenton. I am nine years and ten months old. I am looking for my dad. My mom is Ellie Trenton. She will not tell me his name, but she met him in college. She said he was the son of an astronaut and named after a state capital. I read about you in the magazine. You married the famous model Shannon March. They said you went to the same college my mom went to. They said your dad was a real-life astronaut. You are named after the capital of Alabama. Are you my dad? Please come meet me.

Sincerely,

Cassie Trenton

Frozen with horror, Boston could only gape. The blood congealed in his veins.

Yes, he'd done it now. He'd thought Ellie's name, and look what atrocity had emerged.

Dear God. She'd even dubbed the baby Cassie—the very name he'd chosen.

His stomach churned.

This was wrong. All wrong. It wasn't possible. That baby was *dead*.

He clearly remembered Ellie saying, *"There is no baby. The baby's gone."* She'd been pale and crying; he'd had no reason to think she was lying. *"So just leave me alone, Boston. I never want to see you again. I want to move on and forget."*

"Umm...guys?" came Olivia's voice from beside him. A moment later, Monty tore the letter from his grasp.

Boston lifted his face.

His brother's jaw sagged. "Holy Shit, Boston," he

said, glancing down at the child's scrawl. "This letter was meant for *you*."

Boston shook his head briefly to deny it. "No," he rasped. "It can't be. Ellie...she told me she had a miscarriage."

Chapter Two

Boston missed the address his first two passes down the street—even though his navigation system kept telling him he had arrived—but the third time, he paid closer attention to numbers and yes, there it was, wedged between a pair of three-story homes worth an easy million in mortgage.

The house he sought looked more like a guest cottage. It's floor plan had to be under a thousand square feet total. A single-story building with brown siding and white trim, the place matched the color of the mansion to its left, solidifying his guest-cottage theory. Shrubs and small trees filled the yard and sheltered a good portion of the covered front porch.

To Boston, it wasn't much. The whole thing could easily fit into his garage. But to a woman who'd come from a dirt-poor trailer park in Tennessee, was raised by her spinster great aunt, and had gotten pregnant when she was nineteen, this just might be a dream palace. He could see Ellie settling down here, thinking she'd come out okay.

That didn't mean she lived here, he reminded himself. Just because the return address to that freaky letter was legitimate and led to an actual residence didn't mean any of this was true, even if the facts were too uncanny to give him any sort of hope.

The names, the timing...they all fit.

Hello, my name is Cassidy Trenton. I am nine years and ten months old. Boston subtracted nine years and ten months from his life. Then he took off another nine months, which settled him right smack dab in the middle of April, his senior year at KU, just a few weeks before he and Ellie had split.

His fingers contracted around the steering wheel as a cold sweat filmed his body. Having trouble regulating his breathing, he pulled to the curb and stared at the mini house. Did his daughter live here? Was she inside wondering where he was even as he sat there? Boston's vision blurred, and he concentrated on his oxygen intake before he had himself a full-blown panic attack.

Hello, my name is Cassidy Trenton.

Cassie. God, that was the name he'd chosen. Why, he had no idea. He'd been in meltdown mode back then, trying to deal with reality and ignore it at the same time. It took him nearly three weeks to realize the stress Ellie had to be going through as well and how he was only adding to her troubles with his constant bickering and snide remarks. Wanting to show a little support, he'd stayed up all night, flipping through a baby name book until he'd come across Cassie. At the time, it seemed to fit, so he picked up the phone and called Ellie.

She answered on the fifth ring in a croaking, "'Lo."

"What do you think of the name Cassidy for a girl?" he blurted out without preamble. "Cassie for short."

After a short pause, she said, "Boston?"

"Yeah." God, he'd woken the pregnant woman. "It's me."

"What time is it?"

He had no idea. He hadn't slept in days. There'd been too much to worry about, mainly the confession he had to make to his family that he'd gotten someone pregnant, someone he'd never even told them he was dating...someone he'd been too embarrassed to introduce as his girlfriend.

"It's, ah..." After a quick glance at his wrist, he

winced. "It's almost one."

She made a little mewling sound of distress that went straight to his gut. He loved her little sounds. They'd driven him crazy on too many different occasions. And like clockwork, his body responded. He realized he didn't want to talk to her over the phone. He wanted to be with her, tucked into that stupid single-sized bed she slept on with his body spooned up behind hers and his cheek snuggled to hers.

He closed his eyes and rested his forehead against a nearby wall. "Sorry I woke you," he apologized, realizing how lame he sounded but not sure what to do about it.

She cleared her throat. "It's okay. I went to bed early anyway."

Of course it was okay. She was too forgiving. Hell, she'd probably forgive him for everything else if he'd just let her. But he couldn't. He'd wanted out instead. So in return, karma had bitch slapped him, and now his life was crumbling around him.

"What were you saying?" she prompted. "About a girl."

"I..." His mind went blank. What was the name he'd just chosen? Damn, he was losing it. "I like the name Cassie...for a girl. What do you think?"

"Cassie," she repeated in that sleepy, sexy voice of hers. "Um...okay. Sure. What if it's a boy?"

He paused. Crap. He hadn't gotten that far. To be honest, he thought he'd been doing good finding one name.

"I don't know," he mumbled.

"Well, there's still plenty of time to decide. We don't have to figure it all out tonight."

He wanted to though. He wanted to clear the air between them. Suddenly, he wanted to apologize and get that forgiveness he hadn't wanted before. He wanted to tell her how sorry he was for being a butt in the past few weeks—the past few months, actually. He shouldn't have blamed her or accused her of trying to trick him into anything. He shouldn't have been so hateful. He'd just been so freaking scared. It'd been easier to lash out and get mad. He could deal with mad. He couldn't do scared. He hated being scared.

"Ellie?" he said, his mouth opening to beg her forgiveness right then and there over the phone at one o'clock in the morning.

"Yeah?" she said.

"I..." His mouth opened, but no words came out.

"What's wrong?"

"Nothing," he assured her quickly. "It's just...nothing. I'm sorry I woke you. I'll see you tomorrow at the doctor's appointment. It's at two, right?"

But he hadn't seen her the next day for their check-up. Instead, he'd gotten the call. Ellie had been in an accident. Someone had sideswiped the public transportation bus she'd been riding. She'd ended up in the emergency room and had gone through a miscarriage...or so she'd told him. He'd never actually spoken to a doctor about it.

Boston hadn't seen her again after that announcement. She'd asked him to get out of her life, and he'd been too scared, heartbroken, and relieved to argue. So, he left, never to return and discover if she'd been lying about the miscarriage.

Well, it was time to learn the truth.

He stared up at the house, grinding his teeth. He couldn't move. If Ellie had borne his child, and mother and daughter really lived here, then he wasn't ready to meet the girl. What would he do? What would he say? How in the world would he explain his absence?

He reached forward to start the ignition and book it out of there. But half a second later, he stopped. Closing his eyes and cursing, he rested his forehead on the steering wheel before turning to glance at the miniscule house. He had to know. He wasn't going to leave this town without getting some answers.

With still no idea what to say if anyone was home, he opened his car door and eased out. Starting up the uneven brick walkway, Boston once again studied the small yard. It was void of toys or any sign a child was in residence. But then, Ellie had always been tidy when he'd known her. Then there was also the fact he hadn't seen the backyard. All his sisters kept their children's toys in their backyards.

Running a hand through his hair, he slid off his sunglasses, realizing he still wore them. Ten feet to the truth; his steps kept getting slower. His hands were ice cold; they shook slightly. Five feet and all his questions could be solved.

When he stepped onto the porch, a fuzzy animal darted out from under the steps. Boston breathed out a curse and jumped back. As he watched a fat cat scurry into a neighbor's yard and dash under a shrub, envy filled him. But running and hiding wasn't an option. It was time for answers.

Letting out a long breath, he fisted his shaking hand and knocked. After thirty seconds, he pressed the doorbell and knocked again. Two minutes later, he peeked in the window but couldn't see anything past the heavy curtain.

No one was home.

Not sure if he should be relieved or only more agitated, Boston turned around and jogged off the porch. He was halfway down the walkway when he saw movement from the corner of his eye. He whirled, braced to face anything.

A woman in bright yellow capris and a black blouse threw him off track, however, as she came from the yard of the house to the left, bearing down on him like a female on a mission.

He groaned deep in this throat. Great. A nosy neighbor. That was the last thing he wanted to handle. But with her already headed determinedly his way, he knew he'd look silly if he made a dash for it. So, he plastered a tight smile to his mouth and nodded to her in greeting.

"Can I help you with something?" she asked, glancing curiously at his car sitting at the curb and then back to him. She sounded nice enough, but it was clear she was doing a security check for the home's owner.

Boston opened his mouth, slid his hands into his back pockets, and turned to eye the brown house. "I..."

What could he say? *I'm just wondering if I have a nine-year-old daughter and if she lives here.*

Daughter.

Holy God, the mere word made the hairs on the back of his neck stand on end. Was he a father? Had he been one for nearly a decade?

Then it struck him that this woman would know who lived here. Since she obviously had concerns about strangers lurking in the yard, she'd surely know who owned the miniscule brown house.

Pointing at the front door, he forced a pleasant smile. "I was just waiting for Ellie to get home."

There. Now he'd get some answers. If neighbor woman frowned and said, "Ellie? Ellie who?" he'd know this was some kind of awful prank.

But the woman's shoulders eased at his words. "Oh," she said. Her eyebrows lifted and her gaze quickly traveled down his body. "Are you...a *friend* of Ellie's?"

Boston nearly groaned again. Oh, brother. Not only was she a nosy neighbor, but she was one of those matchmaking busybodies who wanted to know about everyone's love life.

The word, "No," spat out of his mouth before he could check himself.

Neighbor Lady frowned, making Boston flush.

"I mean, I'm..." He floundered. Then he thought of Cassie. "I'm a relative," he finished. If Ellie did live here, then it only made sense Cassidy Trenton existed. That would definitely put him in the role of the absentee father. And yes, one could definitely say a father was related.

Ms. Nosy frowned even more at his answer; he almost rolled his eyes. She wasn't going to back off, was she?

"It's been a while since I've seen her," he offered, hoping to appease her curiosity. "Cassie..." He faltered, cleared his throat, and tried again. "Her daughter wasn't even born yet."

Relief crossed her face as his story meshed with what she knew about the occupants of the brown house. A sickened feeling filled him. It was true then. Ellie lived here with her daughter, Cassie.

"Well, my goodness," the neighbor said, looking suddenly very comfortable with him. "It *has* been a while then, hasn't it?"

Boston nodded and rubbed his hand on his pant leg, hoping she would go away so he could commence a panic attack in peace. But, dear Lord, how could it be true? Ellie had told him the baby was dead. Why would she lie? Why—

"Is Ellie expecting you?"

He lifted his face. The word no was on the tip of his tongue, but he changed his mind at the last second and nodded yes. "But I made it to town a lot sooner than I expected," he lied. "I don't remember when she said she'd be home. Do you..."

"Ellie always gets home at five thirty," helpful neighbor lady answered before he could finish his question. Then she grinned and rolled her eyes. "I swear you can set a clock by Elora Trenton's schedule."

Trenton. So, she was still going by her maiden name. Either Ellie was single or she hadn't taken her husband's name. The Ellie he remembered was traditional. She'd take on her husband's surname if she was married. So, he had to assume she hadn't met someone else and created a child with that person. Then again, why would she name some other man's daughter Cassie?

Boston checked his watch. Fifteen minutes after five.

"Thank you," he offered the woman. "I guess I'll just wait then."

After the woman finally faded back toward her own yard, Boston returned to the porch, where he remembered seeing a wicker chair. The fragile wood creaked and groaned as he sat. Hooking one ankle over his opposite knee, he settled back and waited.

Fifteen minutes later, his foot jiggled impatiently and his fingers tapped rapidly against the wicker armrest. Okay, it was five thirty. Where the hell was Ellie? Where was Cassie? Why couldn't he breathe?

Questions mounted, time ticked on, and Boston continued to wait...and sweat. As sure as the neighbor had been about Ellie's ETA, he grew anxious. Something wasn't right. He remembered her as always being prompt too. So, why wasn't she home yet?

It made him wonder if someone really had pulled a hoax on him. If they had, he wasn't amused. If someone was messing with him, they'd pay. Plotting the demise of his unknown prankster, Boston didn't realize another fifteen minutes had passed until an old Toyota Corolla minus a muffler pulled into the drive.

As the car shuddered to a stop and the engine coughed out its last breath, Boston pushed to his feet. He spotted one occupant—a lone woman—inside. No child sat in the passenger seat or even in the back. Frowning, he moved to the top of the steps.

She didn't notice him. Instead, she opened the driver's side door, slid out, and immediately moved to the trunk to pop it open. He folded his arms over his chest, waiting for her attention.

The lady looked to be the same height and size as the Ellie he remembered. If it was her, she hadn't gained any weight except maybe to grow a few new curves. But after ten years, that was completely possible.

Then it happened.

Before reaching down to retrieve whatever was in the trunk, she pushed a piece of hair out of her face and tucked it behind her ear. The move was so Ellie like, it caused Boston to catch his breath in bittersweet memory of the girl he'd fallen for all those years ago.

It also provided him with a better view of her face.

He sucked in air, forcing oxygen back into his lungs. Oh yeah, his all-knowing gut surprised him with an acidic rumble of recognition. He'd found Ellie all right.

Features that still bore the wholesome girl-next-door had bloomed and turned into the strikingly beautiful TV commercial-mom look.

Her hair appeared lighter. There were now blonde streaks among the dark tresses. She wore the mane shorter than she had ten years ago too. But, wow, this was definitely her.

His stomach tightened as he watched her pull two bags of groceries from the trunk, shut it with her elbow, and finally turn his way.

Ellie, something soft and nostalgic murmured through his bloodstream, startling him with its longing. Ten years melted away and his body grew taut, remembering more than it should. But he knew the sweet memories would drown in bitter reality as soon as she lifted her face and noticed him.

He gritted his teeth, almost reluctant for things to get underway, yet all too aware there was no way out of it now. She was bound to see him any second.

Three, two, one...

****

Ellie was running late.

Her boss, Winston Young, had to be the most forgetful, careless man ever. She'd wanted to clock out early so she could stop by the grocery store and be home in enough time to have supper fixed before Cassie was due back. But Mr. Oh-I-forgot-I-need-a-memo-typed-before-tomorrow had plopped a stack of papers on her desk at four thirty, and she'd suddenly remembered why she couldn't stand lawyers.

They lied and lied and left you nothing but a heaping mess to clean up. And mess was the exact word she'd use for the unorganized pile of junk Winston had left her. She began to understand half an hour later why Winston always talked his clients into pleading out on a case. He probably didn't think he could keep his paperwork around long enough to ever make it to a trial.

After filing the last document into its proper drawer, she'd slapped Winston's last-minute memo onto his desk, wished him a good evening, and hurried toward the exit, tugging her purse strap onto her shoulder as she fled. She didn't even hear all of his, "'Bye then. See you tomorrow," before she shut the door snuggly in his face.

Her quick grocery run proved to be not-so-quick ten minutes later when she stepped foot inside the store and realized they were having a sale on meat. The place was packed, the checkout lines overflowing, and the aisles overrun with customers. Deciding she wasn't going to have time to cook, Ellie snatched two salad meals from the produce section and hurried along.

Cassie would grumble about salad for supper. But they were coated with meats and vegetables and cheese and were about the healthiest quick meal Ellie could buy on the run. And no, Ellie wasn't going to waste time fixing a complete meal. Supper was at six, so she'd have food on the table at six when her daughter made it home from tumbling practice...no matter what.

As she pulled into her drive, she grinned at her perfect little neighborhood and cut the engine of her car that actually ran...most of the time. She hurried to unload her groceries and was just starting to turn toward the front door when she noticed the car parked at the curb.

Living where she did, she was used to pricey automobiles cruising her block. To the left of her house, the Young family owned a loaded Escalade and a Mercedes Benz, and her neighbors to the right drove a Bentley. For a shiny new Infiniti to be parked directly in front of her sidewalk, however, was unusual. She glanced up and down the street, wondering if maybe one of her neighbors was having a get-together, and the Infiniti had merely been looking for a spot to rest. But, no, the roadside wasn't crowded with an overabundance of parked vehicles. Therefore, there was really no reason for someone to park directly in front of her place.

Shrugging off the curiosity, Ellie turned around and started up her front walk. For a moment, she was busy trying to juggle her two sacks of food while digging her house key from her purse. She didn't notice the man until she nearly plowed into him.

She saw the shoes first, a fancy pair of brown suede loafers. They were large, obviously belonging to a male, and partially covered by the hem of tan slacks.

And they were planted on the top step of her porch.

Ellie screamed and dropped her groceries. The shoes moved, taking a step down. Her gaze shot up even as she bent at the knees to retrieve her spilled goods.

And that was where she froze, face tipped up, knees slightly bent, back stooped over, and hand reaching down to snatch her sacks.

Her mouth fell open. "Oh," she breathed in awe as she took in the whole majestic form.

She'd hate to break it to this guy, but if he had anything nefarious in mind, he might want to rethink his life of crime, because honestly, you couldn't really rape the willing.

He was absolutely gorgeous. Tall, dark, handsome, glaringly rich. Too bad all those features turned her off because, well, hello...the way he stared made her think he'd seen her naked and wanted her that way again. Soon.

"Um..." she offered, biting her lip and bending just a little more to grab her bags. "Hello," she finally said and straightened. "Can I...can I help you with something?"

She glanced back toward the Infiniti. Definitely his. Stylish, sleek, a bit conservative while still managing to scream money.

"Yes," he said. "I really think you can help me...Ellie."

That voice.

Ellie whirled back and gaped as the man glided the rest of the way off the porch and took the last three steps toward her.

Oh, God, she knew that walk, that oh-so-gracefully smooth stroll. And that voice. She definitely knew that voice.

Eyes snapping to his face, she searched for familiar features until the young man she'd once known took form in the face of the adult before her. When he sent her a half sneer, half smile, she dropped her groceries again.

"*Boston?*"

Chapter Three

"Been a while, huh?" Boston said, skimming a quick gaze down her body before eyeing the two mangled bags at her feet.

"Oh, my God," Ellie blurted out. "What... How...oh, my God." She covered her opened mouth with her hands and gaped at him over her shaking fingers.

What was he doing here? How had he found her? And why in the world had he come?

There was nothing Boston Kincaid would ever need from her. Things had been cut and dried the last time she'd seen him. She'd told him to leave and never come back, something he'd been itching to do for over a month. So it wasn't like he needed any kind of closure. Everything between them was dead. Door closed, locked, and dead-bolted with its key missing for a full decade. There was no feasible reason for him to return. Unless...

No, it wasn't possible. He didn't know. He *couldn't* know. If he knew, he sure as hell wouldn't have waited this long to come back. But it was the only reason he might ever show up in her life again.

Panic and fear struck; her face drained of color.

His features drew tight and turned hard as if he could read every thought racing through her head. But he merely slid his hands casually into his pockets, achieving that deceptively calm demeanor he'd always been so good at posing.

"Going to invite me inside?" he asked, tipping his head toward her house.

Ellie frowned and dropped her hands from her

mouth. No, no, no. There was no way she'd let him into her home. There were too many pictures of Cassie in there. He couldn't go anywhere near the front door. She had to get rid of him...fast. Slicing an uneasy glance his way, she swallowed as his penetrating eyes nailed her to the spot. God, they were the same shade of blue as Cassie's.

The man was still devastatingly attractive. Ellie bit the inside of her lip and wondered why he couldn't have gotten fat, lost his hair, or developed some kind of nasty twitch. Why'd he have to look even better after ten years? It wasn't fair. And it wasn't helping her concentration at all.

His hair was still inky black but a lot shorter now. And as unbelievable as it could be, she swore his shoulders were even wider. His chest had definitely filled out. He'd always been tall, so at least that hadn't changed. And the aura around him was still—

"Ellie," he said.

As she realized she was just standing there, ogling, and doing nothing whatsoever to scoot him along, her face heated.

"What are you doing here, Boston? How did you..." *Find me.* She paused. How *had* he found her? And why had he wanted to? There could only be one reason, but Ellie was going to deny that explanation for as long as she could. There had to be something else.

"You have some very...*observant* neighbors," he murmured, glancing pointedly toward the Young's house on the left. "Maybe we should go inside before starting this conversation."

Ellie followed his stare and caught sight of Nora in her yard, openly watching them as she watered her plants, drowning her poor roses. She lifted her hand and waved. Boston waved back and gave a nod of greeting. Letting out a groan of misery, Ellie wondered how in the world she was ever going to explain Boston to Nora...and there was no doubt in her mind Nora would badger her until she revealed every detail.

"We have a lot to discuss," Boston told her, turning back with a probing look. "And I don't think you want an audience any more than I do."

Well...that didn't sound good. Actually, it sounded downright threatening. Boston had never been quite this menacing before. Her knees turned to Jell-O.

"What's going on?" she demanded, the hair standing straight up on her arms.

His jaw went stubbornly hard, but when Ellie remained rooted in her spot, he sighed and took his hand from his pocket, holding up an envelope folded between his fingers for her to see.

Ellie's mouth dried out. Eying the letter, she had this urge to snap it from him and tear it into tiny pieces. With no idea what was inside the note, she had a strong suspicion it had somehow brought him here.

"Did you really have a miscarriage?" he asked.

God...there it was.

The earth opened and left her suspended above a deep chasm. Ellie's ears buzzed; her skin turned prickly and cold. This was it. He knew. She had no idea how, but he'd finally discovered the truth.

Life flashing before her eyes, her heart rate accelerated. The man she'd once thought had completely destroyed her was back to do it all over again.

She glanced at the letter and then up into his eyes. A nervous droplet of sweat leaked down the center of her spine, making the back of her shirt cling to her skin.

Licking her dry lips, she held his gaze and croaked, "Excuse me?"

"Did you lie to me in the hospital that day?" he repeated. The question was asked a little less calmly this time.

Ellie shrank back a step, but she frowned as if he were insane. "Why would I lie?" she hedged, glancing back at the note he was now unknowingly starting to crumble in the tightening muscles of his fist.

"That's a good question," he murmured in a steely soft voice. "Why *would* you lie?"

Ellie backed up another cautious step. Shaking her head, she said, "I don't..." Her eyes darted to the letter in his hand. "What is that, anyway?"

"It's a letter," he stated the obvious. "Written to my brother, Monty."

"Written to your...your *brother*?"

He nodded and took a looming step closer. "You really have no idea about this, do you?" He wasn't asking. He stated it as if he were just now convinced of that fact.

"Of course not," Ellie snapped, wanting to back away some more, but remaining stubbornly still. "You're not making any sense. What does some letter to your brother have anything to do with me?" She set her hands on her hips and sent him her best intimidating glare. "And how in the world did you know where I live?"

For an answer, she got a slight smirk. "Well, that was the easy part," he murmured, unfolding the letter. "It was on the return address."

Boston held up the note for her to read. And sure enough, there it was, in her daughter's handwriting, their permanent address. Right above it were the printed words, Cassidy Trenton.

Ellie's mouth dropped. "Oh, my God."

"Who's Cassidy Trenton?" he asked. "And why did she send my *brother* a letter, asking him if he was her father?"

"She *what*?!" Snatching the note from his hand, Ellie ripped the stationary from the envelope. "I can't believe this," she murmured even as she read the words. "I can't..." She pressed a hand to the side of her face. "What in God's name was she thinking? And why would she believe your brother was..."

She glanced up; her words fell silent as she met the deadly expression on his face.

"Still feel like standing out here?" he asked. "Because, at this point, I don't care where the hell we talk. As long as I get some goddamn answers. Right now."

"Okay." Ellie quickly nodded, finally becoming compliant. "Let's go inside." She stepped forward and nearly went sprawling flat on her face as she tripped over the grocery bags she'd dropped.

"Oh," she mumbled, glancing down.

She swept one bag into her arm and reached for the other, except Boston leaned down and snagged it with one hand. She looked up, surprised. His cool blue eyes studied her dispassionately.

She flushed and looked away. "Umm, thank you," she mumbled and hurried past him. With him so close behind her, her fingers shook as she tried to unlock the front door. Leaning her single sack against her hip and chest to help balance it, she made three attempts before she finally slid the key home and managed to get them inside.

As she stepped over the threshold, something wet and gooey soaked through her shirt. She glanced down as she flipped on the interior light and groaned. Yep, she'd completely forgotten about the eggs. Yellow goop seeped through the brown paper bag, leaking down the side.

"Great," she mumbled. This was just icing on the cake.

Dropping her purse to the floor at her feet after she slid it off her shoulder, she backed away and watched Boston fill the room, still holding her other bag of groceries down at his side with one fist. Her eyes lifted, and she blushed as he glanced at the egg stain on her left breast.

"I..." she started, feeling like a total moron. "I need to clean this up. Just...wait right here," she called, already turning away and hurrying toward the kitchen.

Her pulse jack-hammered a mile a minute. Her hands shook uncontrollably as she dumped the rumpled bag on her counter and hauled the mangled egg carton from the top. Filmy egg white dripped through her fingers as she deposited the whole container into the sink.

After rinsing her hands and dampening a washcloth, she extracted more groceries from their death tote, sponging them clean. She'd just wiped a sticky smudge off her plastic salad containers when she was struck anew by the situation.

Her daughter's father waited down the hall in her living room. *Boston Kincaid* was in her house, waiting for answers she didn't want to give. Vision blurring, Ellie grabbed the edge of the counter and coached her breathing back to normal.

Okay, she could deal with this. There was no reason to panic. She should leave the groceries to unpack later and finish her talk with Boston, though, oh God, she didn't want to stop dealing with the groceries. She wanted to continue washing them and putting them away, pretending everything was still normal and her whole existence wasn't being threatened.

Worst case scenario, she'd end up losing her little girl forever. Since that was very unlikely, she should just settle down, because she could deal with anything else he threw her way. But at the mere thought of losing her baby girl...

Her breath hitched. Cassidy was the best thing

that had ever happened to her.

Ellie's pulse doubled, and she became dizzy all over again. Fighting off the black dots blotting her vision, she straightened and smoothed down her slacks. She needed to go out there and confront him before Cassie made it home, which was pretty much any moment now. But as her hands slipped over her blouse, ironing out wrinkles, she encountered the egg mess.

"Shit, shit, shit," she muttered and fumbled to unbutton the shirt.

As she did, she hurried toward the doorway that led onto the back porch, which in turn doubled as the laundry room. Glad she hadn't gotten around to folding the last load in the dryer, she yanked out the first top she saw and shrugged out of the egg blouse. Her fingers tripped over the buttons in her haste to shed it. She'd just lifted her arms to pull the clean, yet wrinkled T-shirt over her head when she turned to reenter the kitchen.

Gasping, she screeched to a stop as she came eye to eye with Boston. Grocery bag still in hand, he'd found his way back and was perched frozen in the opposite doorway across the room, appearing caught off guard by her state of undress. Though ten feet of space separated them, he might as well be touching her by the way his gaze slid down her bra and flat stomach.

Ellie remained frozen for probably a full second before she yanked her shirt the rest of the way down. Boston made a disinterested snort as he stepped into the kitchen to set her second sack of groceries on the countertop. He turned away, keeping his back to her, and examined her mini kitchen.

"The eggs broke when I dropped the groceries," she explained needlessly.

Feeling moronic, she returned to the counter

and wiped dripping yolk off other foodstuff. She made a point not to make eye contact with him. But from the corner of her peripheral vision, she watched him wander toward the refrigerator. Proof of his daughter's existence littered the surface.

Pausing at a picture of Cassie in her soccer uniform, posing with a ball, Boston studied the shot for a good fifteen seconds. Ellie wondered what he was thinking, wondered if he experienced that instant spark of pride she always did every time she looked at her daughter. He turned suddenly as if staring at the picture was too much to take in and zeroed in on a graded math test where Cassie had scored an A+. Slowly reaching out, he tugged the sheet from its magnet.

"Where is she?" he asked.

"What?" Ellie jumped and spun fully toward him, startled to discover he'd lifted his face and was staring at her, waiting for an answer. She focused on the test in his hand and let out a breath. "Oh. Cassie's at..." she was about to spill out her exact whereabouts. One of the carpool mom's would be bringing her home from tumbling lessons any minute now. But she caught herself, realizing she didn't want him knowing too much.

"She's not here," she finished in a bold voice she didn't feel.

He scowled.

She sighed and stopped wiping. "Look, Boston. I don't know what gave her the idea to send that letter to your brother, but—"

"Dammit, Ellie," he snapped. "Is she mine or not?"

Ellie blinked. "Of course she's yours."

"Of course," he repeated on a derisive snort. Every muscle in his face pulled tight as he threw her a look to kill. "Then why did you tell me she died?"

When Ellie jumped at his tone, he paused to

wipe at his mouth, a full attempt to gain some composure. But then it all slipped and boiled over again.

"You told me the baby was dead. You said you had a miscarriage. You demanded I get out and leave you alone. Lord above, Ellie, why did you do that?"

Ellie folded her hands in prayer and pressed them to her mouth. When she moved them away, she met his accusing gaze directly. Why exactly had she lied to him? That was the million dollar question.

At the time she'd thought she was in love. It didn't matter if he'd hurt her and resented ever meeting her; she'd adored him. She hadn't been able to bear the thought of him hating her and holding a grudge against her because she'd accidentally gotten pregnant. He'd been full of so many dreams, had so many plans for his life. Those plans had been important enough to him that he'd gotten rid of her in order to pursue them. Ellie had presumed that if his dreams were that big, then he should go after them. So, she'd cut him loose and taken all the fear and trouble of a baby onto her own shoulders.

She couldn't tell him any of this, however. Not only would he not believe her, but that reason wasn't even valid anymore. She no longer loved him that way. She no longer cared about providing him with an opportunity to follow his life's dream. Lifting her face, she let out a breath and met his accusing gaze.

"I was young and stupid." She waved a dismissive hand for emphasis. "I was thinking with my emotions rather than my brain."

Boston nodded. "And when you grew up?" he pressed, spreading his arms to encompass the room. "You couldn't have gotten this far without growing up at least some. There's been ten years to tell me about her. So, what's your excuse now? Why didn't you get a hold of me when you weren't so young and stupid and emotional anymore?"

Because she couldn't risk the chance he'd try to take her baby away.

Ellie would've regretted ever meeting Boston Kincaid if it weren't for the fact he'd given her the most precious gift in her entire life. Cassidy was her reason for getting up in the morning. Without her daughter...

She shook, not even wanting to think about that possibility.

"What are you so upset about, anyway?" she grumbled, trying to turn the tables on him. "You didn't have to drop any of your precious dreams, did you?"

He straightened. "What's that supposed to mean?"

"Well, just look at you." She motioned to his clothes. "I can see you're successful. Do you think you'd have gotten any of this, that car out there, or your...your whole way of life if you'd stayed here and become a daddy? You wouldn't have been able to go off to law school..." Ellie paused and eyed him. "You *did* go to law school, didn't you?"

Wouldn't that be the kicker if he hadn't. He'd caused their breakup so he could go off to Yale and not have any disturbing ties left behind. And she'd lied about his daughter so he could do just that. Wouldn't it be one big ironic joke if he hadn't even bothered?

But obviously, he had. His jaw hardened as he glared. "What's your point?"

"If I had kept you here," Ellie explained calmly. "If I hadn't lied to you, then you wouldn't have any of this today, Boston. Instead, you'd be some miserable man who blamed everything on me for tying you down and keeping you from your dreams. Well, I refused to be the scapegoat for all your problems. So, yes, I lied. And if it wasn't for that lie, you wouldn't have anything you have today."

"What are you fishing for, Ellie? A thank you?" He let out a bitter laugh. "Don't hold your breath. You kept my child from me."

"A child you didn't want."

Shock froze every muscle on his face. "Says who?"

"Says you. You told me you didn't want the baby."

"The hell if I did."

"You did," she insisted. "You said you weren't ready to be a father. You said—"

"Oh, my God," he yelled. "I was upset. I was afraid. Of course, I didn't feel ready. And don't you dare tell me *you* did. We were both scared out of our minds. Christ, Ellie, that didn't mean I wanted out. I never wanted out of the situation."

Ellie shook her head and wrapped her arms around her waist as if she were cold. "I just...it seemed like a good way to let you go with a clear conscience."

Boston stared thoughtfully a moment. Then he nodded as if he understood. But a second later, he exploded.

"That's the biggest pile of horse shit I think I've ever heard. *Let me go?* You had no right. If I hadn't wanted to stick around, I would've left at the first of it. Did you think I wouldn't want to know my own child? Did you think... Oh God."

He turned away, and she knew he was once again trying to control the onslaught of emotions rushing through him. Running his hands through his hair, he glanced her way. "Damn it. Damn it. I'm so mad at you, I can't even..."

He shook his head and turned away again, setting his hands on his hips.

"I have a daughter," he said to no one in

particular as if he wanted to test the sound of that reality on his lips. "I've had a daughter for nine years and ten months, and I wouldn't know her if I ran into her on the street. I don't know the sound of her voice. I don't know what she looked like when she took her first step or if she..." His voice broke and he glanced over his shoulder to glare at Ellie. "How could you take that away from me?"

Her whispered answer was, "You said you didn't want her."

"You know I didn't mean it like that," he spat out, his voice growing again. "We were both screaming things we didn't mean back then."

"Kind of like how we are right now?"

"No. Right now, I mean everything I'm saying. I'm pissed as hell. You turned me into a...a delinquent father."

She wrinkled her nose. "Delinquent?"

"Neglectful," he restated, sending her a dry look. "Falling down on one's duty. It's a violation of the law to neglect your own child. You've caused me to break the law...*for years.*"

"Oh, brother." She rolled her eyes. "Yeah, you're definitely a lawyer now, aren't you?"

"Damn it, Ellie," he exploded.

"Boston," she cut in before he could go off on one of his self-righteous tangents. "I made a decision I thought was the best for all three of us—"

"Well, it wasn't the right one," he roared. "You never should've goddamn lied to me. You never should've..."

The words died on his tongue, and he froze. His face drained of color as his eyes drilled into a spot behind her.

Already knowing what, or rather *who*, she was going to find, Ellie whirled and gasped, bringing her hand to her heart.

"*Cassie!*" she wheezed in a high voice.

The raven-haired child rooted in the kitchen entrance stared at Boston with wide, frightened blue eyes before swiveling her gaze back to Ellie. She was a beautiful girl, tall for her age, the second tallest in her class. Slim with tanned, golden skin and the perfect face, she'd inherited Ellie's nose, chin, and mouth and Boston's intelligent blue eyes and inky black hair.

"Mom?" she said in a wavering tone as she dropped the gym bag hanging off her shoulder and skittered the last few feet to Ellie's side, once again glancing cautiously toward Boston. "What's going on?" she asked, seeking comfort by snagging Ellie's hand.

Ellie opened her mouth and turned to Boston as if looking for assistance. But her heart dropped into her knees when she took in the vanquished features on his face. He looked completely lost and exposed, a vulnerable train wreck.

Honestly, she couldn't blame him. This was his very first encounter with his daughter, and the girl gaped at him as if he were an axe murderer. Biting the inside of her lip, she fought back the instant guilt. But, hell. She should've known better than to engage in a yelling match with him when she knew full well Cassie was expected home any moment.

"Who is he?" Cassie asked, her voice shaking. "Why're you two yelling at each other? What's happening?"

Boston dragged his eyes up to Ellie. His gaze begged for help. For a second, she thought he was going to cry. Ellie gripped her hand around Cassie's small fingers.

"Cassidy Diane," she stated firmly, ignoring Boston for the moment and turning to give her daughter her full attention. She swiped the envelope off the counter where it had been piled along with all the groceries. Waving it in Cassie's face, she demanded, "Did you write this?"

The child focused on the letter, and her eyes bulged. In an instant, her fear evaporated. She brightened and whirled around to gape at Boston. "Are *you* Montgomery Kincaid?"

Chapter Four

His daughter was talking to him. Boston couldn't wrap his mind around the concept. A part of him had helped create this tiny person. She *was* a part of him. Yet everything about her remained foreign.

Cassidy Diane. Diane was his mother's name. Unbelievable. This child was so...well, she was perfect. Absolutely flawless. Boston couldn't stop staring.

He'd been on the verge of a breakdown for a second there. When she'd originally laid eyes on him, she'd laser-beamed him with a killer glare. Obviously, she was a protective thing. She definitely didn't like him yelling at her mother, that was for sure. The girl had sidled herself next to Ellie and frostily scowled at him with a courage that was, frankly, remarkable.

So much for a good first impression.

But now...now that she knew he was here because of her letter, it looked like she was going to plow that perfect nine-year-old body against his legs and hug him for the next month. Though that thought was preferable to her skewering him through with a lethal stare, it still scared the bejesus out of him just about as much as thinking she might hate him. He was this girl's father, but he didn't know a thing about her. He had no idea what he was supposed to do.

Should he go to her? Was she expecting him to race over and pull her into his arms, tell her how much he loved her and how happy he was they were finally together?

Apprehension spiraled through him.

His eyes rose anxiously to Ellie. For the first time since he'd showed up, she actually looked apologetic for putting him through this hell. Turning away, she drew Cassie's arm toward her, commanding her daughter's attention.

"No, he is not Montgomery Kincaid," she said, voice stern and face set so she looked like a disappointed mother. "Now, answer my question. Did you write this letter or not?"

Boston nearly rolled his eyes. Of course she'd written the letter. They all knew she'd written the damn letter. Why in the world was Ellie beating a dead horse?

Instead of answering, however, Cassie pooched her lower lip in displeasure. She looked up at him with the saddest, gravest expression he'd ever seen. "He's not Montgomery Kincaid? Then who is he?"

He was tempted to say that yeah, sure, he was Monty. At that moment, he'd say anything to put that excited gleam back into her eyes.

"I'm Boston," he croaked, sounding like a complete ninny because he wished he was who she wanted him to be. "Monty's my brother."

His daughter blinked, digesting that news. The slow sweep of those long lashes reminded him so much of Ellie, his guts knotted. God, he did not need a reminder she was half Ellie's too. It brought up all sorts of images of how she'd been conceived, making his chest constrict with a crazy, regretful ache.

If only he'd played his cards right ten years ago. If only he'd been a half-decent person, these two females would be his closest family right now; they'd probably be his entire life. They wouldn't be strangers standing across an unfamiliar kitchen and staring at him with similar stares of wary distrust.

"But why didn't *he* come?" Cassidy asked,

tugging Boston back to the situation at hand. She turned expectantly toward her mother. "I wrote my letter to *Montgomery* Kincaid, not—"

"Cassidy," Ellie cut in, setting her hands on the girl's shoulder and turning her so they were facing each other.

She moistened her lips, and Boston held his breath, realizing this was the moment. She was going to announce the truth. He felt like Darth Vader. A deep voice was going to proclaim, "Luke, I am your father." And little Cassidy Diane Trenton was going to be shocked to her toes.

But instead of confessing his paternity, Ellie said, "Go change out of your clothes. Take your bath and we'll talk about this when you're clean."

Boston exhaled, half relieved, half disappointed.

"But I'm not supposed to take my bath until eight thirty." Cassie protested, sending a mutinous look Boston's way. "And what about supper? Supper's always at six."

"I think you'll live if we do things out of order for one night."

"But—"

"Right now, young lady," Ellie cut in.

Cassie glared at her mother a moment in protest before she caved and flung her long black hair over her shoulder as she spun away to stomp from the room.

Boston watched her disappear from sight. His eyes felt glued opened as he stared at the spot where he'd last seen her. His daughter. He'd just met his nine-year-old daughter. And all he'd said was, "I'm Boston."

God.

His legs gave out and his body sagged. He hadn't realized he'd backed himself against Ellie's cupboards until he reached behind him and caught hold of her countertop for support.

"Boston?"

He looked up, but the closer Ellie stepped, the further away she seemed to get. She reached out like she might comfort him. But she pulled her hand back at the last moment as if realizing what she was about to do.

For a split second, he wished she'd touch him. He ached for some of her sympathy. Hell, he wanted to wrap her in his arms and smell nothing but her hair, soaking up all the comfort he could get. Did she still use that lavender-scented shampoo?

Boston laughed bitterly and wiped at mist that had gotten caught in his eye. There were more important things to ponder here. His daughter was just down the hall, taking a bath.

"She looks just like my mom," was all he could think to say.

Instead of replying, Ellie pulled out a chair and motioned to it. He sat and lifted his face, but she turned away before he was ready for her to leave. She returned seconds later with a glass of ice water. He realized the drink was for him when she set it next to him on the table. Automatically, he drank.

The water cleared his head as much as it did his throat. He gulped every last drop and closed his eyes when he finally had to lower the glass.

"Are you okay?" Ellie asked, moving another foot away as if he might be contagious. "You look like you're going to throw up."

He kind of felt like he might.

"I..." He tried to tell her he was fine. But the words that came out sounded a lot more like, "I didn't think it'd be like this."

He touched his chest, wondering if he was having a heart attack. "To see her for the first time," he added. "I didn't think I'd feel so...I can't breathe." He tugged frantically at the top button of his collar only to realize it was already unbuttoned.

"What do you say to a nine-year-old?" He didn't know the first thing about kids, especially nine-year-old girls. Sure he had nieces and nephews, but this was totally different. This was *his* child.

Automatically, he looked to Ellie for help. But as much as he wanted to beg for her comfort, he wanted to keep yelling at her too. She'd lied to him and purposefully kept his daughter from him.

"I need to put the cold food in the refrigerator," she blurted out, snagging his empty cup and moving toward the sink to wash it and set it back in the cupboard.

Boston sat back in his chair, watching her stash her groceries. She'd just turned to a pantry to put away her canned goods when the back door opened. He glanced over and blinked when a small blond-haired boy strolled inside like he owned the place. Ellie didn't notice him at first, but Boston couldn't take his eyes off the kid.

Who the hell was this? Was he another child of hers, a younger son or something? The idea of Ellie having more children didn't sit well with him, and he wasn't about to explore why. He scowled as he watched the scrawny kid in the thick glasses meander toward the fridge and lug out a gallon of milk.

****

Ellie finally noticed the boy a second later, or rather she noticed Boston watching him. She turned and jumped half out of her skin.

"Keller!" she yelped. "What are you doing here?"

"I'm...getting...a drink...Mama Ellie." The boy panted, out of breath because the milk was too heavy for him.

Ellie hurried forward and took the carton from his grasp. "Well, I'm sure you have milk at home, dear."

"But I'm here to see Cassie. We're going to play

41

the new Pokémon game on her Xbox." He tipped his head back to stare up at her and send her a confused look. "Why should I go home to get a drink and then come all the way back, when I can just get it here?"

Ellie sighed. "Keller, Cassie can't play tonight." She glanced toward Boston. "She—"

But the boy had finally caught sight of him too. His eyes bugged. "Holy cow! Who's he?!" He spun toward Ellie. "Oh, wow. Is he Cassie's dad?"

Ellie's jaw began to fall open before she caught herself and snapped her teeth together. Then she groaned. "Of course," she muttered to herself, shaking her head. "I should've known you were involved in writing that letter."

Keller grinned, proud. "Well, sure. I found his address."

Boston and Ellie exchanged a glance. Boston looked surprised. Ellie was merely bone weary. She turned back to the boy and set her hands on her hips, taking on the aggravated mother look. "*You* found Montgomery Kincaid's address?"

"It wasn't hard." Keller gave a no-nonsense shrug. "All you have to do is pay thirty-nine, ninety-nine on people finders dot com and they just *give* you the address."

Ellie's mouth fell open. "And how did you pay for that?"

Keller started to look a little uneasy. Dipping his head, he mumbled, "My dad has a credit card on his dresser for emergencies."

"Keller!" Ellie sputtered. "Oh, my God."

But the boy was quick to say, "This *was* an emergency, Mama Ellie. Cassie was this close to finding her dad." He held up two fingers, stretching them less than an inch apart.

"But— What...how..." Ellie snapped her mouth shut and gaped openly at the boy. "What even made you two think *Montgomery* Kincaid was her father?"

How had they gotten so close?

"It was in the magazine," he answered.

"The...what? What magazine?"

With a roll of his eyes as if he couldn't believe she could be so ignorant, Keller let out a sigh and trudged across the kitchen. He stood on his tiptoes and reached for a pile of magazines sitting in a basket on the counter. After digging through them a moment, he lifted *Vogue* and showed it to her. The cover read, "Shannon's Out-of-this-World Marriage to Astronaut's Son." Ellie frowned at the picture of the famous model on the cover.

"Shannon March," Keller said. "Right here it says she married the son of a real-life astronaut. And you told Cassidy her dad was the son of an astronaut. There's not a lot of actual astronauts out there, you know," he added as if he were an authority on the subject. "So, it was pretty much a given this could be her dad."

Mouth falling open, Ellie turned toward Boston. "You married *Shannon March*?"

"My brother did," he murmured, frowning as he eyed Keller.

"Oh," she said. Wow. Her daughter's biological uncle was married to a world-known model. How amazing was that?

Boston eyed the magazine as he pushed to his feet and strolled toward it. A bug-eyed Keller handed it over as soon he reached for it.

"We read the article about her marrying Montgomery Kincaid," the boy said. "And when it said he went to the same college as you, Mama Ellie, then we knew...we just knew this had to be her dad. Because you said...you said you met her dad in college and he was the son of a—"

"I know what I said," Ellie snapped, irritated her own words had come back to bite her in the butt. But she'd never thought her daughter would turn into a mini Sherlock Holmes and actually get so close to finding the truth. Then again, she should've known better with a genius savant like Keller as her best friend.

"Keller," she said on an exasperated sigh. "You need to go home now. And don't think I won't tell your mother about borrowing that credit card."

"But..." the boy sputtered as he was nudged toward the exit.

Ellie opened the door and ushered him out. "You can see Cassidy tomorrow."

"But is he Montgomery Kincaid or not?" he asked, peeking around her to get one last look at Boston.

"He's not," Ellie said and shut the door in his face.

She paused to press a hand to her aching temple. She would've liked to follow Keller out the door and escape too, but this had to be dealt with. Regulating her breathing and repeating a soothing monologue in her head as she turned, Ellie caught sight of Boston skimming through the article about his sister-in-law.

He glanced up and arched a non-impressed eyebrow. "I take it you told her about me but never gave her my name."

Ellie sighed. She'd had to give her daughter *something*. Cassidy had been asking about her father a lot lately, and she was as stubborn as all get out. Once the girl wanted something, she worked to get it. And lately, she'd wanted to meet her father. Ellie should've known she'd start looking by herself. She'd definitely gained her sense of determination from Boston, that was for sure.

"If I'd known she was going to pull a Nancy Drew on me, I wouldn't have given her anything."

Boston's gaze iced over. His jaw tightened, but he didn't comment. The boy she'd known ten years ago wouldn't have kept silent. He'd have spat out something sharp and demeaning. But the aged, more polished version of that young man held his tongue.

Instead, he glanced out the window. "Who was that kid?"

Ellie cleared her throat. "Um...that was Keller Young," she answered in a slightly unsteady voice. She noticed a tremor in her hand as she reached for a box of cereal to put away. Not wanting him to see the fear clogging her system, she jerked her fingers behind her back and spun his way as if to check if he noted her anxiety.

She cleared her throat again when she realized his gaze was fixed on her arm tucked behind her back.

"He, ah, he lives next door," she continued, wondering why she was talking about Keller. She needed to get him out of here before Cassie was done with her bath. She needed him gone and as far away from her and her baby as he could possibly get.

But she just kept talking like an idiot. "He and Cass have been best friends since the moment we moved here six years ago."

Boston nodded as if soaking in every detail of his daughter's life he could uncover. "He seems pretty smart for his age."

"Oh, he's a whiz all right," Ellie said. "He could probably pass a high school G.E.D. if he wanted to. All his teachers keep trying to talk him into advancing into special gifted classes. They're always wanting to skip him a grade or two. But he refuses. He wants to stay in the same class as Cassidy."

Boston cocked his head curiously at that news. "He's the same age as Cassie? But she's probably a head taller than him."

Ellie couldn't help but smile. "Actually, he's a month older than her. Yet another reason he didn't want to skip any grades. He's already picked on enough for being so small. Cassidy deflects a lot of teasing for him. I bet he'd come home with a bloody nose every day if it wasn't for her."

"She fights off his bullies, does she?" he asked, looking amused and a little proud.

Something hard and intense thumped into the base of her stomach. But seeing that pleased glint in Boston's eyes made her feel connected to him the way only a pair of proud parents could be. And she couldn't help but remember back to when he'd been her entire world and how much she'd adored him when they'd conceived their daughter together.

Feeling herself soften, she nodded yes. Boston's mouth curved slightly like he was remembering a happier time too. But a split moment later, he paused as if realizing she was the enemy now. His face stiffened into a cool glare and he glanced away, stuffing his hands moodily into his pockets.

Ellie swallowed and dropped her eyes. "So, ah, anyway. You probably need to get back to, ah..." Wherever the hell he'd come from.

Boston's gaze zipped accusingly to her face, eyes narrowed. She bit her lip.

"What about Cassie?" he asked.

"What about her?"

His forehead wrinkled. "She still doesn't know who I am." Ellie didn't think that was a problem. As if reading her thoughts, his scowl deepened. "I want her to know the truth."

Lifting her eyebrows, Ellie said, "Oh, you want her to know the truth, huh? Sure, I'll tell her exactly why we broke up."

An uneasy look filled his face, and he opened his mouth to comment. But Ellie kept talking. "I'll be happy to tell her exactly where things went wrong. And how you were so ashamed of being with me you would never let me meet your family, or—"

"I never—" he started, but she kept talking over

him.

"Or how you thought I was just a gold-digging bitch who purposely trapped you into staying with me by getting knocked up."

"I apologized for that." His face turned gray as if remembering his own words made him physically ill. "As soon as I said it, I told you I was sorry."

Unable to watch the repentant features that looked so truly genuine, Ellie turned and crossed her arms over her chest. "So you did," she murmured, though she was sure he could hear in her voice that she'd never forgiven or forgotten.

A tense moment of silence followed, and finally he murmured, "Is that why you told me you had a miscarriage? Because I was such a jerk?" He sucked in a breath. "Jesus, Ellie, I was a stupid, immature kid who was scared out of my mind. How could you—"

"And what do you think *I* was?" she broke in incredulously, spinning to glare at him. "I was three years younger than you and a lot less experienced in the ways of the world. What do you think it was like for me?"

"Okay." He lifted a hand to hush her. Glancing toward the hallway, reminding her Cassidy was still just down the hall, he repeated, "Okay," in a calm tone that made her want to rail at him all that much more. But how could he keep a level head when all she wanted to do was scream, and throw stuff, and cry?

Hissing out a disgusted breath, she spun away and pressed a hand to her thumping heart. Tears threatened, and she gnashed her teeth to keep them away. But damn it. She hadn't let herself cry over Boston Kincaid since—

"So I was a stupid, immature, *selfish* kid," he revised. "I didn't care about anyone but myself, and I freely admit that. I cannot tell you how sorry I am about how I treated you. I will always regret the things I did and said." He drew out a long, loud sigh. "I mean, God, if I'd known then I'd never feel for a woman the way I felt about—"

Ellie whirled to gape at him at the exact moment he broke off. She gulped when she found an expression of shocked horror on his face as he realized how much he was about to reveal. But that last word of his statement, though never spoken, seemed to hover in the air above them.

Lips parting in stunned disbelief, she could only watch as Boston shook his head like he was trying to deny what he'd just blurted out. His chest expanded as he sucked in a breath. Then he licked dried lips and sent her a wary glance.

"This isn't why I'm here," he stated, sounding a little desperate, as if he was trying to convince himself of that fact more than he was trying to convince her. "I'm here because I have a daughter, and *you* kept her from me. And I want her to know who I am."

But Ellie couldn't process anything past *If I'd known then that I'd never feel for a woman what I felt for* you, you, you, you, you...

She'd never thought he actually cared for her...at least not after it was all said and done, when her eyes had been opened to his stupid, immature, selfish ways...not after she no longer thought she was crazy in love with him. No. Then she'd been able to see how much she *hadn't* meant to him, how it'd only been about the sex for him.

Shaking her head in an effort to clear the racing thoughts, she swallowed and hoarsely answered, "I don't know if that's such a good idea." Then she gritted her teeth, mad at herself by being swayed by his sweet words. It was foolish to believe, even for one second, that he'd actually changed, that he wasn't still that self-centered, immature jerk.

He'd used pretty words to get into her pants back then too, just like he was doing now. But this time around, he wanted something more precious than her virginity; he wanted her daughter.

"And why wouldn't it be a good idea?" he asked, jerking her attention back to the present.

Ellie took a deep breath. "I'll tell you why," she murmured evenly. *Because I don't want you to take her away from me.* "Because she's gone nine years without a father and has done perfectly fine. Letting you into her world so suddenly will only confuse and hurt her. She doesn't need you. She has a great life."

His jaw bunched and his eyes flared. She wondered briefly if he might actually attack her. Then he blew out a breath from between clenched teeth and growled, "Is that why she went behind your back to find me? Because she doesn't *need* me? Is that why she and her little friend scoured magazine after magazine until they found something that fit her daddy's description? Because she doesn't *want* me?" He shook his head slowly. "Try again, Ellie."

Ellie gave a shaky swallow; air wobbled through her lungs. She couldn't remember feeling this scared since—God, this was probably the most frightened she'd ever been. She hadn't even been this frightened when she'd been eight and both her parents had died, leaving her with a great aunt she'd never met before, or when she'd been nineteen and the doctor had placed a new baby in her arms for her to raise alone.

"You can't have her," she said softly and bit back the wince. But damn it, why had she just revealed her deepest fear to him?

He didn't answer her immediately. He merely studied her as if trying to find more secrets she hid. Finally, he said, "Right now, all I want to do is meet her. I want her to know who I am."

"Right now?" she repeated, latching onto that term. "What about later, then?"

His jaw went tight. "You don't want this to get ugly, Ellie. I *am* a good lawyer."

She paled. "Don't threaten me, Boston. This is my child you're talking about. I raised her and fed her. I rocked her to sleep every night and worried about her every day. I was the one to bring her up from an infant and care for her. You don't even know her."

"And whose fault is that?" He blinked rapidly as if trying to wipe away an onslaught of tears. "You didn't give me a chance to mess up," he whispered in a hoarse voice.

Ellie shook her head. "You'd already messed up."

He ran a hand through his hair. "I messed up with you," he reminded her. "Not her."

When she didn't answer, he growled out a sound of frustration. He opened his mouth, but something in the doorway caught his attention and he promptly snapped his jaw shut. Knowing it was Cassidy, Ellie cursed her luck and turned slowly to find her daughter once again standing in the entrance of the kitchen, but this time she wore her nicest dress, white tights—which she always refused to wear— and her glossy black dress shoes. She'd brushed her hair, something Cassie usually made Ellie do since she hated doing it herself, and even put barrettes in the dark locks.

Seeing the girl primp to meet her father made Ellie want to cry. Without wanting to, she gave in.

Every night for the past year, she'd been forced to tell the girl something about her daddy. Not wanting the usual bedtime story from one of her books, Cassie had opted for information about Boston. That was why she'd learned so much about him and been able to find him...because she'd bugged Ellie constantly for facts.

Seeing that hopeful gleam in Cassie's eyes was Ellie's downfall. Her daughter had been dreaming of this for months...years.

"Cass," she said quietly. But the girl paid her no attention.

She strode to Boston. He met her gaze, and Ellie could tell he was holding his breath.

"Are you going to take me to my dad now?" Cassidy asked. "That's why you're here, isn't it? Because he couldn't come himself?" Grinning broadly, she looked down at her dress. "Well, I'm ready to meet him."

Boston sent her a wobbly smile. "You look very nice too."

Ellie wanted to hug him. That was the best thing he could've told the girl.

Cassie beamed. "Is he waiting very far away?"

"Cassidy," Ellie interrupted then. Her daughter ignored her until she said, "Montgomery Kincaid isn't your father."

Cassie whirled around, her eyes wide with denial. "He's not?" Her bottom lip quivered, and Ellie sent her a sympathetic look as she shook her head no. "But...but...why is *he* here then?" Cassie motioned blindly toward Boston. "He wouldn't come if his brother wasn't—"

"Cassie, come sit down," Ellie interrupted, moving toward the kitchen table.

Her daughter didn't budge. "No. I want—"

"I'll tell you the truth about your father," she added evenly, though she had to pitch her voice up an octave to catch Cassie's attention. "Now, sit down."

For a moment, it looked like Cassidy was going to rebel. Then she glanced up at Boston. He hitched his chin encouragingly toward a chair. Finally, the girl slumped into action, but she didn't look happy about it. She probably thought Ellie was going to evade the subject like she usually did.

Easing down into a seat next to her daughter, Ellie reached out and took both of Cassie's hands. From the corner of her eye, she saw Boston edge closer, though he still kept a good distance away.

"Cassie, honey," she started, sounding surprisingly calm considering the way her heart threatened to thump its way out of her chest.

"Listen to me, sweetheart." Her fingers tightened around Cassie's. "Boston is here because he read the letter you sent his brother. You see, he also went to the University of Kansas at the same time as I did. And he's also the son of an astronaut. He...he..."

She paused to glance his way. She hadn't realized saying it aloud would be so hard.

Oh, boy. What if she couldn't do it?

But as soon as she caught Boston's anxious gaze, she felt encouraged. Turning back to Cassie, she said, "Montgomery Kincaid is only your uncle. Boston..." she added, glancing at him again, "is your father."

Cassie's mouth fell open in awe, and she lifted her head to look up at Boston. "*You're* my dad?"

His face had drained of color, and it didn't look like he'd remembered to breathe in the last thirty seconds. But he held Cassie's gaze steady as he nodded.

Cassie slowly slipped to her feet, and Ellie let go of her hand as she watched her little girl cautiously approach the grown man who looked like he was going to hyperventilate any moment. Ellie could honestly say she'd never seen him look so scared.

"Really?" Cassie asked, looking him up and down as if she couldn't believe it.

For a split second, Ellie thought he was going to pass out. But he seemed to collect himself enough to give another mute nod.

Cassie gasped in pleasure. "Can...can I hug you?"

Boston's jaw dropped. He glanced quickly at Ellie as if seeking permission. But before she could give any kind of response, he turned back to their daughter.

Eyes watering, he choked out, "I think I would like that." He made a small sobbing sound as he fell on both knees, and Cassie leapt into his open arms.

Chapter Five

She felt so small in his embrace. Her limbs were toothpick thin, but the girl had muscle, and she put her whole body into hugging him as tightly as she could. He closed his eyes and inhaled her sweet child scent. Her hair was still damp from the bath Ellie had told her to take. The wet locks soaked his collar and cheek. But he didn't care. He was hugging his daughter.

Pulling away so he could see her perfect, heart-shaped face, he wiped at the corner of his eye and sent her a watery smile.

"It's nice to finally meet you," he said, hoping she wouldn't notice how nervous he was, how his hands shook, or how sweat gathered on his brow. When he straightened, her head fell back as she gaped up.

"You're tall." She took a step back to study him. Boston opened his arms to give her an unrestricted view, suddenly uncertain with his body, wondering if she'd find him lacking or—

"Are you rich?" she asked, taking in his tie and jacket.

Boston cringed. Why hadn't he changed out of his work clothes before coming? He'd left straight from EarthNet, wondering why he'd even bothered to go in at all. Sure, he had a pile of projects to finish, but he hadn't gotten any work done. Now he wished he'd changed into something more—God, what did dads wear?

"Ah..." He cleared his throat, not sure how to answer. He didn't want to look pompous and brag about how well off he was, but—

"Are you married?" she broke in, obviously thinking he'd taken too long to answer. "Do I have any brothers or sisters?"

"No," he said, glancing quickly at Ellie and hoping she didn't think it was because of her he'd remained single. "I'm not married, and you don't have any brothers or sisters."

"Where do you live?" Cassie went on, not even taking the time to digest his answers.

Feeling as if he were in an interview, Boston wiped his damp palms on his pant leg. "I live in Kansas City. Er, actually Overland Park."

"Kansas City?" She gaped, her eyes widening. "That place is enormous. Mom took me there once to see some Christmas lights in this really long mall."

He grinned.

"Do you have a Nintendo Wii?"

The unexpected and abrupt change of subject made him blink. "Ah, no. No Nintendo Wii." He hoped that wasn't the wrong answer, because, hell, if it made this little angel happy, he'd buy six of them.

But his daughter didn't seem to care one way or another. "My friend Keller has one," she said conversationally. "When his mom bought it, he gave me his old Xbox."

"I don't have an Xbox either," he murmured.

Cassie's eyes went huge with disbelief. "Really?"

He managed a smile. "Back in my day, there was only a regular PlayStation. And the basic Nintendo."

"Wow, you're really old then, aren't you?" Cassie grabbed his hand. "Hey, want to play on my Xbox? I just got this totally awesome Pokémon game. It's sweet."

Boston lifted his eyebrows. Sweet? Man, he *must* be old. Whatever happened to awesome, and cool, and far out?

When he realized Cassie was waiting for a response, he panicked. His daughter expected him to play a video game with her. He hadn't played one of those things in years. He'd probably be so rusty, he'd die on the first level...if they even had levels anymore.

"How about I watch you play instead?" he suggested.

"You don't want to play *with* me?" she asked, her eyes going large with disappointment.

Boston's heart turned over. The mere thought of letting her down made his breathing catch. "You'll have to show me how," he started. "I don't know—"

"Okay," Cassie said cheerfully. She grabbed his hand and led him down the hall toward her room. He followed willingly, glancing back once to check how Ellie was dealing with this. She watched her daughter with a slight smile. Then she lifted a hand to her eye but dropped it quickly when she caught Boston's gaze.

He turned back to Cassie.

"It's real easy," she was saying as they entered a lavender room edged with a pastel-flowered border. Out of his element, he faltered. But Cassidy looked right at home as she flopped onto a beanbag chair in front of an ancient television and turned on the power, all the while constantly explaining the game.

As she chattered, Boston settled onto the floor beside her and tried to listen to her instructions, though he was too busy staring at her to soak in the rules. She really did look like the pictures he'd seen of his mother at this age. It was remarkable. She was so pretty...and intelligent. He just couldn't believe something so completely perfect had come from his loins.

As they started the Pokémon game, Boston learned tidbits of her life, such as the fact that Nora Young was Keller's mother and babysat for Cassie when Ellie was at work. From his daughter's continued gossip, he guessed Nora had been the nosy neighbor he'd already met.

From just listening, he also discovered Ellie was a paralegal who worked for Keller's uncle. That information surprised him. He couldn't see Ellie working for a lawyer. She'd always acted so disgusted by the profession. Or maybe she'd been disgusted by Boston's drive to become one himself. He'd put law school before her, and that had never settled well.

He shifted uneasily and focused on Cassie. His daughter liked to talk, which was fine with him. He was too nervous to speak anyway.

The one thing that truly surprised him about her, though, was her ability to touch. Physical contact was something he distinctly remembered about Ellie...or rather the lack thereof. Touching had never come easily for Elora Trenton, and it had only made Boston want to put his hands on her all that much more. As one who'd been overwhelmed with a close-knit family, Boston had been crowded by parents, cousins, aunts, uncles and his four siblings. He'd been handled to the point he'd always sought space and privacy.

So, realizing Ellie wasn't used to her personal room being breached had been very strange to him. And it never failed to fill him with the urge to invade. He'd felt it was his duty to be the one to teach her the simple enjoyment of holding hands and giving massages, making Eskimo kisses, butterfly kisses, French kisses.

He could still remember the first moment she'd voluntarily reached for him. It had thrilled him enough to haul her off to the first available private spot and take her against the wall of a public park's bathroom. But God, he'd loved touching Ellie. He used to spend hours just stroking his fingers over—

Not that this had anything to do with their child. Boston was merely surprised Cassidy was so big on touching. She had no qualms about it whatsoever, in fact. She crawled all over him like a little monkey. She automatically set her hand on his knee when she leaned forward; she unconsciously bumped his elbow; she braced her fingers on his shoulder when she stood.

She was constantly touching him, and he loved it. For a man who had always craved more room, he only wanted to move closer to Cassidy. It was just like it'd been with her mother. He couldn't seem to get near enough to those Trenton girls.

It struck him then that Cassidy's ability to touch had probably come indirectly from him. He'd taught Ellie how to get up-close and personal, and she'd in turn passed the learned contact on to her daughter. The thought made him feel better.

Yeah, he might've missed nine years, but a part of him made it to Cassie anyway—a realization that unwillingly brought his mind back to her mother. Ellie obviously didn't hold the fact that Cassie was *his* daughter against the girl. She was a good parent, and she loved and provided for her child despite the child's paternity.

All that made him even more curious about the woman Elora had become.

****

Ellie waited until ten thirty before she approached Cassie's bedroom. All evening, she paced the kitchen, hoping she hadn't made a mistake by not immediately kicking Boston out of the house after meeting Cassie—or God, even letting him inside in the first place.

But the deep sounds of his laughter mixed with Cassidy's higher-pitched voice kept floating down the hall, telling her how pleased her daughter was. And though Ellie still wanted to pack two bags as

58

soon as he was gone and move her and Cassie to Oklahoma in the middle of the night, she was glad Cass could have this moment she'd wanted for so long.

It was time for the "moment" to end though. An hour and a half past Cassie's bedtime and five hours past the moment she'd wanted Boston out of there, Ellie inched toward her daughter's room.

Holding her breath, she tapped cautiously on the door as she opened it.

Two pair of blue eyes glanced up at her and, for a moment, she couldn't breathe. They looked so much like each other.

"Uhh..." Feeling regretful for interrupting, she hesitated. Biting her lip, she said, "Cassie usually goes to bed at nine. And...and she has school tomorrow."

Boston glanced at his Rolex, blinking. "Wow. I didn't realize it was so late."

As he stood, Cassidy clamped her arms around his legs. "Don't go!" she begged. "Please, oh, please don't go."

"I...I'm sorry, I can't stay," he told her, looking bowled over by the idea his daughter wanted him to stick around. "You have to go to school tomorrow, and I have work. Besides, I have to drive all the way back to Kansas City tonight."

"Where exactly do you live?" Cassie asked, looking curious.

Unable to watch their goodbye, Ellie stepped into the hall and quietly closed the door.

****

"...well, that's not so far away," Cassie said.

Boston reached out and sat his hand on her hair. "Not so far at all," he agreed softly. He could visit her just about every day at this distance. "Well, I guess this is goodbye," he said, noticing—in his peripheral vision—that Ellie had slipped back out of the room to give them a private farewell.

Reaching down, he scooped Cassie up, making her eyes go big.

"Cool!" she said. "Mom can't lift me like this anymore."

Boston grinned and gave her an encompassing hug. Cassie wrapped her arms and legs around him, hugging him back.

"When will I see you again?" she asked.

"Whenever you want."

"Tomorrow," she decided.

He nodded. "I could do that."

"Could we go to Chuck E. Cheese's?"

"If you'd like," he answered on a chuckle as he smoothed his hand over her hair again, still amazed he had a daughter. He was touching his daughter.

"Then I want to go to Chuck E. Cheese's," she said.

So it was set.

He was whipped.

Boston could already tell he was going to be one of those soft fathers who spoiled their little princess rotten. And he was going to love every second of it.

After tucking her under the sheets and kissing her forehead, he slipped out of Cassie's darkened room and saw a shadow of movement down the hall, coming from the kitchen.

Ellie.

His mouth went dry, but he started that way, wondering what he was going to say to her. Instinctively, he wanted to thank her. He wanted to show her his appreciation for her help in easing his way into Cassie's life tonight. He was glad she'd given him some time alone with their child. But then he figured she damn well better have...since it was her fault he didn't know Cassie in the first place.

He also wanted to yell at her, cuss her out for keeping him from that adorable, smart, remarkable little girl. He had a daughter, and he'd been absent from nine years of her life...because of Ellie. He wanted to hate her as much as he wanted to share this magical moment with her. He had this strange urge to go into the kitchen, sit down and tell her about all these amazing feelings surging through him.

Boston didn't give into any of his urges, however. Instead, he stopped in the opening of the kitchen and paused.

She sat at the table where it looked like she was paying bills. Though he was curious just how well—or not so well—she was doing financially, he stayed rooted in the doorway. Ellie slipped off a pair of reading glasses that made her look sexily astute. The wary gaze she sent him, however, reminded him how they weren't friends and how he shouldn't be thinking of her cute button nose or large brown eyes.

He didn't want to be attracted. He was still mad at her. Yet, unable to forget the physical relationship they'd once shared, he ached with hungry nostalgia.

"I'm heading out," he said.

She nodded and rested her elbows on the tabletop.

He couldn't seem to move and just stood there, staring at her for another moment.

"Some time," he started, "we're going to have to get together and talk about custody."

Ellie's face drained of color. But she didn't say anything. She merely turned back to her work, ignoring him.

Realizing he'd outstayed his welcome—not that there'd been one from her anyway—he tipped his head in farewell and backed away from the room.

****

Well...he was a father now. He had a little girl who was absolutely perfect. He hadn't realized he'd been nervous over what she'd be like until the relief over having a smart, cute, well-behaved daughter swamped him.

Ellie had done an excellent job raising her.

Ellie.

Boston lifted a hand and pressed his palm to the side of his aching head. God, he didn't want to think about her too. There was too much other stuff going on right now, though he had to admit the last ten years had been kind to her in the looks department. Very kind. She'd been pretty at nineteen, but at...what would she be now...twenty-nine? Thirty? Whatever. The fact remained, she was gorgeous.

Catching her stripping in the kitchen hadn't deterred that conclusion either. Ten years...and his body had still reacted like the horny twenty-two-year-old he'd been so long ago when he'd stepped into the doorway and found her with her shirt off and her arms over her head.

Oh yeah, she'd definitely aged nicely. Her breasts specifically.

Boston had accidentally overheard two of his sisters discussing their breasts after having children. One had complained that hers had shrunk and another was bemoaning the fact that she'd only gotten bigger. Though Boston had booked it out of the room as soon as he'd stumbled across such a conversation—hell no, he didn't want to hear about his sisters' breasts—their words had left a distinct, lasting memory.

And when he'd seen Ellie all shirtless and inviting, he thought, oh yeah, she'd gotten bigger after having Cassie. He would definitely know, too. Once upon a time, he'd imprinted every inch of her body into his brain. And her boobs had *not* been that full ten years ago. These days they'd probably fill his hands to overflowing.

Boston let out an aggravated groan. He'd wanted to test his theory. He'd wanted to stroll over to her, tug that shirt right back off, and cover her with his hungry fingers. He missed her body more than he'd ever missed anything, no matter how much he denied it.

He'd also wanted to give her a disdainful look and mutter something nasty like, "Not interested," or, "Been there, done that." But his mouth had been too dry to say anything, so he'd settled for a snort and forced himself to turn away like he didn't want to bury himself inside her for old time's sake.

As he'd moved off, he'd come across pictures and graded papers on the refrigerator. Instantly, his mind had returned to the right track.

Cassidy.

He was there for Cassie. Not Ellie. Never Ellie. He'd burned the Ellie bridge, then he'd set the whole damn forest on fire so another could never be rebuilt in its place. And then he'd gone and flooded the banks between them. There was no way, no how, he'd ever cross back over. Too much pain and anger and hurt had filled their last few weeks together.

Yet, from the rubble of their ruined relationship, an amazing child had emerged.

Except for those few weeks when he was about to be a daddy, he hadn't thought about having his own child. And back then, he'd been too freaked out to think much at all. Now, however, his mind whirled. He was a father. He had a daughter. And he wanted her.

Already thinking up a contract for parental rights, Boston turned down his street. Tomorrow, he'd have to research custody and child support. God, he probably owed a fortune in child support. He was going to have to calculate that and be prepared in case Ellie fought back. Still deep in thought, he pulled into his drive and sucked in a breath, slamming on the brakes when he found his way blocked.

Damn, he should've expected this. Half a dozen cars—none his own—crowded into his half-circle drive. His parents', his brother's, Cameron and Olivia's automobile, along with all his sisters' cars sat waiting for him.

As he parked behind his parents' Dodge Avenger, the front door of his house opened and the hoard spilled out, making him regret ever giving anyone a spare key.

Staying in his Infiniti a moment after killing the engine, Boston closed his eyes and wondered briefly why he couldn't have been born an orphan. He didn't want company right now. He didn't want all the questions and concerns. He just wanted to lock himself inside his house and quietly digest the evening he'd just spent with Cassie...and Ellie.

But no, there was no way that was going to happen. Not with his family. His door was pulled open and Olivia's voice immediately asked, "Is she yours?"

A dozen people crowded the opened space as he blew out a lungful of air and climbed from the driver's seat. Someone shut the door behind him, and he studied the quiet, expectant faces. It was after midnight, but no one seemed concerned about the time...or even tired for that matter. His yard lamp spotlighted them, and he could tell they were all going to get about as much sleep tonight as he was, which was absolutely zilch.

Relishing the moment of quiet, Boston slid his hands into his pockets before he murmured, "She's mine."

And yes, here it came. The flood of words that poured forth about knocked him off his feet. Everyone spoke at once, yet he couldn't hear anything a single person said.

Glowering at his brother standing beside him, Boston hissed, "Couldn't have kept your big trap shut for one more day, could you?"

Monty opened his mouth to defend himself, but Olivia jumped in. "He didn't spread the news. I did."

Whirling toward her, Boston gaped at his cousin's wife. He couldn't rail at her the way he could his brother, but he did send her an irritated scowl.

"And thank God she did," his mother, Diane Kincaid, cut in. "Who *knows* when your father and I would've learned we have another grandchild." She paused as if suddenly realizing her own words. Then, setting a hand on her head, she looked like she was going to pass out as she rasped, "Oh my God. That makes seven. I have *seven* grandchildren."

Her husband, Lincoln, caught her arm to keep her steady. As two of her daughters reached out to help her as well, Boston clenched his teeth to keep from apologizing.

"I was going to tell you," he said. "Just as soon as I found out one way or another."

"Oh, like you told us when this woman got pregnant ten years ago?" Diane asked, straightening from her near swoon. "Montgomery said you thought she'd had a miscarriage, so you obviously knew you'd gotten her pregnant at one point."

Boston seared an arch look Montgomery's way.

"Hey," Montgomery said, lifting his hands defensively. "They already knew most of it by then. I just filled in the details."

"What's the girl like?" his sister, Madison, asked.

"Where exactly do they live?" Cameron butted in. "What part of Lawrence?"

"How could you not tell us you'd impregnated someone, Boston?" his mother wailed. "We never met this girl...Ellie whoever. I don't even remember you mentioning her. And why in the world did you not stick around long enough to realize she hadn't had any kind of miscarriage? I don't understand how you could have a child and not even—"

"Look, Mom," Boston cut in wearily, setting a hand on his aching temple. "Can I get a rain check on the lecture tonight? I just found out I have a daughter, for God's sake. I need..."

Feeling a little woozy himself, his knees buckled slightly. He caught himself before going down, but a handful of family surged forward anyway, catching him.

"Let's get him inside," his father said, even as his brothers-in-law started to haul him toward the front door.

Shrugging them off, Boston mumbled, "I'm fine." No one seemed to listen until he shouted, "Hey! I can walk by myself."

A dozen pair of hands eased off, but they all stayed suffocatingly close as if expecting him to topple over any second.

"Let's head inside anyway," Lincoln Kincaid said, taking charge of the situation. "There's no reason to discuss this on the front lawn."

And so, everyone shifted toward the house. Monty's cell phone rang on the way. As soon as he flipped it open, he was already saying, "She's his. She's really his daughter!" Boston could only guess it was some aunt or uncle or cousin on the other end of the line.

Once inside, Madison ushered him toward a chair as his other two sisters, Cheyenne and Helena, hurried off together to get him a drink.

"Now, tell us about the girl," his mom demanded, pacing the floor in front of him. "Her name's Cassie, right?"

Boston nodded. "Cassidy Diane Trenton."

"Diane?" his mother repeated, falling to a stop and lifting her head. When Boston bobbed his head in affirmation, she blinked rapidly. Lifting a hand to her face, she wiped her eyes. "She's named after me?"

"What's she look like?" Olivia asked eagerly.

"Did you get to meet her?" Shannon wanted to know.

"I spent over four hours with her," Boston reported.

The room quieted, everyone eager for the news.

"What's she like?" Monty asked.

"She's...she's...well, she's perfect," was the only description Boston could think to give. "Absolutely perfect."

The room sighed in contentment.

"She, uh, she's extremely smart," he added. "I saw a math test on the refrigerator, and she was graded a ninety-eight percent."

"She gets that from me," Diane announced, grinning.

"She looks like you too," Boston said.

"Really?" his mother gasped, squeezing Helena's hand when her oldest daughter reached out.

"I mean, she's got Ellie's features: nose, mouth, and the shape of her eyes. And she's got Dad's coloring with his straight black hair and blue eyes...but she still looks just like those pictures of you when you were that age."

"Oh, wow," Diane whispered, fanning her tear-stained face. "This is so amazing."

"She's in a tumbling class," Boston said, mentioning whatever fact came to mind. "And soccer. And her best friend is a boy who lives next door. Ellie says she's his defender when bullies try to pick on him. And she's got a stubborn streak a mile wide. I could tell that immediately when El had her go take a bath. But she's still obedient. Even though she didn't want to do something, she still did what her mom told her to do. And...and..."

As he realized how badly he was rambling, his

voice faded.

"That's it," Diane said, "I want to meet her. Right now." She actually turned toward the exit as if prepared to leave that very moment for Lawrence.

"Whoa!" Boston said, jumping to his feet. "No one bothers them."

Everyone despised that idea, and they all objected...loudly.

"Hey!" Boston yelled above the roar. "Do you know how intimidating it would be to have fifty strangers invade them all at once?"

"There's not fifty of us. Thirty tops, counting all the aunts, uncles and cousins," someone said just as another person retaliated with, "But we're *family*."

"They still don't know you," Boston argued. "So stay away for a while, okay? As soon as I work out custody with Ellie, I'll bring Cassidy out and you can all meet her one household at a time."

"Your father and I get to meet her first," Diane inserted before anyone else could call dibs.

"Oh, oh! Cam and me second," Olivia said quickly, lifting her hand and wiggling her fingers.

"So, when will you be working out custody issues?" Cameron wanted to know.

"I figure I'll whip up a draft tonight and run the basic plan by Helena in the morning to see what she thinks." He glanced at his older sister, who was also a lawyer.

She nodded in affirmation. "Of course. I'll help any way I can."

"Then I'll approach Ellie tomorrow evening when I go out there again," he added. "Cassie wants me to take her to Chuck E. Cheese's."

"Tomorrow?" Diane gasped. "You're seeing her again tomorrow? Well, good. We'll come with you."

"No! No, I already told you, you're going to scare her."

"Hey, it's a free country. If I show up at the

Chuck E. Cheese's in Lawrence tomorrow, how're you going to stop me?"

Boston sighed, already well aware he fought a losing battle.

Chapter Six

At five till noon the next day, Nora Young swept into Winston Young's law office where her brother-in-law stood over Ellie's desk, giving her last-minute instructions before he went to lunch.

"Table it, Winston," Nora interjected. "Ellie can't work through her dinner hour for you today. I'm taking her out to eat."

"But—"

"The girl's going to shrivel up and starve if you keep denying her a break."

Winston had never been able to stand up to his brother's wife, so he frowned in defeat and turned beseechingly to Ellie. "Well...just make sure this is the first thing you do once you return."

"Of course," Ellie answered and yelped in surprise as Nora grabbed her wrist and tugged her from the office.

In minutes, she found herself seated in the restaurant across the street with Nora, ordering a drink. Blinking herself to the present as she watched the waiter walk away, Ellie suddenly realized her friend had just ordered a cosmopolitan.

"I can't drink alcohol." She whirled toward Nora incredulously. "I have to go back to work after this."

"Oh, honey," Nora murmured and sighed as she reached across the table and patted Ellie's hand in a sympathetic gesture. "That was for me. I ordered you your usual Diet Coke."

"Oh." Ellie sat back in her booth seat and ran her fingers through her hair, wishing she could have the cosmo instead.

Nora made a tut-tutting sound. "Been a long morning?"

Ellie massaged her temples, pressing hard. A throbbing resistance pushed right back. "I don't know what to do, Nora."

"Well, first of all, you're going to bring me up to date. All I know is that Keller came home last night from your place, saying you kicked him out because Cassie's dad was there."

Ellie swallowed.

"And half an hour before you got home, that tall, dark and hot stranger showed up, lingering around your place, waiting around for you like some lovesick puppy dog." She shrugged. "He told me he was a relative and hadn't seen you since before Cassie was born. Course I assumed he meant he was related to *you*, not your daughter. It never occurred to me he might be her *father*."

Ellie dropped her hands from her temples and gaped at her friend. "Wait. What? You talked to Boston?"

"Boston," Nora repeated, lifting her eyebrows in interest. "Is that his name? Hmmm. I like it. Very original. Boston what?"

"What'd he say to you?"

"I just told you. He said he was a relative and hadn't seen you in a long time. Oh, and that you were expecting him but he made it to town earlier than he thought he would."

Ellie snorted. "I most certainly was not expecting him."

"He's really Cassidy's dad?" Nora asked in awe. When Ellie sent her a miserable nod, Nora's jaw dropped. "Wow. Where's he been all these years?"

"Kansas City, I guess."

"And what's he doing there when his daughter's here?" Nora wanted to know.

Ellie averted her face and bit her lip. "I kind of

told him I had a miscarriage."

"You...*what*?" Nora gaped at her like she'd lost her mind, making Ellie flush. "Oh, now I'm going to have to hear the whole story."

Ellie sighed, giving in. "We'd already broken up by the time I found out I was pregnant. Boston went crazy when I told him, accusing me of trying to trap him, of purposely getting pregnant to get him back. He blamed it all on me."

"The jerk," Nora muttered, falling back in her chair. "Why are men such jerks?" Waving her own question away, she leaned forward and confidentially asked, "Okay. Aside from the fact that he's a guy and all guys are scum, why did it end between you two in the first place?"

The answer came to Ellie in a brilliantly clear memory. "He cheated on me," she murmured, though she was already drifting toward the past, sitting in early American history class and listening to Heather Grimaldi talk with her friends about Boston Kincaid, whom she'd spent the evening with at some wild dorm party.

And suddenly, Ellie was nineteen again, in Boston's dorm room, confronting him.

****

"What did you do last Friday when I was working?" she asked, feeling like she had to dive straight to the point or she'd never be able to discover the truth.

Boston wouldn't meet her gaze as he shrugged. "I don't know. Why?"

She shrugged too and had to focus on something else as she said, "So, you didn't meet some redhead named Heather and go back to her apartment with her?"

His silence was the loudest confession he could've made.

Ellie swallowed. "Okay," she said calmly. "I'll

take that as a yes."

Boston shoved his hands into his pockets and stared fixedly out his room's single window. A ray of light glimmered in and reflected a blue-black glow over his hair. He looked so beautiful it nearly took her breath away. But thinking about her beautiful lover with another woman killed her.

He was hers.

"Was that the first time?" she asked hoarsely.

Finally, he lifted his face Their gazes met. "Does it matter?"

Ellie's already broken heart crumbled into dust. Tears rushed up her throat, but she choked them back with a fit of stubborn pride. She'd be damned before she let Boston Kincaid see her cry.

"No," she whispered, looking down at her hands. "I guess it doesn't." She blinked a few times. Her eyes burned but remained dry.

Silence grew thick between them. Boston returned to gazing out the window. Ellie stared at his back and swallowed a lump in her throat that must've been her pride washing down her esophagus because the next words out of her mouth were, "Are you going to do it again?"

His shoulders tensed fractionally. The remaining ashes of her pulverized heart screamed out, begging him to say he was sorry and promise it'd never happen again.

She would forgive him.

In that moment, if he'd repented, she would've forgiven anything.

But he didn't. He hitched a shoulder and softly replied, "I don't know."

Ellie froze. Her blood turned to ice. "So...you're just going to keep cheating on me? Is that what you're saying?"

He whirled around at that question. "Cheating?" he repeated in confusion.

"Yes!" she wailed, throwing her hands in the air. "What do you call it when you're in a relationship with one girl and you go out and—"

"Wait a second," he interrupting, taking a step toward her. "I never said *anything* to you to suggest we were in a relationship. I never made you any promises. What made you think this thing between us was exclusive?"

For a moment, she could only stare at him blankly. Was he kidding?

Then she glared and set her hands on her hips. "Oh, I don't know. Maybe the fact that we have been just *that* for the past seven months. You'd think after that much time, it'd be an unspoken agreement. You didn't have to *say* anything. I gave you my virginity, Boston. I gave you—"

"What does that have to do with—"

"It has to do with *everything*!" she squawked in growing alarm. "I gave you...I gave you—"

"Yeah, you did," he said. "You *gave* it. Willingly. I didn't force anything from you. I didn't demand or manipulate. And I *never* made you any promises. Damn it, Ellie. I thought you understood what was going on here."

She blinked in utter bewilderment. "I don't understand any of this."

Once again, he was unable to make eye contact. He sighed and scrubbed a hand over his forehead until a red mark appeared. "Well, it still doesn't matter," he mumbled more to himself than her. "It's almost May anyway."

"May? What happens in May?" A terrible feeling crept up the back of her neck, making the little hairs jerk to attention.

He lifted his face and sent her an incredulous look. "I graduate," he reminded her. "I leave and go to Yale."

She shrugged. "So?"

"So..." He frowned, obviously not understanding her confusion. "You're staying here."

The fear that washed through her had her gazing at him in frozen horror. Suddenly, she understood everything. "Oh, I get it," she murmured on a nod. "You go. I stay. That automatically means it's over, huh?"

"Look, Ellie." He let out an uncomfortable sound. "You have your plans, and I have mine. You've always known what I was going to do. Why're you acting like—"

"I have to go," she said abruptly.

"Whoa," Boston said, reaching out to grab her arm.

She paused and stared up at him with her dry, burning eyes.

He shook his head in confusion. "That's it, then? You're just going to walk out. No goodbye, no nothing?"

Ellie snorted. She couldn't believe he actually expected her to be cordial. Then again, she didn't know why she was surprised by his assumption. He hadn't planned on trying to make a long-distance relationship work in the first place, which completely blew her mind. So obviously, she didn't know him like she thought she had.

"Gee," she sneered bitterly. "Let me think. You cheated on me and planned on breaking up in five weeks anyway. So, yeah, I'd say that's it." She glanced pointedly down at his fingers on her arm. "Let go."

His grip tightened. "Ellie."

As soon as she looked up, she realized it was a mistake. The utter panic in his eyes had her melting. If he did anything, said one thing to get her back, she'd crawl into his arms and forget what a snake he was. And wouldn't that make her an utter fool.

"I..." he started and paused to lick his dried lips.

Ellie swallowed, waiting. Her crushed heart obviously didn't know it was broken, because it beat hard and fast in her chest, anxious to hear his words to bring them back together.

He wanted to say them. She could see it in his eyes. He didn't want her to go.

But he surprised them both when he disengaged his fingers and stepped back. "Goodbye then."

Three weeks later, she was packing her dorm bathroom and preparing to head home for summer break when she came across her supply of tampons and realized she hadn't had her period in a long time...too long. Absolutely freaking out over the thought she might be pregnant, she'd raced to the drugstore and bought a home pregnancy test. When it came up positive, she rushed back out and bought another. Three tests later, she finally admitted defeat. Sitting on her small bed, she wept.

It took two days to gather the courage to tell Boston. She remembered how chilly the breeze had been on her slow walk across campus to his apartment building. Her cheeks had been windburned; she had her jacket wrapped snuggly around her with her fisted hands buried deep in her pockets. There were deep-purplish hollows under her eyes from lack of sleep when she knocked on his door.

Boston didn't look much better when he pulled it open. His hair was a mess, his clothes were rumpled, and his eyes were bloodshot. But the expression in his gaze when he caught sight of her had her hopes lifting. His face lit like he'd actually missed her as much as she'd missed him.

Had he felt more for her than he'd claimed?

But with his next breath, he seemed to pull taut, like he'd just reminded himself they were no longer together. His eyes frosted over and his lips tightened. "Ellie," he said in an icy tone.

She looked down but just as quickly lifted her head, demanding herself to be strong. "May I come in?"

She thought he might tell her no; then he shrugged as if it made no difference and stepped aside, letting the door swing open. His eyes were hard on her as she passed. Ellie went straight to his bed and sat on the edge before lifting her face. Boston closed the door and leaned back against it, staring at her coldly. He made no move to sit.

Figuring if he wouldn't sit, then she couldn't either, Ellie scrambled back to her feet. For a moment, she merely stood there, wondering how she was going to do this. How was she going to tell him? It all felt too surreal.

When she'd first seen him in Mack's Burger House, she'd thought of him as something unattainable, someone she could never get close to. Then as time passed, and he talked her into that first date, it felt like she was living in a dream. She was with Boston Kincaid. She couldn't believe it. But now it was over and she still thought of their time together as a dream.

The child growing inside her was real, though. She looked at the man with whom she'd shared so many intimacies. He merely glared back. Wincing, she knew, deep down, he wouldn't take the news well.

She hated the fact he blocked the door. She wanted an escape route handy.

"Well?" he demanded.

Ellie took a deep breath, but once she met his gaze, she had to drop her head.

"I'm pregnant," she said more to her feet than she did to him.

He didn't respond. For the longest time, she was unable to lift her eyes. When she managed to look up and gauge his reaction, she sucked in a breath. He was just staring at her as if he hadn't heard her, as if he was in a movie and someone had pushed pause. Then he blinked rapidly and frowned, shifting his gaze to her still-flat stomach.

He jerked from the door so suddenly she yelped. As he strode toward her with a look on his face that made her eyes go wide in alarm, Ellie stumbled a step back and would've tripped over her own feet and gone sprawling if Boston hadn't reached out and caught her. But once he had his hand on her, he yanked her close, melding their chests together.

"Boston!" she gasped.

He gritted his teeth, his nostrils flaring. "You lying little—"

Ellie's mouth fell open. "*What*!? I..." The grip he had on her wrist, which was only tightening, had her grabbing his shoulder. "Stop!"

He blinked at his hold and let go abruptly enough that she fell back. He looked so shocked he'd actually hurt her, he could only gape for a moment. But he shook his head, his face turning an angry red.

"You would stop at nothing, wouldn't you?" he growled. "Well, let me warn you now, Ellie. Trying to get me back by faking a pregnancy is a real bad idea."

Ellie gaped and stuttered, "Wha-wha-what?" How could he actually think she was lying?

He looked away and snorted. "You make me sick."

Ellie's hands fisted at her sides. She wanted to go to him and shake, slap, or pound some sense into him. But she just stood there, stewing. How dare he think she'd made this up?

Straightening her shoulders, she leveled him with a lethal glower and stiffly said, "If you don't want anything to do with the baby, that's fine with me. I'd hate for my child to have a cheating jerk for a father anyway."

With that said, she moved around him and walked determinedly toward the exit. But just as she reached for the handle and began to open it, a palm reached around her and slapped the door shut. She stared at the closed portal and felt her rigid resolve slip.

Behind her, Boston hissed, "What's your game?"

Ellie swallowed and lifted her head a little as she still continued to stare at the door. There was no way she could face him right then. She just knew she'd cry if she did.

"I assure you," she said, proud there wasn't even a tremor in her steady voice, "this is no game."

"I don't believe you."

Ellie snorted. "That's obvious."

"Then why did you come here?"

Unable to take it any longer, she leaned forward and rested her cheek on the door panel. Pressing her hand against the cool surface and wishing he'd let her leave already, she whispered in desperation. "Please. Just let me go."

Boston touched her, and the gentle pressure of his hand on the back of her shoulder was her undoing. The first tear tracked down her cheek. She blinked rapidly, but instead of drying her lashes, the move only caused another droplet to fall.

"Ellie," he whispered. "Stop scaring the shit out of me. What's going on? Why are you doing this?"

She sniffed in the rest of the tears and wiped at her face. "I don't know what to do," she admitted, hauling in a deep, shuddering breath. Finally, she turned and was satisfied to see he was beginning to appear unnerved. "I...it...It seemed like the decent thing to let you know," she said, and her voice broke. "So, I've done my job. Now let me out." She turned and wrapped her hand around the doorknob, but he only leaned his full weight against the door, moving closer to her in the process.

She closed her eyes, trying to block the feel of his warm chest against her back.

"I need proof," he said after a moment. "You're going to have to take a test."

Ellie laughed, a bitter sound. "I've already taken five. They were all positive."

That answer seemed to get through to him more than anything. He shuddered. Now that he knew she'd been just as disbelieving as he was, he had to know she was telling the truth.

"Well, you're taking another," he rasped.

Unfazed, Ellie merely shrugged. "Fine. Whatever."

"Right now."

Ellie looked up at him. "I said okay."

An hour later, he dropped onto his bed and cradled his head in his hands. Ellie stood frigidly by the door, torn between escape and going to him to share their mutual fear. She'd just decided to move toward him when he lifted his face.

"Did you do it on purpose?"

She fell to a stop and tilted her head. "Do what?"

"Don't act innocent, Ellie," he growled. "Did you get pregnant on purpose?"

Her lips parted, emitting a disbelieving puff of air. "Why would I purposely get pregnant?"

"Oh, get real," he snarled. "You come from a rundown trailer park in Nowhere, Tennessee." While he came from money and security, neither of them had to add. "You probably thought you'd struck it big time when I fell into your lap."

For a full ten seconds, Ellie was too stunned to speak. She couldn't believe his crudity, couldn't believe he would think of her this way.

First of all, she didn't need his money. She'd done without, and she could continue to do without. Secondly, she didn't see how she could have even dreamed up a baby trap to keep him in the relationship when she'd had no idea the relationship had been about to crumble. And thirdly, how could he think she'd do something so underhanded as to trick him? Didn't he know her at all after eight months?

There was no way she'd bring an innocent child into the mix if she thought there was any kind of trouble in paradise.

What followed was the biggest, longest, loudest argument she'd ever had with anyone. Names were called, accusations were made, feelings were hurt. Ellie tried to keep up, but Boston managed to do most of the destruction. And when the yelling was over and the smoke cleared, Ellie was still pregnant, and Boston blamed her.

He couldn't tell his parents; he was too humiliated. She'd always assumed he just wasn't close to his family. That was why he'd never talked to her about them, why he'd never introduced her to them. But then she caught him calling his mother once; she listened to him talk to her on the phone and realized they meant a lot more to him that she'd ever thought. She was the one who hadn't meant enough. She was the one who hadn't been worthy enough to meet his hallowed family.

As he hung up from that call and closed his eyes, letting out a long, tired breath, Ellie knew he'd been too embarrassed to announce he'd gotten a no-one girl from nowhere, Tennessee pregnant. Instead, he'd lied and told his mom he was staying in Lawrence through the summer because he'd found a job. He made no mention of Ellie or their baby.

Things changed considerably after that. They'd broken up weeks before, but it was officially over from that point on. He tried to be polite to her, but neither of them could stop the cool distance. And all too often, they fell into the stupidest fights.

After trying to pick out baby names, with him shooting all of her suggestions down, Ellie sighed in disgust. "Well, want *do* you want, Boston?" she growled.

He spat back, "I don't know! Okay? I do not know. All I can tell you is what I don't want."

"Oh?" she asked cockily. "And what's that?"

"Well, for starters, I don't want to be sitting here picking out baby names. I don't want to be seven months from becoming a father. I don't want to tell my parents I've made the biggest mistake of my life. I don't want to miss my first semester at Yale."

Blowing out a stream of curses under his breath, he surged to his feet and stormed off. And hormonal freak Ellie had become, she curled into a ball and cried.

Boston called her that night at one in the morning to apologize. He actually sounded sincere in his regret as he offered her an olive branch by announcing he liked the name Cassie. But there was still that note of desperation in his voice, telling her loud and clear how trapped he felt; he just wanted to be free of it all. He wanted out, and he wanted to attend Yale.

Getting into a bus accident the next day had been like providence. Ellie hadn't really been hurt. She'd barely gotten jostled, but the encounter had made her bleed and fearing for the baby, she'd agreed to go to the hospital. She'd been looked over and immediately cleared. She'd actually been waiting to be signed out when Boston had rushed into the emergency room where she was lounging on a cot.

She hadn't planned on lying to him. It'd been a spur of the moment thing that surprised her even as she did it.

There was a mixture of guilt and concern in his eyes when he stepped into her hospital room, like he felt as if he'd wished this kind of tragedy on her and now that his wish was granted, he realized how wrong it had been to want it. But he came to her anyway, slowly, like a repenting sinner approaching the confessional.

"How are you?" he asked softly.

All she could do was nod and close her eyes. His trembling hand on her brow made her start crying all over again. When she looked up at him, he actually looked scared. "What about the baby?"

The idea hit her so suddenly, she didn't even really have time to change her mind before she asked, "Have you told your parents yet?"

He looked distinctly ashamed before he slid his gaze away and mumbled, "Not yet."

"Good," she rasped. "Because there's nothing to tell them anymore."

Boston whirled back in shock. "What?"

"There is no baby," she lied. "The baby's gone."

"You...you had a miscarriage?" She couldn't quite read how the news hit him. He looked struck, sure, surprised to say the least. His eyes seared into hers, so she could plainly see the thoughts and feelings flash through him. But they moved and changed so quickly, she doubted even he knew what was going through his head at that moment.

She turned her face aside. "I just want to be left alone, Boston. I want to finish college, go home to my aunt, and forget this ever happened. And you have to leave for me to do that. So, please...just go. I never want to see you again. I want to move on and forget."

He stared at her with wide eyes, clearly unable to believe she was sending him away. For the briefest of moments, he looked hurt. If he'd kept that expression, if he'd done one thing to give her an ounce of consolation, she probably would've broken down and told him the truth.

But after taking a deep breath and clearing his

face of all emotion, he nodded once and turned away. Ellie watched him leave; his stiff, straight back was the last thing she saw...for ten years.

****

"Well, I can understand why you did it," Nora said, jerking Ellie to the present.

She hadn't realized she'd spilled out most of her story aloud until her friend added, "You had a child to protect, and this jerk who'd just cheated on you was making a huge fuss. If you want my opinion, I'd say you did the right thing. If you'd kept him from going on to Yale and passing his bar, he would've held that against you for the rest of your life and made all three of you miserable. I swear, Mendel resents Keller and me, and we weren't even forced on him. We actually *planned* on getting married and starting a family. It's not my damn fault he suddenly realized this isn't the life he wanted..."

Nora fell quiet and her eyes flashed guiltily toward Ellie's, as if she'd just realized she'd gone off on her own tangent. Forcing a smile, she reached out and took Ellie's hand. "You did the right thing," she assured her. "You and Cassie have done beautifully without him."

Ellie nodded but bit her lip because she couldn't keep the doubt from plaguing her. A week ago, she would've agreed wholeheartedly with Nora. Boston had been so mad at her; he would've made a crappy dad. But now...now that she'd seen him ten years matured and then seen how happy Cassie was meeting him and actually liking him, she wasn't certain of anything. She'd do any number of things for her daughter. She might even let Boston Kincaid back into her life to make her little girl happy.

"Might" being the word of the day.

"Did you know Keller was the one who found him?" she asked.

After she explained the boy's involvement, Nora

84

merely shook her head and grumbled, "I told Mendel not to leave that credit card lying around. The idiot." But she didn't look too upset. Rather she looked proud of her genius son. "I swear, someday, the FBI is going to show up on my doorstep because they've caught him cracking into top secret files. He's too smart for his own good."

Ellie nodded sadly. "He probably should've skipped those grades when the principal came to talk to you about raising his level of education."

Nora sighed. "I know, but when he found out Cassidy wouldn't be coming with him, he refused. He won't do anything without her."

Ellie had to agree. "They are quite a pair."

Nora nodded, and the two fell silent. Ellie realized they'd drifted off onto the same thought pattern when Nora sighed and asked, "So, what're you going to do about Mr. Daddy?"

Ellie let out a breath. "I have no idea."

Her first instinct was to pack up Cassie and get them as far away as they could go. But her daughter would hate her forever if she did that. And Ellie knew the child needed a male figure in her life. But did that man have to be Boston?

"I'm kind of hoping he forgets about us and never comes back again."

Chapter Seven

Boston took off work early in order to spend more time with his daughter at Chuck E. Cheese's. But when he reached Ellie's place and knocked on the door, no one answered. Immediately disappointed, he shoved his hands in his pockets and scowled at the entrance as if it was personally keeping his child from him.

It was a Wednesday afternoon, and Cassie should've been out of school by now. She hadn't mentioned any after-school activities she had to be at today when he'd talked to her last night, but that didn't mean she wouldn't be at one of them.

Moodily wondering what he was going to do until five thirty, he toed a brown, wrinkled leaf off the porch and watched it flutter into the yard. He didn't want to skulk around Ellie's house two afternoons in a row. It reminded him too much of the days when he was so anxious to see her, he'd always show up early for their dates only to wait in the hall outside her dorm room until she was ready.

Boston groaned and ran his hands through his hair, feeling an antsy trepidation. He just wanted to see his daughter, damn it. He didn't want to think about her mother.

"Hey, Cassie!" a boy's voice yelled from the next door neighbor's backyard as if answering Boston's unspoken prayer. "Watch this."

The sound of his daughter's laugh followed moments later.

Amazed he could actually discern her laugh, Boston stood in frozen wonder for a second. Yes, that was definitely his little girl howling with giggles. As euphoria filled him, he leaped off the cracked, uneven steps and started off. Following the sounds of Cassie's voice, he strolled back between the two houses.

In the neighbor's backyard, he found Cassie and her friend, Keller. Sitting on the deck at the table under a large umbrella and reading a book lounged the nosy neighbor who'd come over to grill him the day before.

Boston stopped and took in the scene of Cassidy climbing a ladder to a huge tree house. Keller had already reached the top and was watching her ascend, waiting impatiently from the looks of it.

As Boston moved closer, no one noticed his presence. He was fully in their yard before Cassie finally glanced over and saw him. She'd just reached the top of the ladder and was about to disappear inside the tree house when she glanced back.

"Dad!" she screamed, her excitement lighting up her entire face.

Nora lifted her face and let out a startled yelp. Dropping her book, she leapt to her feet and started off the porch just as Cassie scurried back down the ladder.

Being called "Dad" for the first time sent a shiver though Boston. Good Lord. He really was a dad. And he kind of liked it. He'd never thought he'd cherish the idea of having children. Sure, he'd figured he'd probably get married some day and eventually start a family. But he'd just thought of it as part of life. Now, here he was, a father, and he loved the sound of Cassie calling him "Dad."

Forgetting about the babysitter, Boston started toward his child.

Nora reached the edge of the porch just as Cassie reached him. His daughter ran toward him full force and threw her arms open as Boston swooped down to catch her.

It felt good to hold her. Incredibly good. He couldn't help but wonder what it would've been like to hold her the minute she was born, to feel how weightless she was and look into her newborn eyes. A bitter resentment filled him, but he pushed it down and focused on appreciating the nine-year-old she had grown to be.

"You came!" she said, burying her face in his collar a second before pulling back to beam up at him. "You really, really came!"

Boston laughed at her obvious excitement. "I said I would," he answered, a little upset she had to doubt him.

If only Ellie hadn't sent him away, his daughter would never have any reason to think he couldn't keep his word.

Cassie glanced over at the two on the porch. Her friend, Keller, had climbed down the ladder as well and hovered next to his mother.

"Keller," Cassie called. "Nora. This is my dad."

Boston set Cassie down and turned to the woman.

The regal-looking lady stared back, blinking repeatedly. "Well, my word," she said. "Cassidy kept saying her father was going to come see her today, but I thought...Ellie didn't mention any of this to me."

"We're going to Chuck E. Cheese's," Cassie announced happily, taking Boston's hand. Her fingers were so small and soft, he looked down at their connection, startled. He was holding his daughter's hand like it was the most normal action in the world.

Looking up, his chest swelled. "You must be Nora."

She gave him a slight nod, returning, "And you must be Boston." There was a cool edge to her voice today; she wasn't quite as accepting as she'd been yesterday when she thought he was merely a long-distance relation. Yeah, he thought bitterly, Ellie had definitely gotten a hold of her. And probably told all.

Realizing she was Team Ellie, and probably knew more dirt about him than most people did, he turned away uncomfortably and focused his attention on Cassie. "Are you ready to go?"

She started to hop up and down. "I've been ready since last night," she nearly exploded.

"Cassie," Keller said from between gritted teeth as if he was trying to get her attention.

Cassie glanced at her friend. "Oh, yeah," she added to Boston. "Keller wants to come too."

"Keller!" Nora gasped in appalled shock.

Boston studied the small boy who hovered by his mother's legs and stared disappointedly down at his shoes. His heart went out to the poor kid.

"Cassidy wants to spend time alone with her father," Nora berated. "You can't just—"

"Actually," Boston said, cutting in and grinning at Nora, "it's fine. I'm pretty sure most of my family will show up, and there're a lot of cousins his and Cassie's age. So, really, it's no problem if he came along."

Truth be told, he'd like to get on Nora Young's good side. And if that meant taking her son to Chuck E. Cheese's, he'd do it.

But Nora glanced at him as if he were insane. "Are you sure about this?" she asked hesitantly. "His bedtime is half an hour earlier than Cassie's at eight thirty."

No, he wasn't sure about anything anymore. But he merely said, "It's fine. Really."

"Well, all right then," Nora relented, and the two children cheered, dancing around each other. "Let me get you some money for Keller's—"

"Don't worry about it," Boston said, lifting a hand to stop her. When she paused to send him a surprised look, he smiled. "I can cover it."

Nora blinked a couple more times before she matched his smile, flushing a bit in the cheeks. "All right then," she said, quickly turning away from him as if embarrassed. "You two have fun with Mr...." She frowned slightly when she realized didn't know his last name.

"Kincaid," he told her, sticking out his hand and realizing he'd just won over the neighbor lady despite what Ellie had probably told her. "But, please, call me Boston."

****

"He *what*?"

Ellie stared at Nora with wide eyes, thinking her neighbor had to be joking...*praying* she was joking.

Nora paused. "He took the kids to Chuck E. Cheese's," she said slowly, as if talking too fast might get her into trouble. "Why are you looking so alarmed?" she added, starting to look exactly that way herself. "That was okay to let him take her, wasn't it?"

Ellie pressed a hand to the side of her head. Her daughter was gone, and she had no idea when she'd be home...*if* she'd be home.

"When did they leave?" she asked, walking in a slow circle to beat back the panic.

Boston had taken Cassidy. He'd come and gotten her and just...taken her away. She couldn't believe it.

"I...uh, it was between three and five. I don't know. God, I thought you knew he was doing this. You didn't mention anything at lunch, but...Cassidy knew about it, and he didn't act like it was some covert, undercover outing or anything."

"I had no idea," Ellie said numbly. She looked at

Nora with such a pale face the woman reached out as if to catch her before she could fall.

"I am so sorry, Ellie," Nora gushed. "I just...well, hell. I was reading a book one minute and the next, this complete hunk was staring at me and smiling and...damn, I couldn't think." She paused to look at Ellie in awe. "I always knew you had excellent taste, but I thought that was just about clothing sense and shoes."

"Nora!" Ellie moaned. How could she talk about Boston's looks now? Her daughter was missing.

"God, I'm sorry," Nora started again, realizing they had a real problem on their hands. She cupped her face with her fingers. "It's just that I even talked to him yesterday, and he didn't have that effect on me. But then again, yesterday, he didn't smile. Today he did, and it was like...oh, wow, El. That man has some smile."

Ellie didn't need to be told this. She was already well aware of the power behind his stupid, charming smile.

"I think all I could do was stammer, blush and drool. I probably would've handed over my house, car, and kidney if he'd asked. I guess I *did* hand over my kid, now that I think of it. And— Oh, my God!" Nora stopped blabbing and froze with a look of utter horror on her face. "He took Keller too," she said as if just now realizing that fact. "You don't think he'd keep Keller too, do you?"

Suddenly, she looked about as sick as Ellie felt.

****

The parking lot at Chuck E. Cheese's was packed, but Ellie spotted Boston's Infiniti among the family vans and SUVs quickly enough. She found a spot three places down and whipped in, jerking to a halt. In the passenger seat, Nora was out the door before Ellie had even tugged her key from the ignition. Though her friend was sprinting toward the entrance of the restaurant, Ellie could only sit there a moment and try to calm her breathing.

When Nora told her Boston had taken Cassie, she'd thought she would pass out from the fear. She'd feared she might never see her baby girl again. But now that she was staring at Boston's car and knew he'd at least been honest about where they were going, her fears subsided substantially. The relief was so overwhelming, she felt like crying, but for an entirely different reason, a more powerful reason. Moisture actually beaded at the corners of her eyes.

He hadn't been trying to steal her little girl. He'd merely wanted to spend some time with her. And that was the only thought that kept her from leaping from the car and racing Nora inside. Cassidy had wanted to meet her father for months now, and it wasn't just one of those passing wants either—this was a deep-seated need, consuming her entire nine-year-old body.

Ellie'd be lying if she denied dreaming about Boston returning to them and making them a complete, happy little family: mother, father, and baby. She'd always wanted to see him look at Cassidy with an emotion she herself had felt so many times.

But that was a stupid pipe dream; this was reality. And in reality, he'd taken her daughter away without telling her. The urge to kill him was so strong, she stayed in her car with both her trembling hands covering her mouth until the anger cooled a few degrees.

She blew out a breath, smoothed out the wrinkles on her blouse and slowly exited the automobile, reminding herself Cassie was okay. Boston hadn't stolen her. Everything was fine...for now.

As soon as she opened the door to the

restaurant, she could hear her neighbor yelling.

"*You lousy son of a bitch.*"

Obviously, Nora'd had no problem finding him in the crowded joint. Picking up her pace, Ellie hurried forward as her friend ranted on.

"How could you trick me and convince me to send my *son* out with a complete stranger? You made me think you'd cleared this whole outing with Ellie first. I thought it was okay. I thought it was *planned*. But no, you just stole two children away from their homes. How were we supposed to know when you were bringing them back? You never said when you were—"

"Yes, I did," Boston quickly cut in.

He stood in front of Nora with his arms lifted as if to restore peace to the kingdom. Surrounded by a table full of more strangers who looked like they were probably his family, he'd obviously been watching Cassie and Keller and a few other children playing a video game not far away until he'd spotted Nora barreling toward him.

"I told you I'd have them back by eight thirty," he said, looking frankly panicked by the enraged female glaring at him.

"The hell you did," Nora growled.

"But..." Looking truly puzzled, Boston scratched his head. "You said Keller's bedtime was eight thirty. I assumed—"

"Well, that's what we both get for assuming," Nora retorted. "Because I never, *never*, would've let you walk away with Keller, or Cassie either for that matter, if I'd known you hadn't talked to Ellie about this. I can't believe the nerve..."

As she continued to rail, Ellie started toward her daughter. "Cass," she called. Once she got the girl's attention, she snapped her fingers and pointed to the floor in front of her. "We're leaving...now."

Just as Cassie froze with her face showing that

all-too-familiar expression of a tantrum about to start, Boston stepped away from the still-bickering Nora.

"Whoa," he said, grabbing Ellie's arm. Behind him, his alarmed-looking family had all come to their feet and moved supportively closer.

Ellie pulled her arm from his grasp and glared. "What made you think you could just take off with my daughter without even *asking* me?"

Boston opened his mouth, but no words came out... He honestly looked too stunned to speak.

"I came home from work tonight and I had no idea where she was. And even after Nora told me you had her and where you'd taken her, I had no idea how long you were going to be gone. Or *if* you were ever going to bring her back."

Boston's jaw tightened, making his words strained. "I didn't realize I had to run it by you every time I wanted to see my own child."

Ellie let out a disgusted breath. "Yes!" she yelled. "You do."

"Why?"

"Why?! She's my daughter. I have to know where she is."

"Oh?" he drew out the word slowly. Then he glowered. "You mean, like you let me know where *my daughter* was for the past nine years?"

Ellie probably would've wound back her arm and hit him square in the jaw if the older woman behind him hadn't tugged on his arm and jerked him around.

"Are you telling me you didn't get permission to take Cassidy tonight?"

"Permission?" he said incredulously. "She's my child. I don't—"

"Yes, you damn well do," the woman growled sternly, and Ellie suddenly realized this matriarchal figure was his mother. She looked too much like

Boston not to be. When she turned her attention to Ellie, Ellie instinctively moved a leery step back.

But the woman gave her a beseeching look. "Please excuse my son," she begged. "Sometimes, he just doesn't think."

"What? You're siding with *her*?" Boston yelped. "Jesus, Mother. She purposely kept my daughter from me for damn near a decade. I think I deserve one night."

But Diane Kincaid merely lifted a hand to shush him. "*She* is Cassidy's mother," she argued. "She's been the one raising this child. She's your daughter's ultimate guardian and caregiver. Legally, you have no right to her, and you know that."

"Yeah," Boston snorted. "Because... she...kept...my child from me. Did you not hear that the first time?"

"Boston," his mother said calmly. "You're the lawyer here. You should know better. You have no claim to Cassidy. I doubt your name's even on the birth certificate."

"It's not," Ellie cut in, earning a scowl from both Boston and his mother.

"She could have you arrested for kidnapping," Diane finished. She and her son glanced Ellie's way again, obviously wondering if she'd do just that.

"I just want my daughter," she told them. Turning, she grabbed Cassie's hand and said, "Come on. We're going home."

"What?" Cassie exploded. "No! I want to stay. What does he mean you kept him from me?"

Ignoring her daughter's final question, Ellie glanced toward Nora, who was standing with a quivering Keller cowered next to her. Her friend gave a slight, supportive nod.

Boston stepped forward. "But she hasn't even eaten yet," he entreated.

"Can't she stay long enough for supper?" his

mother added.

Her daughter wrapped both arms around her left leg. "Please, Mom, please."

Ellie glanced at Cassie...then Boston. Then she turned her attention to the dozens of curious people standing behind him, watching the show with avid interest. They were going to think she was the Wicked Witch of the West.

But she didn't care.

Tightening her grip on Cassie's hand, she said, "Let's go," and turned away from Boston and his family.

She should've known better, but when her daughter wailed out her disapproval, Ellie still winced at the volume. Cassie hadn't thrown such a royal fit since she was four, but she truly outdid herself now. Thrashing and screaming, she dug her feet in and struggled against Ellie's hold, fighting for all she was worth.

"I want to stay with my daddy," she cried over and over again.

It'd been a few years since Ellie had held her child, but she tried to pick Cassie up anyway. The girl immediately flailed her limbs out, catching her right in the face with a swinging elbow.

"Cassidy!" Boston chided in shock. He stepped forward as soon as Ellie cried out. While she was busy touching her bruised cheek, he bent down in front of their daughter and took her arms. "Calm down."

"I want to stay with you," she howled.

"I know," he said softly. "But right now, you have to go home. I'll see you soon."

"When?" Cassidy demanded to know.

Boston glanced up toward Ellie as he quietly repeated, "Soon." He sucked in a breath and got back to his feet. "Be good for your mom, okay?"

Cassie was still rebellious, but at least Ellie was

able to drag her to the car after that.

It was a quiet trip home. Even Nora and Keller didn't dare speak. Not until Ellie had pulled into her drive and parked did her friend glance over and quietly say, "I'll talk to you later," before she hustled Keller across the yard to their own house.

"Into the bathtub," Ellie told her daughter.

"But—"

"*Now.*"

Ten minutes later, she sat in the darkened living room, bawling into her hands. She hated this. She hated hurting her daughter. She hated being mean. But damn it, she was the injured party here. Boston had scared her to death tonight. He'd taken off with her child. Why was everyone mad at her like *she'd* done something wrong?

When the doorbell rang, she surged to her feet, needing Nora's support more than anything. She didn't even stop to wonder why her friend was at the front door when she always came to the back until she'd already opened the portal. When she found someone who was completely not Nora, she tried to slam it shut.

Boston stuck his foot in the jam just in time. "Ellie. We need to talk."

"I don't want to talk to you," she said and was totally horrified when a sob seeped out.

"You can't run from this," he murmured, his voice a little too coaxing for comfort. "We need to figure out what we're going to do."

At the moment, she hated him for acting so rationally. She still wanted to rail, and scream, and cry. How dare he make her feel even more unhinged with his calm, collected demeanor?

"*We're* not going to do anything," she growled, putting more weight into trying to shut the door. But the man must have an iron foot. He'd didn't budge.

"I can't just turn around and leave, El."

"Yes, you can. You've done it before."

He sighed. "Will you at least let me come in to apologize?"

She cracked off a harsh laugh. "You don't want to apologize."

"Yes, I do. My mother was right. I didn't think today. I...hell. I guess I assumed you already knew I was taking her to Chuck E. Cheese's. Please believe me when I say I never meant to scare you...or your neighbor."

"Apology accepted," she said quickly. "So, now you can go."

"Ellie, I'm not going to leave. Not this time."

"Then what do you want?" she said with a shaky voice.

"For starters, I'd like you to stop crying."

"I'm not crying," she muttered and wiped at her wet cheeks.

She could actually hear his amused smile. "There's more than an apology I need to give you," he murmured. "I had my sister Helena work up a custody agreement today. She's a lawyer too."

For a moment, Ellie stopped breathing. Custody agreement?

"I...here," he said, sounding suddenly uneasy. There was a sound of crinkling paper, and then a legal sheet was thrust through the three-inch crack in the door. "We wouldn't have had the problem we did tonight if we'd come up with some kind of agreement. So, look it over and tell me what you think."

Ellie spent a minute just staring at his hand, the same long, talented fingers that used to touch the most intimate parts of her body but were now handing her a legal battle. Slowly she reached out and slipped the sheet from his grasp. Her chest physically hurt as she dropped her gaze to the document. After glancing over it, which was fairly easy for her since she worked in a law office and understood such forms, she lifted her eyes.

"Every weekend?" she uttered. "You want her every weekend?"

Why didn't he just demand one of her lungs? Actually, those might not be such a difficult organ to give up. At the moment, the damn things seemed to be malfunctioning; she found it nearly impossible to breathe.

Blue eyes peeked through the open slit. "I thought that was more than fair. You'd still get her a majority of the time."

"But *every* weekend?" Ellie repeated in horror.

"What?" Boston demanded. "What's wrong with it?"

"It's just that weekends are the only chance I really get to spend time with her," Ellie argued even though she knew that was a mistake as soon as the words left her mouth. Showing any kind of weakness to Boston was bad.

"Well, that's a whole hell of a lot more than I've ever gotten to spend with her, now isn't it?"

"But...she only met you yesterday," Ellie reasoned. "She doesn't know you well enough to—"

"And just whose fault is that?" he shot back. "If you hadn't lied to me, I wouldn't be some stranger who—"

"Oh, you wanted to go, Boston. Otherwise, you would've stuck around long enough to know there was a baby. You—"

"I left because you ordered me to go!" he roared. "Do you think I wanted—"

"I know exactly what you wanted," she cried out loudly in order to be heard over his yelling. "And it had nothing to do with me. Now get out and leave us alone."

Before she realized what was happening, Cassidy came charging into the living room. Ellie jerked in surprise. "Cass—"

Wet hair swinging behind her and her long nightshirt hanging down past her knees, Cassidy bulldozed her way toward Ellie.

"Leave him alone!" she screamed, flying forward. She pushed Ellie in the stomach with all the strength she had, making Ellie lose her grip on the door, and causing Boston to spill inside.

Surprised, Ellie leapt back and blinked rapidly. If Cassidy had pulled out a gun and shot her, she couldn't have felt more hurt and betrayed. Horrified because tears immediately filled her throat, she could only stand there and gape as her child laid into her.

"This is all your fault," Cassie snarled, her eyes full of lethal accusation, making Ellie feel exposed and ripped open as her daughter pushed on her stomach again. "If you'd just told him about me all along..."

Cassidy would've gone on and on, but surprisingly Boston was the one to stop her.

"Hey, hey," he said softly and crouched next to the nine-year-old, taking her face in his hands. "Let's not get mad, okay? Why don't I tuck you in? I want to tuck you into bed again. Okay?"

Cassidy blinked at him. The tension in her face slowly eased, and she finally nodded. "Okay."

Boston gave a slow smile. "Good," he answered and straightened, reaching for her hand. He cast an unreadable look Ellie's way before walking their daughter down the hall.

Unable to stay in the living room where his cologne still lingered, Ellie paced to the kitchen and wilted into a chair. She shook so hard, her fingers jerked uncontrollably as she covered her mouth.

Cassidy was the only person she had left. That little girl was her life, her only family, her very soul. Ellie would be nothing if Cassie left her. And to have

Cassie so mad at her...someone might as well stab her in the stomach and drag the knife across her abdomen.

It felt like she'd just sat in the chair when Boston strode back down the hall. Ellie popped to her feet. He paused when he saw her.

"Thanks a lot," she growled.

He frowned, clearly confused. "What?" he asked. His expression added, *What'd I do?*

"That's the second time today you've played the good guy, and I had to star as the wicked witch."

His body went taut as he tightly answered, "Hey, it's not my fault you fill the role so—" But he broke off before he could finish the insult.

Blowing out a breath, he ran a hand through his hair and glanced down the hall, quietly saying, "Look. I'm going to leave that form here." He nodded toward the custody arrangement. "And let you think about what would work best for you."

"I don't have to think about it," Ellie hissed just as quietly. "You can't have her every weekend." God, she didn't want him to have Cassie at all.

He sighed, long and low. "Then what do you suggest?"

Never was the immediate response Ellie wanted to give. She didn't want to part with her daughter, even for one day each decade.

But she licked her lips and diplomatically answered, "I could settle for one weekend a month."

"One weekend a *month?*" he sputtered. Then he instantly calmed and glanced down the hall as if to make sure Cassie hadn't heard him. Turning back, he whispered harshly, "Fine then. One weekend a month. And for the first nine years I've lost with her, you owe me two hundred and thirty-six days. I'll just take those now on the other weekends I'm not scheduled to have her."

"Well, then you owe me sixty thousand dollars

for ten years of child support," Ellie shot back.

That caused him to pause. Tilting his head thoughtfully, he murmured, "Hmm. I calculated a hundred and twenty grand. But..." He shrugged. "Do you want that in one lump sum or monthly payments?"

She glared at him for calling her bluff. "I don't want your money. I want my daughter every weekend."

"You're already getting her during the week. Two out of seven days sounds pretty freaking practical to me. You still have the majority."

"Look, Law Boy, I can't be away from my daughter that often. It's just not possible."

"Well, then thank God this isn't about you. And don't call me Law Boy anymore. You only did it because you thought it annoyed me, but all it ever did was turn me on."

Ellie gasped and took a surprised step back. Unconsciously her gaze went to his crotch. She was utterly bowled over to find his pants stretched tight over a huge bulge.

Boston gritted his teeth, turning so she couldn't see the proof of his attraction. "But guess what," he growled. "That part of my anatomy doesn't make the ultimate decisions in my life anymore. I don't care what my dick wants. I don't even care if you're willing...*I'm* not interested. I'm still pissed at you. And I want Cassie *every* weekend. Personally, I think that's being more than fair. It's not like I'm asking for full or even evenly split custody."

"Well, it's impossible," Ellie answered. "And I'm not just thinking about myself. Cassidy's life is here. Her friends are here. She has activities and ball games on weekends."

"And I have a car. I know how to drive. If she has somewhere to be, I can take her just as easily as you could."

"Oh, come on. You're not going to want come all the way back to Lawrence for a—"

"Right about now, I'd go to Italy to get her a pizza," he boomed, advancing until he'd neatly trapped her in a corner.

Ellie gritted her teeth and only had to glance at his face to see just how true his words were. He *would* do anything for Cassie, which made her jealous. There'd never been a point he would've done anything for *her*.

Instantly upset because he'd never loved her how she'd always wanted him to and even more pissed because he'd caused her to experience such a petty feeling as jealousy, she had this irrational urge to slap at him until he bled.

Unaware of just how close he came to bodily harm, Boston blew out a breath and spiked his hands through his hair. "Don't fight me on this, Ellie," he said, restraining his temper and once again talking in a hushed voice. "You *don't* want to take it to court."

Her face drained of color. "Once a month," she repeated firmly.

He was silent, studying the way her hands shook. She couldn't hide her bubbling, erratic emotions at all, and she hated that.

"Every week or we take it to a judge," he reiterated.

Trapped between him and the counter and needing more space, Ellie jerked by, turning her back to him as she moved. But the space was so narrow, she grazed him, making him suck in a breath.

He leapt backward as if she'd just struck him with lightning. She frowned and was about to ask him what his problem was when she remembered the bulge. Lips parting, she lifted her face.

Boston ground his teeth and spun away from

her. Shoving his hands through his hair yet again, he groaned to himself, "I need to get out of here."

Though she fully agreed, Ellie couldn't help but feel a spurt of satisfaction at the overwhelming effect she obviously had on him. It was nice to know she had a little power there, when she didn't anywhere else. It was even nicer to know she wasn't the only one here affected by the other's presence.

"Will you please just sign the agreement so I can leave already?" he asked from between gritted teeth.

Ellie glanced at the legal form she'd tossed onto the counter. Every weekend really wasn't the worst thing he could've demanded. But, still. *Every* weekend? The very thought of being away from Cassie that much made her skin clammy and moist.

"No," she said, unable to meet his eyes.

Though she didn't dare look his way, she could feel him glare. He was so quiet she could only guess what kind of dirty gesture he was making. But in a surprisingly calm voice, he said, "If I asked for more, and we took this to court, I'd get it. This isn't an unreasonable offer, Ellie. It's not like I'm trying to take your daughter away from you for nine years or anything."

She lifted her face. He stared at her intently for a moment before he said, "This isn't over." Then he turned and started from the kitchen only to jerk to a stop at the doorway.

As he slowly came back around, the strangest sensation dropped heavily into the base of her stomach. The way he looked at her, thoughtfully yet a bit savagely, like a lion right before pouncing on its prey, made her skitter a step back, her butt ramming into a knob on one of her kitchen drawers.

"What?" she said.

He gave a single, brief shake of his head. "I just realized I was running away because I was afraid of my attraction to you."

She swallowed, only to realize her throat had gone dry.

As he advanced a slow, meaningful step forward, she reached back to clutch the corner of the countertop for support. "So?" Her voice was unsteady and her eyes huge.

"So...we're going to see a lot of each other in the years to come. Whatever decision we accept on child support, Cassie is still going to tie us together for the rest of our lives. I refuse to let you intimidate me every time I'm around just because we have a sexual past."

Her eyebrows rose. "*I'm* intimidating *you*? Oh, please."

Even his slow smile was predatory. "It wasn't always bad between us," he said, creeping close enough Ellie had to lift her face to meet his gaze.

Her breathing escalated and her nostrils expanded as she dragged in his all-too familiar scent. God, why did he have to smell so delicious?

"And every time you take your shirt off around me," he continued, "or press your ass against my erection, I'm bound to remember just how *satisfying* those not-so-bad times used to be."

Scowling, Ellie opened her mouth to argue each of his points. It hadn't been her intention to turn him on or drudge up any bittersweet memories either time, and the bastard knew it.

But Boston merely lifted his hand and set his index finger on her lips, hushing her. "I don't care if they were accidental incidences or not. They're still playing havoc on my concentration. And my judgment's going to be skewed until I get past this. But...if I could convince myself you're not as good as I remember, I'm sure I'll be fine, and we'd finally be able to discuss whatever we need to discuss in a more professional, unaffected manner."

"Just what are you suggesting, Boston?" Ellie

said, gaping. "That we have sex one last time to get it out of our systems?"

His smile bloomed into a half chuckle. "That would be nice, sure. But I doubt we'd have to go as far as that."

"Then?"

Grin falling, he turned all business in the blink of an eye. "A kiss. All it'll take is one kiss. Then I'll know it's only in my head."

"Oh." Ellie's shoulders loosened and she tilted up her chin. "Well, in that case...go ahead." She was amazed she could act so casual about it when the idea of him pressing his mouth to hers made her heart thump hard against her ribcage.

Boston looked similarly amazed. Instead of dipping his head and pressing his mouth to hers, he lifted his eyebrows. "Well, aren't you a little too willing to comply." Leaning even closer, he whispered, his breath caressing her lips with each word he uttered. "Let me guess. You're having the same disturbing memories."

"No," she rushed out her answer. She wanted to shove against his chest to give herself some room. But she refused to let him know how much his proximity affected her, though, damn it, the glint in his eyes made it clear he already suspected.

"I'm just worried Cassie will notice and get scared if you keep going around...half cocked like you are."

He grinned. "Half cocked? Cute pun." Reaching out, he wrapped a piece of her hair around his finger, growing fascinated with the ringlets her locks made as he slid his finger free.

To keep herself from smacking at his hand and giving away even more of her apprehensions...and desires, she snapped, "Can you just get it over with already?"

His surprised blue eyes met hers. "No." His grin

smoldered, hot and languid. "I have to do this right or it won't work."

She sighed and closed her eyes. "Whatever." Tilting her chin up again, she prayed he wouldn't notice the way her pulse ticked heavily against her throat. "Take all the time in the world then. I don't care."

"You have to kiss me back too," he argued. "Or—"

"I said fine," she grit out.

After a moment, nothing happened. Then he spoke. "Open your eyes."

Though she didn't want to, she found herself following his order as her lashes flickered apart. "Why?"

"I want you to know who you're kissing."

Like she could forget. Ellie watched him warily as he licked his lips and shifted close enough to crowd her against the kitchen cabinets...cool wooden doors at her back; hard, hot Boston at her front.

"Ready?" he whispered.

"Yes." Damn it, would he just do something before she imploded?

Suddenly, there he was. He slanted his mouth down—no hesitation, no pausing to think it through, just steady determination—and their mouths connected. She let out a sob of release, closed her eyes, and bowed her back until her breasts pressed against his chest.

He groaned deep in his throat and cradled her face with both hands, pressing his thumbs against the apex of her jaw as if to force her mouth open in case she tried to reject the push of his tongue. But rejection was the last thing on her mind. She sucked the wet warmth between her teeth and drew from his taste, holding him tight, probably yanking out half his hair she gripped him so hard.

They made love to each other's mouths, diving

deep in the recesses of their souls as they mated, tongue to tongue, breath to breath. Ellie couldn't seem to get close enough and clung to him, clutching his shoulders for dear life. He growled out a sound of similar frustration and picked her up, setting her on the countertop to fit himself between her thighs and press close to her heat.

She gasped and wrapped her legs around his hips, cradling his erection to her core.

"It's you," he rasped against her mouth between each kiss, his hands crazily running up and down her body as if to convince himself of that very fact. "It's you. God, Ellie, I can't believe it's really you."

"Boston," she moaned, throwing her head back so he could nibble his way down her jaw, using both teeth and tongue to lavish her throat.

Reaching the base of her neck, he buried his nose in the top opening of her blouse and held her tight a moment as he breathed in her essence. "Jesus, you still smell the same. Your hair, your clothes, your skin."

"So do you," she said, kissing his jaw and running her hands through his thick black locks.

His fingers fumbled as he opened her shirt. "You and your buttons," he panted, sounding impatient yet tenderly amused. "I swear, I bought you an entire wardrobe to replace all the buttoned garments I used to rip off you."

She grinned and nipped her teeth at his earlobe. "You did." And she'd kept every one of them, storing them away in a box at the back of her closet.

She expected him to lift his face, look her deep in the eyes, and tear the two sides of her shirt apart...for old time's sake. But when he pulled back to grin at her, his fingers slowed, carefully continuing to release one fastening at a time. After watching himself work for a moment, his eyes slid up, and their gazes connected. She felt the punch of longing deep in her gut.

The last button came free, and Boston easily separated the two sides, letting out a breath as his gaze swept over her. "Why didn't I ever realize how much more sensual it was to savor my prize and unwrap it slowly...one button at a time?"

Ellie shook her head, unable to speak, her mind blank of words. His blue gaze held her captivated.

"You're stunning," he said and lowered his mouth to press a warm kiss to her chest, right where her heart beat against the swell of her breast.

Stirred by such a sweet act, she skimmed her fingers over his cheekbone. He closed his eyes and rested his face on her chest, pillowed by her breasts. He wrapped his arms around her waist, and she hugged him back. They remained that way nearly a whole minute before his muffled voice came from her cleavage.

"These grew."

His hand came up to investigate the change in her breasts.

He pulled one free of its bra cup to study its fullness a moment, gently rubbing his thumb over her hard nipple before he dipped and took the throbbing peak into his mouth.

Ellie gasped and clutched the back of his head tight. "Boston. Oh, God. Please."

After moving his attention to her other breast, his fingers found the top button of her slacks. He drew the zipper down. Tensing with eager expectation, Ellie wanted to thrash her head from side to side and moan out, *yes, yes, yes*. But all she could do was tighten her grip on his head as he bit down on her nipple. She arched her hips up when he slid his hand over her stomach and into the waistband of her panties.

His fingers grazed her pubic hair until they encountered an old scar. Pausing, he broke free of her breast, looking confused. Then he leaned forward to examine the mark. After frowning at the foreign blemish that hadn't been there the last time he'd breached her panties, his eyes lifted in question.

"C-section," she answered his silent query. "I'd planned on a natural birth, but...there were complications."

Boston's eyes snapped open wide...alert. "Are you okay?"

She smiled, loving his concern. "I'm fine. Now."

"Now?" Latching onto that word, he wrinkled his brow in concern. His gaze fell to her scar, and his fingers traced it again in a gentle, loving caress. "What happened?"

"Placenta previa. Problems with the placenta," she added at Boston's blank look. "It wanted to come out first, which would've put Cassie in danger. So, they gave me a spinal block and cut her out. It wasn't as bad as it sounds," she was quick to tack on when his face paled. "The doctor handled it beautifully, and Cassie was delivered just fine."

But Boston didn't look reassured. "I wish I could've been there."

Ellie swallowed and closed her eyes. When he pulled his hand from her underwear and zipped her slacks closed, her lashes shot open.

He looked distant and reserved as he took a step in reverse. "I *should've* been there, Ellie."

"Boston," she started. She wanted to reach for him but didn't dare.

As if he could read her thoughts, he shook his head and turned away, running his hand through his hair as he put distance between them. "This didn't turn out like I thought it would." He sighed and glanced blindly across the kitchen before he sent her a leery, untrusting look. "I guess we're just going to have to get used to my attraction and learn to deal with it. Because I won't ever touch you again."

With that, he turned on his heel and strode from her kitchen.

From her house.

From her life.

Chapter Eight

After hearing the front door open and close, Ellie yanked her top back together, slid off the counter, and hurried toward the living room. The room was dark, so she felt safe in going to the window and lifting a curtain. From the streetlamp's glow, she watched him walk stiffly yet steadily around to the driver's side of his Infiniti.

In the sparse lighting, he looked so much like the boy with whom she'd fallen in love. His hair was still pitch black and his form was that same slim, sleek build. It tore her up to see him like that. Once upon a time, he'd smiled whenever he'd seen her. And now...now he scowled as he sent one last glare up at her house before sliding into his car. It was almost shocking how drastically their relationship had changed.

But the one thing that remained the same and surprised her the most was his physical response to her. She couldn't believe they'd both gotten turned on so easily. It wasn't a good kind of shock, though. His instantaneous attraction to her had been one of the main things that had drawn her to him. The man could've had any girl he wanted back in college. Heck, he still could snag any woman. But he'd wanted Ellie. It'd been so flattering she'd been powerless to deny him anything.

The fact that this hadn't changed in ten years was going to make her struggle that much harder. Ellie closed her eyes and snorted out an ironic laugh. Harder. Oh, yeah, she could say that again.

Outside, his car engine started. Her eyes flew

open. As he pulled away from the curb, she rubbed her fingers over the ache in the center of her chest. There was something else that hadn't changed. It still hurt to watch him leave.

Gritting her teeth, Ellie dropped the curtain. As the cloth fell over the window, she backed away and slid her hand down until she clutched her churning stomach. She continued to step in reverse until the backs of her legs bumped the sofa. Though she wanted to sink into the soft, comforting cushions and cry, she opted to walk down the hall and check on her daughter.

Surprisingly, Cassidy was fast asleep. Though she hadn't done so in years, Ellie slipped into the room and tiptoed to the bed. She pulled back the covers and crawled onto the mattress with her baby. Cassie's sweet little-girl smell enveloped her and she closed her eyes. Instantly, she smiled, thankful she was here, thankful she'd ended up so blessed.

Ellie hadn't lived an easy life. Since the time she was eight and her parents had died in an automobile accident, she had grown up in a home where food came sporadically, if at all. She'd lived with her deceased grandmother's older sister, and Aunt Eadie didn't have the greatest memory. Ellie had practically raised herself.

From the moment her daughter was born and that tiny little life had been placed in her arms, totally her responsibility, she'd sworn Cassie would never live the way she had. Her daughter would always have a meal on the table, and she'd always have a structured, orderly life where she could take part in as many after-school activities as she wanted. Plus she'd grow up in a neighborhood where she could play out in the open in a safe environment and attend a nice, reputable school.

So far, Ellie had been able to provide all of that; she wasn't about to lose slack now. Most of her good fortune had come from luck. The house she owned, or at least would own after another twenty-five years of payments, could actually be accredited to her louse of a boss. Winston's brother, Dr. Mendel Young, had wanted to sell his guesthouse for years and when it went on the market, Winston mentioned it to Ellie.

Like a dog to a bone, she'd jumped on the chance to live next door to doctors and bankers. It didn't even matter that her home was only an eighth the size of every other house on the block. It was hers and didn't have wheels under it. She adored it.

She lived in a beautiful, safe community with a wonderful neighbor friend in Dr. Young's wife, Nora. Even their son, Keller, was a blessing to have nearby. From the moment the two children had met, they'd been best friends.

So yeah, Ellie pretty much adored this life she'd built up all by herself. She might've had grand dreams when she'd lived in Tennessee, but she'd never really thought she'd get this far. Hard work and pure determination actually did pay off sometimes.

As she listened to Cassidy's even breathing, she was helpless but to remember the man who had helped her create this gift. It was like meeting him for the first time all over again. She'd fought so hard not to like him, not to fall for him. But she'd failed miserably.

She couldn't let that happen again. She refused to trip into Boston Kincaid's seductive web one more time. This round, they were enemies. It wouldn't do to lose sight of that.

He wanted to take her daughter.

Remembering the look on his face, however, when he'd seen Cassidy for the first time and the way he'd treasured her body tonight, touching her like he'd actually missed her, Ellie gnashed her teeth even harder. Closing her eyes, she swallowed back the guilt over keeping father and daughter apart. Though she tried to stop it, her mind wandered further into the past, back to Cassie's conception, back to when those good times started to turn not so good.

****

It was early April, and Boston was in a mood. He often became irritable and tightly wound when he had a big test or a paper deadline to make. The man was the ultimate worrywart. Ellie teased he was going to have an ulcer before he hit twenty-five. But his mood swings had never turned her off before. She'd always delighted in the fact she could pull him out of his doldrums. That was one of the reasons she'd been so drawn to him. Because he'd been so positively affected by the mere touch of her hand.

As one who'd never been comfortable with getting close to other people, she could curl up to Boston and have his body humming in seconds. It was unreal how near she always wanted to be to him. He was like a drug, and she'd become addicted. So addicted, in fact, the first time he'd pulled away from her had felt like a bad overdose.

She went to his apartment to visit. It was a rainy Saturday afternoon. Though she'd been scheduled to work, another waitress had begged to switch shifts with her. So, Ellie unexpectedly had the entire day off. She could've caught up on a little homework. But she went to Boston instead.

After tapping on his door, she heard his muffled call, "'S open." So, she grabbed the handle and entered.

He sat on his bed, one leg tucked under him, the other hanging over the mattress as he tapped his toe on the floor to the tune on the radio and worked from an open textbook in his lap.

He glanced up briefly. When he saw her, he

didn't smile as he usually did. In fact, he looked a little sick. His face drained of color, and a haunted expression crossed his features so quickly Ellie convinced herself she'd imagined it. Still, warning bells went off.

"Hey," he said stoically and immediately dropped his face to return his attention to his homework, tapping his pen against the textbook.

"Hey," she murmured in reply, closing the door behind her and easing closer to his bed. Something was wrong, ergo, she immediately wanted to fix it and soothe him back into being the guy she loved so much.

"I got off work today. Angela begged to switch schedules so she could go out with some new guy tomorrow night."

"Hmm," he responded, not even bothering to sound interested.

Wanting to cheer him the quickest way she knew how, she sat down on the mattress and scooted closer. "Anyway," she went on. "I was thinking...since I have the entire afternoon off..." She left the invitation open ended.

Spotting a lock of his hair obstructing his view from reading, she reached out to brush it out of his eyes. But before making contact, he shifted his face away. Ellie's fingers froze and her body constricted with pain. He'd never rejected her touch before. Swallowing, she quickly pulled her hand back to her lap.

He glanced over. When he saw the hurt on her face, his eyes filled with regret, and he opened his mouth as if to apologize. But then he forced his gaze away and mumbled, "I really need to study."

"I'll help," she offered and once again reached out, intending to slip his book off his lap. She'd grown accustomed to helping him study. And he'd always gratefully appreciated her efforts, especially when they did the strip off, where she peeled of a piece of clothing for every question he answered correctly.

But for a second time, he rebuffed her and jerked the book away before she could get it. "Damn it, Ellie," he snapped and lifted his face to send her an irritated scowl.

Her mouth fell open; she could only gape at him in agonized surprise.

His annoyance fell flat when he caught her gaze. He gritted his teeth as if supremely conflicted. Then he sighed and closed his eyes, letting his head fall back to bump against the headboard.

"Look, I just want to be alone and study this for a while, okay." His tone was mildly apologetic. Though the word "sorry" didn't cross his lips, he opened his eyes and said it with his expression.

Ellie had no idea what was wrong, but she was vividly aware of the fact that this was the first time she hadn't been able to pull him from a mood. It shocked and scared her and made her think she'd done something wrong, something to upset him. Not wanting to look clingy and beg him to talk to her, she nodded wordlessly and scooted off the bed.

"I'm sorry I bothered you," she murmured and hurried from the room. She ran all the way back through the lazy rain to her dorm room, where she shut herself inside and wept the rest of the afternoon.

Boston appeared the next day. Once again, dismal weather filled the campus with a slow, miserable warm rain. Ellie had dried up from her tear fest and was doing homework when the soft knock came. After scooting off her bed, she went to the door and checked the peephole. Her heart about thumped out of her chest when she saw Boston standing there, his hair glistening with raindrops.

Pulse racing, she flipped the deadbolt and flung

the door open. He lifted his face, and they both froze, taking a good ten seconds to just stand there, soaking in the sight of each other.

Finally, Boston asked, "Want to go for a walk?"

Neither seemed to care how wet it was outside. Ellie merely bobbed her head and answered, "Let me put on some shoes."

He stayed in the hall and watched her through the open doorway as she plopped onto the floor and jerked on a pair of sneakers. The fact that he didn't come inside told her things still weren't kosher. But Ellie didn't care. He was here. He was attempting a reconnection.

She assumed he'd tell her what was wrong, what she'd done that had upset him. She'd been wracking her brain for twenty-four hours, trying to think up something she might've said to displease him. But she couldn't think of anything. All she knew was that she loved him, and thinking he was upset with her hurt her to no end.

Ellie was surprised when he remained strangely mute as they started their walk. He didn't seem to want to talk. He only wanted to walk.

So, they walked.

It was ten minutes into their stroll before he even took her hand. Still no words were spoken; he merely slipped his damp fingers through hers and held on. Ellie closed her eyes briefly and tightened her grip in quiet support. Another ten minutes passed. He led them to a deserted memorial park and into a thick copse of trees off the beaten path.

When he slowed to a stop, Ellie looked up. He turned to her slowly and blinked as if surprised to see her.

"You're all wet," he murmured, realizing it for the first time. He lifted his hand and wiped a stream of rain off her cheek.

Her heart warmed. "So are you," she told him

and brought her hand up to mimic his actions.

He closed his eyes and moved his face against her fingers, delighting in her touch. Lightly catching her wrist, he held her hand still as he pressed his mouth against her palm and kissed her, licking the rain off the inside of her fingertips.

Ellie's loins tightened and her spirits lifted. "Boston," she whispered.

He inhaled loudly, smelling her scent. When he opened his eyes and looked at her, she felt the zap in every pore of her being.

"I'm sorry," he whispered, looking regretful like he'd never looked before. "God, I am so sorry."

Then he reached for her face. She eagerly reached back. They made love right there, in the slow rain with no protection. No umbrella. No condom. Boston had been inside her without a condom before, but he'd always pulled out at the last moment.

This time, he didn't. He didn't even seem to realize he had nothing on to prevent a pregnancy. And Ellie was too glad he wasn't upset anymore to remind him otherwise. She didn't want him to stop. So, she held him close and continued to participate in the most erotic, prolonged event of her life.

He said sorry a few more times; she assumed he was apologizing for his mood the day before. It took her a week to learn there was so much more he'd been trying to beg forgiveness for. Yes, she found out exactly why he'd withdrawn from her the Saturday before. And it had nothing to do with her own failings.

She entered her American history class at nine the next Monday morning and was startled to hear a couple of girls mention Boston's name. They didn't just say Boston, either. They said Boston *Kincaid*. There was no way they were talking about someone else.

A chesty, lithe redhead by the name of Heather Grimaldi described him to a tee and went on to enlighten her friends how she'd picked him up at a party the week before. Then she bragged about how she'd gotten him to go back to her room with her. She hadn't been able to go into much more detail before she sighed with delight and slumped down in her chair, smiling dreamily at her companions.

"Oh my God, that man can kiss," she said. "He has, like, the softest mouth ever." Then she giggled and added, "I can't wait to see him again."

Sick to her stomach, Ellie jerked to her feet and raced from the classroom before the professor even entered to start his lecture.

****

Moisture running in droplets down her face, Ellie realized she'd unknowingly started to cry as she'd drifted off into sleep. Sucking in a tear, she wiped it away with the back of her hand and then reached out to stroke the still slumbering child's hair next to her. Her beloved Cassie, who'd been conceived in the rain, lay peacefully asleep. Focusing on that, Ellie reminded herself she had someone to truly love now. Life was still good, and she was still happy. The simple reappearance of Boston into her world wasn't going to ruin that. She wouldn't let it.

Hoping a good night's sleep would fix the little pity party she'd had when she'd crawled into bed with Cassie, Ellie woke the next morning with a headache. Sleep had fixed nothing. In fact, sleep hadn't even come. She'd just lain there, awake and miserable, listening to Cassidy snore.

Groggy and sore, she rolled off the small mattress and took her shower. She was cooking sausage links and toasting bread when her daughter stumbled into the kitchen.

"Morning, sweetheart," she greeted her, her back to Cassie because she was busy flipping the links and trying to press all the grease out of them with her spatula.

Cassie didn't answer, but she'd never been a bright and shining morning person, so Ellie wasn't concerned about it—until she turned around to butter the toast. She slid a smile her daughter's way only to pause when she found the girl scowling.

"Honey, what's wrong?"

Cassie kept glaring. "You yelled at him again after he tucked me in last night, didn't you?"

Ellie's mouth fell open, speechless. "Yell" wasn't exactly the word she'd use for what they'd done.

"Why do you hate him?" Cassie said. "He just wants to be with me, and you keep pushing him away. Why do you want to keep my dad from me?"

Her daughter looked so tormented, Ellie's heart crumbled.

"Oh, baby," she said, dropping the butter knife and kneeling in front of the chair where Cassie sat. "No. I never wanted to keep him from you."

"Yes, you did too! You told him I was dead. You—"

"That wasn't because I wanted to keep him from you, Cassie. I..." She what? Suddenly at a loss for words, she stared at her daughter blankly.

Had she wanted to keep the two of them apart? From the very moment Cassidy had been born, she'd been Ellie's. Cassie was Ellie's one great accomplishment. Her daughter was her life and her world. Had she subconsciously been hogging that wonder all to herself? Had she purposely driven Boston away so she didn't have to share with him?

Cassidy was still staring up at her, waiting for an answer that Ellie couldn't give.

"Eat your toast," she mumbled and plopped the hard bread on her daughter's plate.

Cassie stared down and glared at her food, refusing to touch it.

And thus progressed their relationship. Three days later, Ellie felt like a damn recorder. Once again in the kitchen, mother and daughter filled the room with a hostile silence. Ellie stuffed her mouth with a forkful of Hamburger Helper and chewed relentlessly, though it tasted like cardboard to her.

She scowled at Cassie, who sat slumped in her chair, arms crossed over her chest, refusing to eat. This argument they had going was proving to be their longest yet. When Ellie tried to corner Cassie and get her to talk, Cassie would turn around and ask Ellie questions about Boston that shut her mother up in seconds.

But Ellie wasn't sure how to tell her little girl she'd never meant to hurt her by pushing her father out of their lives. She'd thought she'd been protecting her child, shielding Cassie from possibly having a dad who only regretted her existence.

It became a battle to even get Cassie ready for school in the mornings. The child rebelled against everything Ellie told her to do. And so, the silence had started.

Worried about her daughter trying to starve herself, however, Ellie pointed her fork at Cassie's plate and growled, "Eat your green beans."

Cassie glared at the plateful of food. "I hate green beans."

"That's why there're only three on your plate," Ellie reasoned calmly. "But they're good for you, so...eat."

"No."

"Cassidy."

"Why do you always tell me what to do?" Cassie snapped, jumping out of her chair and glaring across the table, her small hands fisted down at her sides.

"Hmm," Ellie answered with a thoughtful look. Pressing the handle end of the fork against her chin, she answered, "Maybe it's because I'm your mother."

Okay, so this probably wasn't the best time for sarcasm, but she was sick and tired of all the antagonism already. She and Cassie had never quarreled this long before.

Cassie's chin quivered, she looked so mad. "Andy in my class," she said, staring straight into Ellie's eyes, "he lives with his dad. His mom was really mean, and he told a judge he wanted to live with his dad, so—"

"Well, that's not what's going to happen to you," Ellie interrupted, her skin going cold all over. But dear God. She hadn't expected her daughter to pull that kind of comment out of her hat.

"Why not?" Cassie asked, her jaw set and her eyes hard.

"Because that's blackmail, and I won't allow it," Ellie said. She quietly set her fork down as not to bring attention to the sudden shaking in her hands.

"What's blackmail?"

Ellie closed her eyes briefly. "It's using something against someone to get what you want," she answered, sending her daughter a warning look. "It's selfish and mean, and I'm not going to let you try it."

But Cassie looked determined, which caused a warning shot of fear to roar up the back of Ellie's spine.

"Why'd you keep my dad from me?"

"Cass—"

"Why?" Cassie screamed, stomping her foot.

"I don't know how to explain it to you," Ellie answered as honestly as she could. "But I was thinking about you when I made my decision. I did what I thought was best for the both of us at the time."

Cassie didn't understand that answer. She shook her head. "No, you weren't. You weren't thinking about *me*. I hate you. I want to go live with my dad." She spun around and clomped down the hall to her room, slamming the door once she reached it.

Tears clogging her lashes, Ellie reached across the table, stabbed Cassie's three green beans and jammed them into her mouth.

Chapter Nine

Boston Robert Kincaid was the son of an astronaut.

The day Boston told Ellie this tidbit, she gave him her virginity. Those two details didn't have anything to do with one another, of course. She didn't sleep with him because of his slight claim to fame. No, it was more the fact that he'd opened up to her about a part of his life that had seduced her into giving him her body.

He wasn't sure why, but Boston had held himself back on their first few dates. He usually didn't exercise such restraint. If he wanted a girl and knew she wanted him, he pursued relentlessly. But for some reason, it seemed important to hold off with Ellie. He craved her with every breath, so a lacking libido wasn't the problem. It just felt better to tease first, to put it off for as long as he could. And it wasn't just put he was teasing.

Torturing her with restraint was fun, sure. He loved to kiss her until she clung to him, breathing with this little catchy sound that drove him insane, and then he'd pull away, run his fingers over her face and tell her goodnight. She'd just stare at him with that confused, adorable, dazed look of hers, wondering why he'd stopped.

Oh, yeah, he liked to tease Ellie. But teasing himself was just about as fulfilling. Or *testing* himself, as he called it. He wanted her, wanted her more than he remembered wanting anyone. So, he tested himself, to see how far he could go before he couldn't hold back any longer.

He lasted two months.

They went out on their chaste dates at least twice a week—usually more—and he always, always kissed her goodnight. The best part: he was the one who usually pulled away and ended the kisses. He started them, and he finished them. And afterward, Ellie was putty in his hands...until the afternoon she pushed him past his limits.

Walking hand in hand—and Boston was proud of the fact that he'd just gotten her used to holding his hand—he escorted her up to her dorm room. He stayed behind her, dipping his head and kissing the back of her shoulder as she unlocked her door. After peering inside and discovering her roommate was gone, she invited him in.

He had her on her bed about two seconds after the door was shut and locked behind them. Twenty minutes later, he pulled the brakes and stopped the kissing. But he couldn't seem to pull away and leave. So, they just stayed there together, wrapped around each other on her small single-sized bed, thoughtfully listening to each other's settling heartbeats.

Boston closed his eyes as he ran his fingers up and down her arm and reveled in the softness of her cheek on his chest. As much as his dick throbbed, primed for action, he thought he could fall asleep there like that—it felt so good to simply hold her.

From the silence, Ellie said, "Tell me something about you. Something no one else knows."

"You tell me something about you," he countered, not wanting to talk about himself.

"I asked first," she pressed.

He grinned even as he sighed in disgust. The woman's stubbornness could frustrate him to no end, but it was one the things he liked best about her.

"I don't know," he started reluctantly. "I can't think of anything that at least one person doesn't

126

know."

"Just tell me something...something that makes you unique."

"Oh, now wait a second. You want me to confess something embarrassing, don't you? Something like I wet my bed till I was thirteen."

"Did you?"

"No."

She laughed and pinched his chest. Boston growled and rolled over on top of her to pin her to the bed. Snagging her wrists, he pulled her hands above her head and loomed above her.

She merely grinned up at him, looking like there was nowhere else in the world she'd rather be. A split second later, he forgot about paybacks. Need filled him, and he barely murmured, "I'm going to have to put those busy little hands of yours to better use," before he set his mouth to hers.

He panted, body straining for more, by the time he pulled away. Unable to properly catch his breath, he rested his forehead against hers and closed his eyes. It was getting harder and harder to stop every time.

"Tell me something about you," Ellie urged again on a whisper.

She was still under him, with his body fully on top of her, his engorged fly pressed between her legs. He couldn't stop thinking that if they were naked, he'd be inside her.

"Tell me anything," she said.

"Ah..." He blew out a breath. Concentration was nearly impossible. "My dad was an astronaut," he said, thinking it was probably the only unique aspect of his life.

"Ha, ha," Ellie said dryly and pushed lightly against his shoulder.

Boston lifted his face in surprise. "No, I'm serious."

She rolled her eyes. "What in the world would some astronaut be doing, living in Kansas?"

Boston sent her an unamused look. "Thanks a lot, El," he muttered. "I try to tell you something for real, and you laugh at me."

"Oh, pul-lease," she argued. "There's no way. You're so full of it." She frowned at him, clearly annoyed.

"Google it if you want to," he challenged. "His name's Lincoln Kincaid. He made two trips into space. You can find him on the NASA website."

She rolled her eyes. "There's no way the son of a distinguished astronaut would be living in Kansas and going to some public state college. No way."

"I'm going to Yale next year," he reminded her. "I've already been admitted. I only came to KU because it was just about the closest decent college I lived by."

"Whatever." Ellie pushed against his chest again as if she wanted him to get off her.

"Why don't you believe me?" Boston asked, tightening his grip on her arms and not letting her get away.

"Because it's a ridiculous claim, that's why."

"You know what? It is a little ridiculous, so why would I make up a story like that? Especially since you can prove it right or wrong with a little Internet research."

"I'll tell you why. You want to impress me so I'll sleep with you."

Boston laughed. He glanced down at her heaving chest that was pressed against his. "I don't have to make up some stupid story to get that," he murmured. "You'll sleep with me anyway."

Ellie's eyes filled with outrage; she struggled a little harder to get free. But he merely leaned down and pressed his mouth to her throat. "I could've had you a month ago," he said and gave a husky laugh when she moaned and arched against him. "You know I'm right."

Giving up her attempts to break free, Ellie latched her arms and legs around him. He closed his eyes and deepened the kiss. "Then why haven't you done anything about it?" she asked as her fingers found their way under his shirt.

"I'm trying to be...oh God...uh...patient. Yeah, I'm trying to be...damn, Ellie, what're you *doing*?"

He threw his head back and let out a moan as her hands undid his zipper after they'd removed his shirt.

"Patient?" she asked, wrinkling her nose at the word. "What for?"

She rolled him onto his back and finished easing down his straining fly. When the open space filled with nothing but hot, hungry Boston, she reached out and touched him through his boxers.

His body jerked, and he tried to sit up, but she pushed him back down. He stared up at her as she slid his jeans the rest of the way down his legs.

Ellie quietly repeated, "Why are you trying to be patient?"

Boston shook his head and gritted his teeth as she discarded his underwear next. "I don't know," was all he could think to answer. With her, fully clothed, leaning over a totally naked him and staring at his penis like she wanted to lick her way to the tasty center, he couldn't come up with one reason why he'd ever wanted to be so damn patient.

"Well, then," she murmured. "If you can't think of some earth-shattering reason why I shouldn't go down on you, then..." She glanced at his straining shaft. "Do you mind?"

Mind? His body bowed and his hands fisted around the sheets under him...and the woman hadn't even touched him yet. "Be my guest," he rasped.

Unable to help himself, his gaze followed her fingers as they slowly reached out. He started to shudder an inch before contact. When she finally slid one index finger down the full length of his erection, he nearly exploded.

Boston let out a groan, and Ellie's gaze flashed anxiously to his as if afraid she'd done something wrong. Her fingers snapped back to her chest.

"Don't stop!" he demanded, pleaded, begged in one breathless pant.

"S-sorry," she said and quickly wrapped her entire hand around him.

Her fingers were cold like she was nervous, but he didn't care. He closed his eyes and let out a long, loud sigh. She stroked slowly, her touch soft and her grip loose. It drove him mad. In seconds, he was arching and straining for more. For harder, rougher, wetter.

"Ellie," he said in that pleading, demanding voice again. Her eyes lifted once more, inquisitive. "Enough teasing," he bit out. He was going to push her hand aside and finish himself if she didn't hurry.

"Oh," she said and nodded. Thinking she was going to tighten her grip and quicken the pace, he was surprised when she leaned down instead and licked him from base to tip.

"Oh, *God*!" he shouted and arched his back nearly a foot off the bed. "El..." he choked out hoarsely, gripping two handfuls of her thick brown hair.

Her technique left a lot to be desired. She went too slow, didn't suck hard enough, and her teeth scraped him till he winced even as he moaned with pleasure. If he'd had any idea it was her first blow job, he would've given her an A for effort and enthusiasm. As it was, he was so close to the edge, he feared he was going to shove her face down and gag her if she didn't hurry.

To avoid just that, he reached for her and pulled her head up and off him. "Stop," he rasped urgently.

She lifted her face, her eyes wide with worry and surprise. "What's wrong?"

"My turn," he rasped, sitting up and pushing her down onto her back in one smooth move.

He'd never undressed a girl so quickly before. But he jerked her shirt over her head and peeled her jeans and panties down so fast she giggled.

"Shh," he told her, ridding her of her bra. "You're not supposed to laugh at a guy when you have him naked."

"I'm not laughing at you," she said, eyes glittering with glee. "I'm laughing *with* you."

"Smartass," he said and grinned as he covered her warm naked body with his. His erection brushed the inside of her thigh, making her shudder.

"God, you feel good," he whispered and ran his hands up her body, cupping her breasts as he leaned down to kiss her.

He wanted to push inside her right then. He was there, at the entrance, and his tip was wet with moisture, beyond ready to glide into that hot, wet cave and hibernate for a solid hour. But he held back, slipping his tongue inside her mouth instead and making love to her there. Turnabout was fair play, he thought, and broke himself away from her lips a moment later to ease down her body, kissing nipples and a belly button on the way.

"Boston!" Ellie yelped in alarm as he hovered over the apex of her legs. "W-what are you doing?"

"I told you," he answered. "It's my turn." And then he licked her.

Ellie bucked and gurgled out a scream. She grabbed his hair and nearly yanked the locks from their roots. But he wasn't deterred from his task. He entered her with one finger as he continued to stroke her with his mouth. When she arched and gasped even more, he added a second finger. Going crazy under him, Ellie kept chanting his name and talking about God and hell. He didn't catch a lot of what she cried out, but the tone definitely had him feeling pretty incredible.

He wasn't prepared for her to come so quickly. When she pulled her body taut and began to spasm, he jerked in surprise, a little disappointed it was already over. He'd just started to really like her taste. But, all too soon, she subsided, her breathing erratic and heavy. Boston lifted his head. The sight of her debauched, naked body still quivering from his mouth had his arousal growing double in size.

She met his gaze with dazed, glazy eyes. "B-Boston?"

He had to be inside her right then. Surging upward, he made them one even as he took her mouth with his and buried all ten fingers in her hair. She was so wet and ready for him, he shouldn't have met any kind of resistance. So, when he did, making her cry out in pain, he stumbled to a stop.

Fully imbedded inside her, he let out a breath and looked down into her face. "Oh, God," he whispered in scared, amazed and frightened awe. "You're a..." He couldn't even say the word.

She smiled and touched his face. "Not anymore."

A virgin. She'd been a virgin all this time, and he hadn't had a clue. Hell, why hadn't she said anything? Why hadn't she told him so he could go slower...so he wouldn't hurt her so bad?

"Does it still hurt?" he asked in concern, glancing down at their joined bodies. But the view only made him want to thrust for all he was worth.

Even as she bit her lip, she shook her head and said, "No. I'm fine."

"Don't lie," he said and kissed her lightly.

Ellie wrapped her legs around his hips and moved up against him. "Ellie," he gritted out, grabbing her hip to still her. He pressed his forehead to hers. "Why didn't you tell me?"

"I didn't want you to be nervous."

Boston choked out a laugh. But then it struck him. She was right. He would've freaked. But how in the world would she know he'd be nervous?

"I've never been anyone's first time before," he stated, only supporting her claim even more.

"Well, you're going to get an "I" for incomplete if you don't finish. Right now."

Smiling, Boston kissed her again and moved. He didn't get any "I"s that night. He finished just fine, four times in fact before he left Ellie's bed the next afternoon. It was his first night of marathon sex, but it certainly wasn't his last. With Ellie, he became an absolute nympho, wanting to bury himself inside her all the time.

****

Ten years later, the very memory of record-breaking sex with that woman could have him salivating in seconds.

"Bos? Yo, Boston. Earth calling."

Boston blinked and focused his attention on Cameron, who was sitting across the desk from him in Boston's office and staring at him as if he were insane, which obviously he was if all he could think about was Ellie.

For the past six years, he and Cameron had been partners in running their business, EarthNet, though to be fair, Cameron was the brains of the operation and Boston was technically only his attorney. But Cam tended to get irritable when Boston tried to call him boss, so they'd settled on the term partners, when in truth, all Boston handled was the legal end of things. Cam made the ultimate decisions.

"Dude, where were you?" Cam asked, frowning. "I've *never* seen you space off that bad before."

"Sorry," Boston mumbled and tried to remember what they were discussing. It was seven in the evening and he'd been stuck in this office since five thirty that morning, escaping for only fifteen minutes to fetch some food at noon. He was starving, and horny, and didn't want to think about work.

"So...good daydream?" Cameron asked curiously.

Boston shifted, moving so Cam couldn't see his arousal, though he wasn't sure why he bothered. There was a desk between them, hiding anything embarrassing.

"Do you think wanting to see Cassie every weekend is asking for too much?" he wondered aloud, instead of spilling his secret memories.

"Every weekend?" Cameron asked, looking seriously thoughtful for a moment. Then, "Actually, yeah, I do."

Boston scowled and straightened. "Hey, you're supposed to be on my side here."

"I am," Cameron argued. "But come on, Bos. What do you know about little girls?"

"I know Madison and Helena and Cheyenne's daughters love me." All his nieces and nephews loved their Uncle Boston.

"That's because you only play with them a few minutes when you see them," Cameron countered. "You don't take any of them home with you. You don't have to discipline them or provide for them, feed them, or clothe them. Face it, bud. Neither of us have any idea what it takes to be a father. That's why kids start as babies. They know as little about being a kid at that point as we know about being parents. Ergo, we all learn and develop together. You don't just pick up a nine-year-old girl one day prepared to be a dad."

"Hey, it's not my fault I wasn't there—"

"I know," Cam said sadly. "But that's how it is, okay? That's why I think you need a learn a little more about her and how to be a father before you can spend so much time with her."

"And how am I supposed to learn if I don't get to see her every weekend? Not being able to practice isn't going to help me learn squat, Banks."

"So, go over and spend time at her place, in her environment. Watch how her mother treats her and learn that way."

Boston nearly swallowed his tongue. There was no way, no how, he was going to spend that much time around Ellie. He'd...well, he'd implode or something. Damn, he was already thinking about sex too much as it was.

Scowling at Cameron for his logical advice, Boston shoved out of his chair and moved to the window, where he rested a shoulder on the curtain-lined frame.

"And...he takes up the Boston Kincaid moody pose," Cam murmured. He laced his fingers together and rested them on his stomach as if waiting for Boston to come back with a smart-mouthed comment.

But Boston ignored him. He stared out at a trio of women taking a smoke break in the parking lot. One lady had just lit up, and as she sucked in her first breath, a heady look of pure ecstasy crossed her face. Then she exhaled and her shoulders slumped, draining of tension. Smiling, she said something to her coworkers, making all three of them laugh. Boston felt envy as he watched the relaxation seep into her.

"I think I should take up smoking," he announced.

Cameron arched a curious eyebrow. "So now you think you need a vice to help you with... What exactly do you need help with, Kincaid? You seem to be dealing with the fact that you've got a daughter pretty well to me. You like her, she likes you. And you haven't mentioned any problems getting around her mother..."

At Boston's sharp glance, Cam shut his mouth and stared. Then a telling grin spread across his face. "Ah," he murmured, eyes twinkling with mischief. "So, it's your baby's mama bugging you, huh?"

"No," Boston bit out moodily and moved his shoulder in an antsy manner to find a more comfortable position where he leaned. But that didn't work. He still wanted to crawl out of his skin.

"In the excitement over Cassidy's existence, I've forgotten there's an ex-flame involved in all this too."

Cam was quiet a moment, as if waiting for Boston to open up his closet and start pulling out the bones. But Boston remained silent. So, Cam let out a little sigh and said, "You know what I think?"

Boston lifted his face and turned to give his cousin an incredulous look. "Do I look like I care what you think?"

Cam ignored him. "I think you were way serious about Cassie's mom."

Boston's jaw bunched. "Don't go there."

"Why not?" Cameron asked. "We're best friends. If you can't tell me, who can you tell?"

"No one. And let's keep it that way."

"So, how long did you see her?"

Boston didn't answer for a minute. Then he moved restlessly back to the window and muttered, "Eight months."

Cameron fell out of his chair. Literally. Boston turned to frown at him.

From the floor, Cam's jaw fell loose. "Eight...oh my God, you stayed with *one* woman for eight months? Jesus, Kincaid, how is it possible I never knew about her...that no one in the family knew about her?"

Boston scowled. "You were busy mourning your

136

first wife, and I was away at college."

"Yeah, but Monty would've been in college too at that time. Why didn't he—"

"Okay, fine. I purposely kept her a secret!" Boston cut in sharply. "You're right. It was different with Ellie, and it scared the hell out of me. I wasn't used to getting that serious with a girl. So, refusing to let anything go too far with her, I intentionally never introduced her to anyone in the family to convince myself she wasn't that important. Are you satisfied now?"

Cameron just sat on the floor and gaped.

"Will you get up!" Boston snapped and turned away to frown out the window.

Cameron stood slowly, wiped himself off, and calmly sat in his chair. Then he shook his head. "Holy Lord, Bos. You totally fell in love with her, didn't you?"

Boston's eyebrows pulled down low over his eyes. "No," he was quick to spit out. Then he swiped a harassed hand through his hair. "God, I don't know. But if I ever fell for anyone, it would've been her."

"So, why'd you break up?" Cameron asked curiously. When Boston didn't immediately answer, he said, "Oh. Right. I forgot. She got pregnant. You both freaked. Then, when she claimed she had a miscarriage, you were so relieved there wasn't a baby, you took off out of there. End of story."

"That's not quite how it happened. We'd already been broken up a few weeks by the time she told me she was pregnant," Boston admitted quietly. He closed his eyes, and the memories swelled. The guilt washed over him, a wave of nausea wracking his body.

"So, then why did you break—"

"Cameron!" Boston nearly shouted. "I just told you, I'm not going to talk about this with you."

"But—"

"Look, it's over between us. We split because of irrevocable differences, and there's no way, no how, we'll ever get back together...*especially* after she went and kept my daughter from me for nine freaking years. The only contact I'll ever have with Elora Trenton will be over custody for Cassidy. Got it?"

Frowning, Cameron opened his mouth. Before he could speak, Boston's iPhone rang.

Grateful for the distraction, he dug it from his pocket and stared blindly out the window. "Kincaid," he growled.

"D-dad?" came the sobbing reply.

"Cassie?" Boston jerked around in surprise, making Cam surge to his feet. "What's wrong?"

She sniffed and whimpered a moment. Then she wailed, "Can I come live with you?"

"What's wrong?" he repeated, envisioning her broken and bleeding and alone in some dark alley. "Where are you?"

"I'm at home. And I don't want to live here anymore. I hate her so much. She's mean and...and...she won't let me do *anything*."

Boston let out a breath. The adrenaline thrumming through his body didn't shut off so quickly though. He pressed a hand to his jack-hammering heart.

"You had a fight with your mom?" he was finally able to ask.

"Mmm-hmm," Cassie whined pathetically.

Boston's shoulder's dropped. God. Talk about giving a guy a heart attack. He'd thought something was honestly wrong with her.

Sniffing, Cassie asked, "So, will you come get me?"

Chapter Ten

Ellie was cleaning, trying to work off her bad mood, when the doorbell rang. Still upset with Cassidy, who'd barricaded herself in her room hours ago, Ellie had gone on a cleaning rampage and was currently replacing all the newly washed towels she'd never used back on the top shelf of her hall closet.

She didn't want to take Cassie's threats to heart. But if Boston heard one word of their daughter's new wish to live with him, she'd probably lose the girl for good. She had to think of a way to calm the nine-year-old before she spoke to her lawyer of a father...before she went off the handle and did something to get herself taken away from Ellie for good.

Frowning as the gong echoed through the house, Ellie dusted her hands off on her hips and started toward the entrance. She'd just hit the living room when Cassie barreled out of her room.

"No!" Ellie said sternly. "Back into your room, missy."

"But—"

"Back," Ellie repeated.

Sending her mother a look from hell, the nine-year-old stormed back into her room and slammed the door. Ellie sighed. Though her nerves were about to snap in half, Ellie forced herself to remain calm. Cassie was just in a mood. Give her a day or two and her temper would cool. Then Ellie would go into Cassie's room, sit on her bed, and they'd have their mother-daughter talk, working everything out. They always worked things out. They were a pair, a team.

Nothing could keep them apart for long.

Bolstered by that thought, Ellie opened the door and froze. Boston lifted his face, and their gazes held fast.

"Oh, God. What're *you* doing here?" she blurted out, instantly sick to her stomach.

No, no, no. He couldn't come here tonight. Not with Cassie in the mood she was in. Okay, Ellie trusted her daughter to want to stay once she was calmer and more rational. But she had no idea what Cassie would do if she saw her father *now*.

Boston quietly studied her a moment before answering. "Cassidy called me."

Ellie's face drained of color. Clearing her throat, she reached for the doorframe to keep from passing out flat on her face. "She...what?"

He nodded. "She asked if she could come live with me."

Ellie's stomach contorted with pain. No. He couldn't take her baby girl. He just couldn't. Folding her arms over her chest, she cocked her brows and said, "So, you've come to pack her up and leave together, just like that, hmm?"

Boston sighed. "No. I came because... Damn it, Ellie. Will you let me in?" When Ellie didn't budge, he lifted a hand to signal peaceful intentions. "I only want to talk to her."

And convince her to leave me so she can go live with you, Ellie wanted to snarl. But she kept silent. No, she couldn't say anything to really tick him off, or he'd have Cassie out of here in seconds. Realizing she'd have an even bigger fight on her hands if she tried to keep the two of them apart right now, she reluctantly stepped aside.

Obviously, Boston had been expecting the fight. Hesitating, he paused and looked at her. Then he nodded a brief thanks.

Stepping carefully over the threshold, he glanced her way one last time as if he expected her to change her mind. Then, he passed through the living room and started down the hall. Ellie moved to the hall entrance to watch him. He knocked softly on Cassie's door and opened it. When Cassie's ecstatic cry echoed back, Ellie cringed. Boston disappeared through the doorway and shut himself inside with his daughter.

That was when Ellie decided it was time to have her breakdown.

She hurried to the kitchen, out the porch/laundry room, through the back door, and onto the patio. There was a tattered old picnic table sitting on the cobblestone deck. She collapsed onto the bench, clutched her stomach, and looked up at the house, wondering if Boston was busy helping Cassidy pack.

She could fight him. And she could fight Cassie. But there was no way she could fight them together. If they wanted to be with each other, there was no way Ellie could deny it. Cassidy was the most important person in the world, and if Boston was what she truly wanted, Ellie knew she'd grant it. Even if it destroyed her in the process. She'd die for her daughter if she had to.

****

Cassidy was lying on her bed, staring at the wall when Boston tapped on her door and popped his head inside.

"Hey," he said quietly.

She glanced over, looking moody and rebellious. But when she saw him, her eyes shot open. "You came!" she screeched and leaped off the bed.

Boston slipped inside and softly closed the door behind him. He barely caught Cassie as she launched herself into his arms.

"You really came," she repeated in awe and

nuzzled her face in his shoulder, wrapping her arms tight around him.

"I told you I would," he murmured and stroked her hair as he carried her to the bed. Boston sat and settled her on the mattress next to him. He pondered idly as he did so, wondering if he would've kept her nestled on his lap if he'd known her for the past nine years and ten months. If he was familiar and comfortable with his daughter, would he have set her next to him like she was someone else's daughter and kept that polite distance between them? Or maybe he would've kept her close and continued to run his hand comfortingly down her back.

A wave of regret hit him. He'd missed so many years.

He waited a beat for the anger to follow, the resentment against Ellie. But he didn't experience it. Instead, he focused on Cassie, intent to make up lost time.

"Now," he said. "What's going on between you and your mother?"

"Nothing," Cassie mumbled, ducking her head. "I just want to come live with you."

"Well, I don't think nothing happened," Boston said, staring down at the top of Cassie's hair. "I think *something* definitely happened."

"She's so mean," Cassie finally admitted, lifting her face to show Boston a rebellious look. "I can't do anything because of her. She treats me like a little kid."

Boston checked the impulse to say, "But you are a little kid."

"I hate green beans, but *she* makes me eat them. My friend Ally gets to stay home from school at least once a month because her mom is so cool. But my stupid mom makes me go every day. I have to take a bath when she tells me to and eat what she tells me to. And she kept me from you. She always makes me do stupid stuff that's *good* for me. I'm sick of it. Maybe I don't want to brush my teeth every night. Maybe I don't like *healthy* food."

Boston swallowed back a quick laugh. His poor little girl. She had a first-rate mother, and it was driving her crazy. He opened his mouth to tell her she should be grateful instead of so unappreciative, when she blurted out, "And It's *her* fault you didn't know me all these years."

Boston paused.

"If she hadn't lied to you, you wouldn't have left. It's all her fault."

His chest tightening, Boston sighed and rubbed his face. He didn't even bother to ask how she'd learned so much about the weeks after her conception. "No," he said. "It's not *all* her fault. Cassie, I..." He lifted his face and winced in apology. "I said some things"—and did some things—"to make your mother think I didn't want to stick around. She had a reason to do what she did."

Maybe not a good one in his opinion, but she'd had one.

Cassie looked up at him with wide eyes. "But you *did* want me, didn't you?"

"Yes," Boston answered immediately. "Of course. And I want you to come live with me more than you'll ever know. But I think you should stay here with...with your mom."

"Y-you do?" Cassie said, her eyes going wide with hurt.

As much as he wanted to pick up her suitcase and say, "Let's go," he knew that wasn't the right decision. Children of separated parents had it hard enough as it was. It wouldn't help anything to create such an open war with Ellie about this. Picking that fight with her after the Chuck E. Cheese's outing and letting Cassie catch them at it had been an eye-opening experience. Unmarried or not, he and Ellie were this child's parents, and they needed to appear as a united front.

So Boston swallowed his pride and nodded. "Yes," he said. "You need her right now. And no matter how mad you are, you love her, and you'd hate to be without her." He paused when he saw her face turn hard and unyielding.

"Just tell me who'd make chocolate chip cookies with you?" he asked because he remembered Cassie talking about how she loved to make cookies with Ellie. "And who'd go before-school shopping with you every year?"

"C-couldn't you?" the girl asked, looking up at him with wide questioning eyes.

He melted. "Well, yeah. I probably could," he relented with a nod. "But it wouldn't be the same. That's special stuff you do with just your mom. You and I are going to make up new stuff to do together. And that'll be *our* special time."

Reaching out, he took both her hands and squeezed firmly. "I promise someday I'll take you home with me and you can visit my house for a while. Okay? But you have to stay here too. You have to make up with your mother."

Cassidy frowned at that suggestion. "I don't want to make up with her." She jerked her hands from his. "I hate her."

Boston blinked in surprise. He didn't much like the fact that his sweet, innocent young daughter could be so spiteful.

"Please let me come live with you," she begged.

His heart filled with an emotion that seemed to consume him to the point of explosion. He just wanted to scoop her up and let her have whatever she wanted. But she was being a brat, and Ellie's words echoed through his head. *That's the second time tonight you got to play the good guy.*

"No," he heard himself say, sounding stubbornly

resolute and, surprisingly, just like he could remember his own father being. "You said some very mean things about her. Things that would hurt her. I can only imagine what you told her to her face. So you're not leaving this room until you can apologize to your mother."

Cassie's face filled with surprise. Then anger. Crossing her arms over her chest, she growled. "Fine. I didn't want to leave anyway."

****

Boston eased quietly out of Cassie's room, slightly sick to his stomach. Worried he'd just lost his one chance with her, he paused to swallow down his rising panic. Then he huffed out a breath and walked through the house until he saw Ellie through the back window. Blowing out another breath for an entirely different reason, he opened the door to join her. He wasn't sure why he bothered. Both Trenton girls despised him at the moment. He should leave. But he felt drawn to Ellie, and leaving was the last thing he could do.

It was a cool evening with a slight breeze. Ellie sat at a picnic table, huddled inside her bulky jacket. For a moment, she looked so much like that college girl he'd fallen for, he couldn't even breathe.

Then she lifted her face and that was it. All the anger he'd felt over the past week evaporated. In its place, a strange ache wrapped around his chest and pulled taut.

Light from the kitchen window reflected on the wet gleam on her cheeks. He didn't like seeing her cry. It made him feel helpless and clumsy. He just wanted to go to her and pull her into his arms and tell her—

Instead, he shoved his hands into his pockets. "There. Now we're both the bad guy," he said and moved to sit on the bench seat opposite hers.

Ellie unobtrusively tried to swipe at her cheeks.

145

"What?"

Boston tilted his head back so he could stare up at the sky and not her. "She begged to come live with me, but I said no. I told her she couldn't even leave her room until she apologized to you."

"You what?"

She sounded so surprised, Boston straightened and gave her a helpless shrug. "It sounded like something a dad would say."

He wondered if it'd been the wrong thing, though. He wondered what he should've said. The temptation to ask Ellie what he should've done almost suffocated him. He was so uncertain, even his own skin felt uncomfortable.

But then he noticed a slight smile on her face. "That's exactly what I told her too," she finally murmured.

His heart thumped against his ribcage in a crazy little beat. He wanted to reach across the table and take her hand.

Unable to keep the anxiety at bay, he asked, "Do you think she'll ever talk to me again?"

Once again Ellie sent him an amused smile, making his pulse even more erratic. "Cassie might be quick to throw a fit, but she's just as quick to get over it. She'll probably be calling you tomorrow and begging you to take her back to Chuck E. Cheese's."

"And would you let me?" he asked softly.

She didn't answer immediately. Boston held his breath, hoping he hadn't just started another fight. He didn't want to fight tonight. Not when he felt such a kinship with her.

But Ellie didn't grow upset. She lowered her eyes to her tightly clasped hands in her lap and answered, "You know, you could've taken her away for good tonight. I was so upset, I probably would've let her go with you if that was what you'd both wanted."

He swallowed. "I was tempted to tell her yes."

Ellie looked like she was going to start up crying again. Boston was grateful she managed to keep the tears at bay. It was hard enough as it was to sit across from her and not move toward her. Her face was already blotchy from bawling, and he was once again filled with the urge to hold her.

"I love my daughter," she said in a hoarse voice, "But tonight, I couldn't have fought her...not you and her both."

Boston swallowed, not sure how to respond.

"I thank you," Ellie whispered. "For whatever reason you decided to convince her to stay with me, I thank you. From the bottom of my heart."

He lifted his gaze. "A little girl needs her mother," he said. "And you...you're a good mother, El. I only have to look at her to know that. She's the most amazing child I've ever met. She's perfect. You've done an excellent job raising her."

Ellie's face contorted even more, but she still didn't cry. "Thank you."

"No matter how much I want to be with her," he added with great reluctance. "You were right when you said she doesn't need me. She'd be fine without me." Then he shook his head. "She wouldn't be fine without you."

When she didn't respond, Boston worried he'd revealed too much. But he also realized he couldn't have Cassie without Ellie's help and support.

"You've really changed since college, haven't you?" she murmured.

He gave a soft, surprised laugh. "God, I hope so."

Ellie pulled her feet up on the seat so she could hug her knees. "You know I can't live with losing her every weekend, don't you?"

Boston sobered and let out a long sigh. So, they were back to square one, were they?

"What about every other weekend?"

Cradling her head in her hands, she closed her eyes. "I...I'm sorry, Boston. I know you're trying to work with me, but I...I can't. I just can't do it. It's like we're talking about taking my oxygen away."

Boston closed his eyes and ran his fingers through his hair. "Will you be honest with me if I ask you a question?"

After a moment, she gave a hesitant nod.

"Do you..." The asking was tough for him, and he had to pause before he continued. "Do you think she'd be better off if I did leave and never came back? I mean, I'm not going to mess her up by suddenly becoming involved in her life, am I?"

****

For a moment, Ellie was too stunned to speak. This wasn't the Boston Kincaid she knew at all. The college boy she'd dated would never have given her such an advantage, never exposed his vulnerable side. He didn't question himself.

The man really had changed.

Determined not to let that affect her, she asked, "Would you leave if I said yes?"

The achy look he sent her made her want to start crying again. "I want to say yes," he said. "I only want what's best for her. But from the first moment I saw her, I don't know..." He shook his head, as if dazed. "It was like...*bam*, smacking me in the center of the chest and taking my breath. That little human was a part of me. And suddenly, I wanted...I wanted to be a father. *Her* father. I wanted to be a part of her world. But..." He paused to lick his lips. "I don't want to hurt her."

Ellie felt herself fall into a hole she'd sworn to herself she'd never fall into again. She looked at Boston Kincaid and wanted to be loved by him. He honestly seemed like a different man from that twenty-two year old she'd once known. He'd matured.

Loosening toward him, she admitted, "If you want the truth, then no, I don't think she'd be worse off with you in her life." Then she bit the inside of her lip, wondering what the hell she was doing. This was her one chance to get rid of him, and she wasn't taking it.

Boston looked about as shocked by her declaration as she felt about making it. But he laughed in relief and grinned at her like he thought they were mending fences when, yeah, that probably was what they were doing. Neither of them had yelled all evening. That had to mean something.

"So, what happens now?" he said.

Ellie was about to answer, "I don't know," when it struck her. "I think you need to get to know Cassie better before you can take her anywhere by yourself. I mean, tell me honestly, what do you know about nine-year-old girls?"

Frowning, he said, "Nothing, but—"

"Plus, if I saw you with her a few times, and was convinced she'd be okay, then I'd probably feel better about letting her go with you overnight somewhere."

He paused, looking truly shell-shocked now. "You mean, you want me to come *here*...with you around...to see her?" He looked like he might prefer a root canal.

"Not especially," she admitted. "But it's the only compromise I can think of at the moment."

"Fine, then," he said and nodded a little too quickly for her comfort. "I'll come here. When do you want me?"

Right now...in the bedroom, flat on your back. The answer popped into her head so suddenly, she actually blushed for thinking it. Glancing away in absolute mortification, Ellie cleared her throat. "Umm...how about Saturday. Anytime. We'll be here all day."

"Is eight too early?"

She shook her head.

He smiled. "It's a d—ah, it's a deal then." Pushing to his feet, he held out a hand. "Thank you, Ellie."

"Thank *you* for what you did tonight."

Their hands met across the table in a formal manner. But his warm flesh connecting with hers still caused her skin to tingle.

"I just hope she doesn't hate me now," he murmured as he slowly pulled his palm from hers.

It took Ellie a moment before she figured out to whom he was referring. Then it struck her. Cassie.

"Oh," she said a little breathlessly. "No. Cassie will be okay. Trust me."

He still looked uncertain. "I wish I could mend fences with her before I leave," he murmured. But then he hitched a brave smile Ellie's way and added, "I'll see you Saturday."

Ellie opened her mouth and almost made a huge mistake. It was on the tip of her tongue to invite him to stay and find out for himself just how okay Cassie was going to be. But that would be the error of all errors. No, she didn't want to be Boston Kincaid's enemy, but befriending him wasn't smart either.

"I'll see you Saturday," she returned, feeling lame.

And for the first time in over ten years, they separated in peace. Ellie sank against the picnic table and cradled her head in her hands, wondering if being on good terms with him might be more dangerous than keeping him as an enemy.

When the back door cracked open, she jumped and surged to her feet, ready to throw herself at him. But thank God, it was Cassie coming out to join her and not him returning.

"Cass," she said.

"Mommy," the girl spoke in a trembling voice. "I...I'm real sorry for the things I said to you. I..."

"Come here," Ellie said.

Her daughter dashed forward, throwing her arms open. Ellie pulled the child into her lap, and they hugged.

"It's okay," Ellie murmured, kissing her hair. "I love you. No matter what, I'll always love you."

As the girl settled against her and they began to talk out their problems, Ellie felt a spurt of regret that Boston hadn't been able to get the same make-up session she was having. He was missing out on one of the greatest gifts a parent could have. And for the first time in a good long while, she wished she hadn't kept him from his little girl.

Chapter Eleven

That Friday night, a thunderstorm rolled over Lawrence. It was bad enough Ellie and Cassie hurried to the Young's house to stay in their basement for the worst of the squall. Keller and Cassie sat cross-legged on the floor playing Go Fish as the adults hovered by the high basement windows and watched strong winds and rain roll in.

In the midst of the windiest weather, a loud crack of thunder hit so close, the windows shook and the air was filled with an electric charge that made the hairs on Ellie's arm stand on end. The lights went out and a huge thud was heard, followed by a crashing sound outside.

Ellie and Nora let out small startled yelps as the two children screamed and leapt toward each other, groping in the dark until they found one another. Mendel, who was actually home for the evening, cursed until he found a flashlight and flipped it on.

The mothers immediately sought their children to comfort them, and Keller's father tried to peek out the small, foggy windows to see what had happened.

"Tree got hit by lightning," Mendel announced. "Took out the electric wire."

"Was it our tree house tree?" Keller asked, hurrying toward his father and trying his best to see out the window, but he was so short he couldn't see anything. Dr. Young didn't bother to answer his son but went to find his cell phone so he could call in the outage.

Ellie peered out the window to see which tree had fallen.

"It's not the tree house," she assured the children.

Cassie and Keller cheered and hugged each other, dancing in a circle and celebrating until Mendel told them to hush.

Rubbing at her chilled arms, Ellie glanced out the window again and swallowed when she took in the sight of the tree that had fallen.

Half of the massive trunk had landed in her yard.

****

Boston arrived to quite a scene Saturday morning. He could hear Cassie and Keller in the backyard, only for their voices to be cut off by the sound of a chainsaw firing up. He strolled around the side of the house and came to a surprised halt when he found them. The two kids chased each other, playing tag as an adult male in the Young's backyard sawed at a huge fallen tree. Boston gaped at the mess until he spotted Ellie alone in her yard, wearing a pair of worn jeans, an old college sweater, and gardening gloves. Her face was red with exertion as she tried to drag a single large limb toward a pile she'd already gathered.

He lifted his eyebrows, thinking she had the makings for one hell of a bonfire.

Nora Young stood near the man with the chainsaw, trying to talk to him. He had to shut off his engine to hear her.

"You're going to cut up the limbs on Ellie's side too, right?" she asked.

Giving her an annoyed frown, the man grumbled, "I don't think I'll have the time."

"But she can't—"

Turning his back on her, the man started his saw again, cutting off the rest of her words.

Nora glared for a few moments, her hands set on her hips. But then she shook her head and turned away to march toward Ellie's yard.

"I'll help you, El," Boston heard her call. She grabbed another end of the limb, and together the two women were able to drag the partial tree to the pile Ellie had already collected.

Boston sighed, realizing exactly what he'd be doing for the rest of the day. He started toward Ellie when Keller finally spotted him.

"Hi, Cassie's dad," he called and dodged just as Cassidy was about to tag him.

At the boy's greeting, Cassie stopped running and grinned, waving madly. "Look. Our tree fell down." Then she barreled into his legs and hugged him.

Boston sucked in a breath and knelt down to give her a full hug. Okay, so Ellie had been right. Cassie was quick to get over her anger. But it still felt good to know for certain she didn't hate him.

Pulling back before he got emotional, he forced a grin. "So I see." He stayed kneeling beside her because he liked being close. He enjoyed it when she was happy and affectionate like this. It'd been the same way with her mother.

Glancing unconsciously toward Ellie, he was surprised to find she'd stopped her work and was watching them. She gave him a small smile when their gazes met, and he immediately straightened to his feet.

Ellie dragged off her gloves as she strolled his way. "I completely forgot you were coming today."

Boston jammed his hands in his pockets because they were itching to reach for the stray hair clinging to her cheek. He forced his attention to the felled tree. "Hmm, I have no idea what might've caused you to forget."

Ellie gave him another smile and looked over at the tree as well. "Yeah, a storm passed through last night."

"I saw that on the Weather Channel. But I didn't realize it'd been so bad."

He took an instinctive step back as Nora Young joined them. The last time he'd talked to her, she'd been ready to tear his head off. Not sure if he was still listed on her bad side, he held his breath until she spoke.

"Thank God you're here. Ellie's been on the phone all morning trying to get a hold of a yard-cleaning service. But with the storm that came through last night, they're all tied up." She looked at him expectantly.

He opened his mouth to respond but Ellie broke in, "Boston's only here to visit Cassie. I'll take care of the yard myself." She glanced at him with a meaningful look. "One of the services should call me back any minute." When a ringing came from her back porch, she brightened. "That's probably one of them now." She turned away and hurried to her deck where she'd left her portable phone.

As soon as she was ten feet away, though, Nora whirled to him.

"I'd like to apologize for absconding with your son the other night," he said before she could speak. "I honestly had no intention of scaring you."

She blinked a few time, clearly startled by his remorse. "Well," she said, clearly not sure what to say. "I guess if Ellie's forgiven you, so can I. I actually *gave* you permission to take Keller to Chuck E. Cheese's, and besides, he's back now. No harm, no fowl. I'm willing to let bygones be bygones. If..." she added archly, making him lift a curious brow. "You give Ellie a hand with cleaning up her yard."

For a moment, he could only blink at her. Then he finally asked, "You actually think I'd let her take care of a mess this big by herself?"

"Haven't you before?" she asked, glancing Cassie's way.

Biting back a nasty retort, Boston cleared his throat and quietly answered, "I don't think you know enough about me to make that kind of observation."

Her eyes narrowing a little too perceptively on his face, she said, "Or maybe I know too much."

The chainsaw in her own yard stopped and the man running it yelled, "Keller! Stop playing around and come pick up these sticks." Then he glanced Boston and Nora's way. "Nora. I need you."

"Be right there, dearest," Nora called back, her voice so sweet, it sounded fake even to her husband, who scowled before returning to his chainsaw and starting it again.

"That's my husband, Dr. Mendel Young," Nora murmured to Boston, watching her husband work. "He's a cheating bastard too."

She turned to Boston, eyebrows arched in challenge.

He gave a slight nod of defeat. "Then I guess he and I will get along fine together, won't we?"

"I was right," Ellie said, breaking into the conversation as she hurried over, a bit breathless from her rush. "That was a lawn service calling me back."

"And?" Nora asked.

Looking momentarily uncomfortable, Ellie glanced toward Boston before answering, "They can be here in two weeks no problem."

"Two *weeks!*" Nora exploded. "Oh, Ellie. That's awful."

"Got a chainsaw?" Boston asked.

Ellie's head snapped around. She stared at him as if he were crazy. "No."

He nodded even as he pulled his iPhone from his pocket. Dialing a number, he returned his attention to her as he waited for someone to answer.

"Boston, you don't have to worry about my yard," she started. "Why don't you take Cassie somewhere and spend the day with—"

But he held up a finger, cutting her off. "Hey, beautiful," he spoke into the cell, grinning as he did so. "Can I talk to your loser husband?"

After pausing to wait a moment, he spoke into the receiver. "You using your chainsaw today? Yeah, Ellie's got a tree down in her yard. It's pretty big."

He glanced her way and said, "Sure, we could use that...or better yet, grab Monty and bring his trailer. There's enough tree here for a few ricks. Great. Thanks. Oh, and stop by my place on your way to grab an extra pair of work clothes for me."

After rattling off Ellie's address, he disconnected and turned toward the women. With a proud nod, Nora grinned and was off toward her own yard. Ellie didn't look so grateful.

"Got a trash bag and a rake?" he said before she could start.

She nodded. "Yes, I have a rake. But I don't want you to worry about any of this. This is my yard, Boston. It's not your problem."

He turned away and called, "Hey, Cass. Come here."

The girl had been in the Young yard with Keller, picking up twigs and sticks. But at her father's voice, she hurried his way. As she approached, he knelt down to talk on her level.

"You want to make some money today?"

Lured by that offer, she moved closer. "Sure."

"Uncle Cam and Uncle Monty are going to be here soon. We're going to help your mom clean up this yard. It sure would be a big help if you could rake all the small twigs into a pile. I'll pay you ten bucks an hour."

"Okay," she said brightly.

"And if you do a good job," he added, tugging playfully on her ponytail as he pushed back to his feet, "I'll make sure you get pizza for lunch."

"All right!" she cheered.

"Then get to work, young lady," he said, clapping his hands. She hooted and raced off toward the small shed by the back of the house.

"Good Lord, Boston," Ellie commented, clearly amused. "Ten dollars an hour? I would've raked the yard for half that."

Boston turned to her, his smile growing. "Oh, I have other plans for you."

****

By noon, Ellie was sweating her butt off. It'd taken a good hour for Boston's brother and cousin to arrive. The two men had been impatient for an introduction, refusing to start any work until they met her, which threw her for a loop. She hadn't expected any of Boston's family to want to meet her, much less be excited about the prospect. So, this...eagerness they had to simply talk to her caught her totally off guard.

She would've thought they'd be more anxious to see Cassie. But she soon learned they already had.

"You didn't get a chance to meet either of these two the other night at Chuck E. Cheese's," Boston started. "But this is my cousin, Cameron Banks, and my brother, Monty."

A little sick at the realization that these two strangers had seen her in her prime—chewing Boston out—she gave them a small smile, hoping they didn't think she always acted as bitchy as she had at the pizza parlor. But they both surged forward with warm smiles, making her jerk and take a leery step back.

Just as Montgomery stuck out his hand, Cameron butted him aside with an elbow and took her fingers, tugging them to his mouth. After pressing his lips to her knuckles, he glanced at her with a devastating, yet ornery smile.

"It's an honor to finally meet you," he murmured

in a husky voice.

Ellie blinked, not sure how to take this green-eyed hunk who couldn't seem to stop grinning at her with the orneriest look in his gaze. She glanced hesitantly toward Boston and was surprised to find him scowling at his relative.

"Banks," he growled. "That's enough."

"What?" Cameron asked innocently. "You flirt with my wife nonstop. I think I'm entitled to—"

"Don't even think about finishing that sentence," Boston warned.

"You're such a moron," Montgomery told Cameron, shoving him back with his own elbow so he could gain Ellie's gaze.

The jostling for her attention made her blink in bewilderment. At best, she would've hoped they'd attempt to be cordial. But this...this was downright flattering.

Montgomery once again stuck out his hand. "You probably don't remember me, but I had a class with you in college."

"Calculus," she answered, taking his fingers.

He beamed, his smile spreading wide. "Hey, you do remember."

How could she have forgotten? She'd been in love with his brother at the time.

"You knew my brother?" Boston asked, sounding startled, as he shifted a somewhat accusing look her way.

Simultaneously, Monty and Ellie turned toward Boston. "We never actually met," Montgomery started. "Remember? I said so the night we received Cassie's letter?" But Boston wasn't paying any attention to him.

He was too busy pinning Ellie with narrowed eyes. "But you knew who he was?"

Ellie gave a slight nod. "I knew he was your brother," she affirmed.

His mouth dropped. "Why didn't you ever tell me?"

Her back went straight and her shoulders squared righteously. "You never bothered to tell me you had family on campus, so I didn't think you wanted me know about him."

"*What*? That doesn't make any—" He must've realized he was about to start a fight if he said one more word, because he sighed and ran his hands through his hair. "I didn't realize I'd never told you about Monty," he grudgingly admitted.

"Oh, come off it." Ellie let out a harsh laugh. "Every time I asked about your parents or your siblings, you changed the subject. Every time I asked about your childhood or home life, you buttoned up."

He shook his head in denial. "I never purposely kept my family from you."

"Yes, you did. Because clearly, I wasn't important enough to meet them. You put me right in my place from the very beginning, and I was just too stupid and blind to notice it."

Okay, so the fight was on anyway.

"Now who's the moron?" Cameron asked Monty. Ellie whirled around to find both of Boston's relatives grinning with their arms crossed as they watched avidly.

"Don't worry, El. We're cheering for you," Montgomery assured her, looking way too amused.

"And how dare you not tell her about *me*." Cameron turned toward Boston, setting his hands on his hips in outrage. "I think I should've been mentioned at least once a day. I'm your best friend, for crying out loud."

"Not then you weren't," Boston grumbled.

"I can't believe you never even told her I was going to school with you," Monty exclaimed. "And why didn't you ever introduce her to *me*?"

Boston balled his fists in a threatening stance.

"Will you two go away?"

"But you just told us to get our butts over here," Cameron reminded him.

Growling out a sound of frustration, his cousin sneered, "Just...go cut the tree, will you?"

"Geez," Cameron muttered, tugging on Monty's arm and pulling him away from them. "Someone forgot to take his anti-anger pill this morning."

As soon as they were far enough away, Boston turned to her. Ellie held her breath, bracing for the explosion.

"Ellie," he started as if he was going to spill out a whole crap load of pathetic excuses. Then he stopped himself and shook his head miserably. "I was awful to you," he said in a tired voice. "I know that. But I paid for it big time by losing you. My sentence has been served. So, I think we should get to start over with a clean slate. Today, I just want to help you clean your yard."

Ellie folded her hands over her chest, suddenly upset he was once again making her out to be the the wicked witch, and he was the good guy, only wanting peace. Her jaw was still hard with resentment, and she knew she couldn't speak, so she merely gave a terse nod.

It was unfeasible to believe he thought losing her had been the worst punishment possible, so of course she kept replaying that line over and over in her head. He could've kept her if he'd wanted. She'd been such an idiot back then, she would've let him back if he'd said sorry. But he hadn't.

And she'd be the fool if she believed his fancy little words now...except...he wasn't the same person anymore. He'd changed. In everything he did, she could see how he'd changed. Which made her even more confused.

"Come on," he told her, holding out a hand. "I'm going to show you how to use a chainsaw."

Ellie met his gaze, not sure what to do, what to believe. But it didn't take long for her to be held captive by those blue orbs. The man had a look that would turn her into his little puppet.

"Get over here," he urged, almost playfully, a smile hovering over his lips. "You're going to work for your lunch, woman."

Drawn by the challenge in his statement and the excitement in his eyes, Ellie followed him to the back of Monty's truck, where a third unused saw sat, waiting for them. Glancing toward her daughter, she grinned when she caught sight of Cassie diligently raking sticks. Montgomery and Cameron had already moved to the main trunk and were slicing away, wood chips flying past their shoulders.

"I'll get it started," Boston offered, making Ellie arch a brow.

"Oh, no you won't," she said. "If I'm going to work this thing, I'm going to learn how to do every step."

He grinned. "Well, okay then. Come here."

She strolled forward, not knowing what he intended until he was standing behind her and helping her hold the chainsaw with both hands, practically embracing her as he did so.

"Just relax," he said after explaining the procedure. "You're as stiff as a board."

"And just how, pray tell, am I supposed to get comfortable with you back there, like that?"

That caused him to chuckle. She swore he moved in closer behind her.

"So, you're saying this would be an inopportune moment to mention that's my sweatshirt you're wearing then," he murmured in her ear. "And the last time I wore it, I was inside you."

Ellie leaped away from him, almost causing him to drop the chainsaw. He fumbled for a moment, trying to keep his hold on the machine. "Jesus,

Ellie," he yelped.

She could only gape at him, grabbing two handfuls of her gray top with the faded KU Jayhawk printed across the front. It was huge, and old, and comfortable. And hers, damn it.

"This isn't *your* sweatshirt," she insisted.

He grinned as he set the chainsaw down. "Yes, it is." He reached for the hemline to poke his finger though a fraying hole. "I snagged this on a tree the day we had sex in the rain. Don't you remember that afternoon?"

She swallowed. "How could I forget? That's when Cassidy was conceived."

His jaw dropped. "Was it really?"

She bobbed her head, feeling like a moron for revealing such a thing. "It's the only time we did it without total protection," she added, her face heating for letting another remembered intimacy slip.

He ran a hand through his hair and cracked off a surprised laugh. "Well, I'll be damned. That explains that then."

Her brow wrinkled. "Explains what?"

"I thought it was the rain that made that time so..." He broke off and sent her an uneasy look. "I tried it with other women after that, but it was never the same. Now, though, I think it was Cassie. We created something important that day. That's why it was so...out of this world."

Ellie knew her eyes were wide as she stared up at him. But holy cow. Goosebumps spread up the back of her neck, and a rising heat crawled up the inside of her thighs.

"I'm going to go change," she rasped and spun away.

He caught her arm. "Don't." The plea was simple and quiet, but it stopped her in her tracks.

"I always wondered what happened to this

sweatshirt. But I'm glad it stayed with you...and Cassie."

Ellie's lips parted in shock. "Boston," she whispered.

"Hey, you two!" Cameron called, pausing to point in their direction. "You're not going to get any work done, just standing there, making googly eyes at each other."

Boston dropped his hand from her arm, but she still felt the warmth and pressure where his fingers had left their impression.

"Let's cut some wood," he said.

And thus started a day of labor like she'd never experienced before. Forget Tae Bo. It didn't even signify compared to the workout she received now. Sweat dripped off her temples in buckets. Her arms were so tired from lifting the chainsaw, her muscles quivered every time she gunned the motor.

It was a quarter after twelve when she finally couldn't take it anymore. She shut off the engine and set it on a log, afraid her arms were going to shake off her body. They felt like limp noodles.

Boston sidled up to her seconds later, holding out a bottle of water. She took it appreciatively and chugged without grace.

"Why don't we switch," he offered, hefting the saw.

"I'm fine," Ellie said, though, no, she wasn't.

He ignored her stubborn pride with a shrug. "Hey, if I don't get a turn, how am I supposed to show off my muscles for..." He met her gaze with a slow smile and belatedly finished with, "Cassie?"

Ellie rolled her eyes and sent him a reluctant grin. "Then by all means," she offered. "Knock yourself out, Law Boy."

The name no sooner left her lips when she remembered and slapped her mouth shut. His words from over a week ago filled her head. *Don't call me*

Law Boy anymore. You only did it because you thought it annoyed me, but all it ever did was turn me on.

Her eyes skidded to his. His teeth flashed as he smiled. Oh, yeah. He'd definitely heard her. Caught by his gaze, she felt restrained by his blue eyes.

But the moment was soon broken by her daughter. "Mom, I'm starving."

"Yeah, so am I," Cameron said, wiping sweat off his brow with the back of his wrist as he strolled closer and glanced Boston's way. "Are you going to allow us a lunch break or what, slave master?"

Boston and Ellie exchanged glances. "I did promise Cassidy pizza," he admitted.

"Pizza?" Montgomery perked to attention, setting down a limb he was hauling to join the group. "I think I could eat a large pepperoni all by myself right now."

After digging some cash out of his pocket, Boston turned to Ellie. "Would you mind picking up a couple?"

As he held out the money, she frowned and shook her head. "I'll pay," she offered, glancing toward his brother and cousin. "It's the least I can do."

"No," Boston said. "This one's on me."

"Boston," she started on a tired sigh. "You've already done enough today."

"Ellie," he countered just as stubbornly. "I *want* to pay."

"Good God," Cameron broke in with a disgusted growl. "*I'll* pay if it'll get you two to stop bickering. I'm wasting away here. Need food. Must eat soon."

"Oh, fine," Ellie ground out, snagging the money from Boston's hand. Turning from the annoying men, she glanced at her daughter. "Go see if Keller and Nora want some pizza too."

Chapter Twelve

As it turned out, both Keller and Nora not only wanted to eat with them, they also wanted to ride with Ellie and Cassie to pick up the pizza.

"Oh, Lordy. I needed a break," Nora groaned and then let out a moan of delight as she slipped into the passenger seat of Boston's car.

Ellie still couldn't believe she was actually going to drive such a nice automobile. But he'd parked behind her, blocking her in the drive, and when she'd asked him to move his car so she could get out, he'd merely tossed her his keys and instructed her to take the Infiniti.

"Mendel is driving me insane," Nora grumbled. "I'm telling you, that man's not a doctor. He's a dictator. Actually, scratch the 'tator, and *that's* what he is. Move that, pick up this, cut that. Kiss my ass. I was just about to murder him when you saved us."

Chuckling, Ellie started the engine and sucked in a breath as the smooth motor hummed to life under her. In the backseat, the two nine-year-olds were chatting away about what they were going to do with the money they were earning today. After Cassidy told Keller how her father was paying her to pick up limbs, Nora had felt obliged to do the same for her son.

"Looked like you were having fun over there with all those power tools and sexy men, though," Nora commented and then yawned, closing her eyes and resting her head back against the car seat rest.

"Nora!" Ellie hissed in alarm and glanced in the rearview mirror to make sure Cassie hadn't heard.

Those "sexy" men just happened to be her father and two uncles.

"Oh, they're not paying attention." Nora snorted. "Kids never listen to adults. But you've got to admit, good looks run in that family. I mean, holy crap, El. I don't really think it was all that hard labor making me sweat. It was Boston and his brother and cousin."

Sputtering out a surprised laugh, Ellie shook her head and turned into the pizza parlor's parking lot.

"Well, admit it," Nora pressed. "It's not a sight you see every day. Those three look damn good all sweaty and dirty."

"Okay, okay," Ellie broke in, still unable to control her chuckling. "I agree. Now, hush." She parked the car and as her passengers piled out, she reached for her purse. But when she did so, she paused, taking note of the cubbyhole in the center console.

Grinning to herself, she pulled the money Boston had forced on her from her pocket and tucked it into the change holder. There, she thought, pleased with herself. He wasn't paying for anything today.

She stepped lighter as she followed the crew inside and was finally able to admit that Nora had been right. Boston looked great in the old jeans and sweatshirt Cameron had brought over for him. It reminded her of how he'd looked in college.

Too bad it wasn't July, instead of November. The heat might've forced him to peel off his shirt while he worked. Even so, there was something about men and power tools that was beyond yummy. He kept pausing throughout the morning to pay attention to Cassie too, which made him that much more attractive. Once he'd picked her up and held her over his head so she could pull a dangling limb hanging broken from a high branch.

Another time, Ellie had caught sight of him teasing Cassie and then grinning at her as he tucked a leaf behind the girl's ear. It was so similar to a time in college when he'd plucked a flower out of the campus flowerbed and slipped it behind Ellie's ear. Her heart jumped like crazy.

She'd spun away from the scene and promptly severed a large limb to alleviate the pressure building in her chest. But it hadn't seemed to help because she could still hear laughter across the lawn; Boston's and Cassie's both. And she'd ached for something she knew she shouldn't.

****

After pausing for lunch, everyone set back to work. Cassie and Keller were tired of raking and went inside Keller's house to play video games. By late afternoon, most of the mess was cleaned in both yards. As Cameron and Monty cut the last large limb, Boston hauled stacks of wood to the already overflowing trailer. Ellie tried to assist him, though she could only carry one block at a time.

Every once in a while she could hear Nora and Mendel arguing in their yard. Cameron, Monty and Boston grinned at each other as they listened.

"They're better than watching a soap opera," Cameron admitted and started his saw to cut his way through a limb connected to the main trunk that was sticking up in the air. Ellie bent over, too busy picking up another log to notice where she was standing.

But she heard Boston's sharp call loud and clear.

"*Ellie!*"

She glanced up just in time to see him charge toward her. It wasn't until she noticed the panic on his face that she caught motion from the corner of her eye. The limb above her cracked and began to fall...on *her*. The log she'd just lifted slipped from her fingers and she cringed, bracing for the impact.

It never came.

Boston hurled himself toward her, his hands lifted to catch the tree. He cursed as he did so, and she could only imagine how much it injured him to save her. As the branch settled over them, he gritted his teeth and held the wood off them, straining with all his might. Leaves and limbs covered Ellie and Boston like an umbrella, cocooning them inside.

Boston continued to hold the large limb above them; Ellie knew it had to hurt.

But he still immediately glanced at her in concern. "Are you okay?"

"Yeah," she answered, breathing hard. "Are you?"

He nodded, but she could see it in his eyes. He wasn't comfortable at all.

"You guys all right in there?" Cameron asked from outside the branches.

Boston's gaze stayed on Ellie. She stared back at him with wide eyes. They were close. Boston had his hands up, holding the branch off them. He looked down at her like it would be nothing to tilt his head a little and press his mouth to hers. Ellie stopped breathing, waiting for him to do just that.

"Yeah," he finally answered Cameron. "But could you get this damn tree off us?"

Ellie abruptly snapped back to reality.

"Oh, my God," she cried. "I'm sorry, Boston. Are you sure you're okay?"

"I'm fine," the words came from between gritted teeth.

Cameron and Monty lifted the branch together and pushed it to the side. As soon as it was gone, Boston dropped his arms, sucking in a breath. He pressed his palms together as if trying to hide them. But Ellie saw blood seep through the cracks

"Boston, no," she breathed, snatching his wrist. She pried his hands apart and turned them up, only to gasp at the sight of torn and raw flesh. Biting her lip, she looked up at him with concerned eyes.

"They're okay," he said.

She shook her head. "No, they're not. Damn it, this is my fault. If I would've just looked where I was going in the first place... You should've let the tree fall on me."

As she was talking, berating herself and him too for getting hurt on her account, she kept a hold of his wrists and began dragging him toward the back entrance of the house.

Boston followed meekly and only once said, "Ah...El? Where're we going?"

"I'm going to patch you up," she huffed, still furious with herself.

"Ellie." He laughed uneasily as he followed her inside. "I'm fine. Really. It's just a couple scratches."

But she was determined. She didn't let go of him until they were in her bathroom. She closed the toilet seat and ordered him to sit.

"Yes, ma'am," he murmured, all the while giving her an amused look.

Turning on the water, she reached for his fingers again and didn't even notice how easily he handed them over. She plunged his hand under the warm stream, getting her own fingers wet in the process. Cringing at the blood that filled her drain, she muttered, "Just a couple scratches," and grabbed a washcloth. After thoroughly cleaning one palm, dabbing out chunks of bark and dirt, she took care of the other, continuing to grumble to herself as she opened the medicine cabinet and searched for some ointment and gauze.

He sucked in a breath as she applied the salve. Ellie couldn't help but wince right along with him.

"Sorry," she whispered and leaned over to blow

on the cuts, her long hair falling over her shoulder and caressing his wrist as she did so. He sucked in another breath, this time for an entirely different reason.

She straightened abruptly and cleared her throat. Carefully keeping her eyes off him, she opened the gauze and began to wrap his hands.

"So, am I going to live?" he asked quietly.

Ellie risked sending him a brief frown. "It's not funny," she admonished. "You hurt yourself because of me."

"Well, if I knew I was going to get this kind of attention for it, I would've injured myself a long time ago," he said and then laughed. "Jesus, El. You don't have to turn me into a mummy."

"Hush," she said and taped off the end.

Once she turned away to store her ointment and supplies back in the cabinet, she felt him push to his feet. He moved closer. She knew because she was suddenly enveloped by his smell and his very heat.

Ellie swallowed and finished putting away her first-aid kit. They were too close. The already miniscule bathroom grew even smaller, and suddenly she couldn't breathe so well. Slowly, she pushed the cabinet door closed and met his gaze in the mirrored reflection.

"Ellie." He touched her back lightly.

She jumped. Mortified by her own response, she covered her mouth with both hands and spun toward the exit. But she didn't even get one step before he took her arm.

"Ellie," he said again, his voice soft and entreating.

"Boston, I'm sorry. But I can't—" she started, turning toward him, merely to let him down easy. But when his blue gaze latched onto hers, the words died in her throat.

"You can't what?" he asked.

She shook her head, unable to even remember what she'd wanted to say.

"Oh." The word puffed from his mouth, and his warm breath caressed her cheeks.

His gaze darted to her lips and back to her eyes. Then slowly, so frustratingly slowly, he bent his head, stopping an inch from her mouth as if waiting for permission to proceed.

Ellie exhaled, closing her eyes and tipping her face up. Soft, warm lips pressed against hers, gentle enough she wondered if she was imagining it, dreaming it. But then he made a sound in the back of his throat. His hot mouth moved over hers fully, slanting and stroking his tongue boldly between her teeth.

He cupped her jaw, his warm fingers heating her skin. She sank against him, wrapping her arms around his neck. His middle nudged hers, and the press of his erection through his jeans made her sob. God, she wanted to moan aloud. *Thank you, thank you, thank you.* She'd been craving to do this again for nearly two weeks.

He backed her up half a step until her bottom hit the edge of the sink vanity. Then he lifted her, setting her on the counter, and ran his hand up her thigh, touching her through denim.

"Oh, Lord," the words were pulled from her. She arched, throwing her head back and gasping again while his mouth and tongue moved down the side of her throat. "Boston."

He pulled back slightly to look at her. No words were uttered, and that seemed to be the most poignant thing he could've ever said. His gaze spoke volumes. Ellie reached for his face and dragged him back.

His breathing was ragged, but then, so was hers. His mouth scorched, his tongue slid like wet silk into her mouth, unforgiving as it sought hers.

"I can't stay away from you. Why can't I stay away from you?" he rasped, burying all ten fingers in her hair. "God, I want you."

Her eyes fluttered open. She was kissing Boston again. It was so familiar, she almost wept with longing. She could remember this so well. He kissed the same, touched the same, smelled the same. And she'd missed him.

"I want..." she started, only to get caught on a gasp of pleasure.

"Yes?" he urged, his voice low and thick.

"I want—"

"Yo, Boston," a male voice yelled from the back door. "You alive in here?"

Ellie jerked backward, pressing a hand to her heart. Boston bit out a curse and closed his eyes.

"Kincaid?" Cameron called.

"Just a sec," Boston answered on a loud growl. He glanced at Ellie, his eyes unreadable before he opened the bathroom door and stepped into the hall.

"Whoa," she heard Cameron say. "You really did hurt yourself."

"No," Boston answered. "Ellie went gauze happy, that's all."

Pressing a hand to her heart, Ellie slid off the bathroom sink's vanity, inhaled a lungful, and stepped into the hall. "He'll thank me tomorrow when his hands feel fine and aren't raw and burning," she informed Cameron.

Cameron grinned at her and immediately turned back to Boston. "So, did you ask her if Cassie could come for Thanksgiving yet?"

Ellie froze and Boston grew stiff next to her. She looked up at him as he gave a slight shake of his head, opening his mouth and looking way too guilty.

Glancing menacingly toward his cousin, he bit out, "No, I haven't yet."

Cameron blinked at the killer look he was

receiving and glanced quizzically toward Ellie before returning his clueless gaze to Boston. "What?"

Boston closed his eyes and whispered an obscenity.

"Ah..." Looking distinctly uncomfortable, Cameron backed from them and pointed toward the exit. "Monty and I are almost done. We're just going to...yeah." He turned and hightailed it out of there.

Silence followed. Ellie heard Boston shuffle uncomfortably.

"Ellie..." he started.

Whirling toward him, she held up a hand to stop him. "Next time you want something from me, just ask. Okay? Don't go groping me in the bathroom, thinking it'll butter me up—"

"Whoa," he cut in, grabbing her hand and tugging her toward him. "Just stop. What happened in there had nothing to do with—"

"Oh, don't even bother, Boston. You don't really—"

"Jesus, I knew you'd jump to the wrong conclusion. That in there was not some deliberate scam to soften you up. And goddamn you for suggesting it was. I'm not that twenty-two-year-old jerk I was ten years ago. How many times do I have to tell you?"

He whirled away from her, hissing indecipherable words to himself before he paused and lifted his face. "I understand you're going to have problems trusting me now. But I didn't even use that kind of underhanded trickery back then. So, I don't think I deserve this now."

Ellie opened her mouth to comment, but he still had plenty to get off his chest. "I know I was awful to you. I *know*, okay. But every single physical moment we shared was real. Jesus, that's why it was so hard to—"

When he stopped talking, she couldn't help but

ask, "So hard to what?"

He shook his head, unable to look at her. "Nothing."

Turning away, he started to stride down the hall. But he'd gotten no more than five feet from her before he paused and let out a long, miserable sigh. Slumping with his back to the wall, he shoved his hands into his pockets and stared down at his feet.

"I've forgiven you for keeping Cassie from me," he murmured. "I know you had your reasons, but you *did* do wrong by me. And I've gotten over it. Completely." He lifted his face and glanced her way. "It's vital that we at least try to get along. We have a child together, Ellie. We need to form some kind of unity. But before we can accomplish that, you have to at least attempt a little forgiveness on your part."

Too choked up to talk because, damn it, he had a point, Ellie could only nod.

"Do you believe I wasn't trying to mislead you in the bathroom?"

Again, she nodded.

He blew out a breath. "Good. That's a start at least."

He was quiet a long moment, and there was no way Ellie could speak.

Finally he pushed away from the wall. "I still have very strong feelings for you, Ellie. I'll always want to act on them. But believe me when I say I won't force my unwanted attentions on you and *grope* you again. Okay?"

With that said, he spun away and left the house.

It was Ellie's turn to sag against the wall. She covered her mouth and tried not to be affected by his words. But then she wondered why she was trying so hard. Why did she have to hold a grudge?

For too long, she'd shrouded herself in hurt, built up an armor against suffering that kind of pain again. Ten years ago, he'd destroyed her and ruined her idea of love. But he was right when he'd said they had no hope for even an amiable future if she couldn't even try to let some of that bitterness go. There was a nine-year-old girl whose happiness depended on it.

Realizing what she had to do, Ellie straightened and left the hallway. As soon as she opened the back door, she saw him crouched down by Monty's truck and hugging Cassie goodbye.

"When am I going to see you again?" Cassie asked, her eyes huge and sad.

"How about next Thursday?" Ellie spoke, slipping her hands into her back pockets as she approached the group, her gaze moving unconsciously toward Boston.

Both father and daughter turned and glanced up in surprise. "What?"

"What do you say, Cass?" she asked, ignoring Boston. "Want to spend Thanksgiving with your dad?"

Cassie's eyes grew wide. "Can I?" she asked, clearly excited about the idea. "I can't wait to see Libby and Cora again."

Ellie smiled, guessing Libby and Cora were probably cousins close to Cassie's age. She laughed as Cassidy squealed in delight and hugged her father again.

"This is going to be so much fun," Cassie exclaimed. She'd never been to a true Thanksgiving before. It'd always been just her and Ellie. But now that she had a large family, she was going to get something Ellie had only dreamed of.

Cameron and Monty demanded that Cassidy hug them as well before they left. And as Monty swooped the girl up in the air, making her shriek in delight, Boston shifted closer to Ellie.

"Thank you," he murmured quietly.

She nodded mutely. In the next moment, he was

enveloped by his brother and cousin, talking guy stuff before the two men waved farewell and piled into their extended cab pickup.

Ellie walked Boston around to his car and remained standing in the front yard, watching his Infiniti disappear down the street. Cassidy had drifted off long ago to look for Keller, but Nora appeared from the yard next door, strolling Ellie's way.

When the older woman reached her, she slid her arm over Ellie's shoulder and sighed peacefully as she watched Boston's car leave as well.

"You're going to forgive him, aren't you?" Nora finally murmured.

Ellie's shoulders slumped.

Nora chuckled. "Yeah," she agreed. "I probably would too."

Chapter Thirteen

Thanksgiving came with a crisp breeze, chilling the air and filling Ellie with a desolation she refused to think about until after Cassie was gone.

This was going to be her first holiday totally alone.

After her parents had died, she'd always had Aunt Eadie. Though her grandmother's sister hadn't been the ideal caregiver, she'd at least tried to give Ellie holidays. For one Thanksgiving, the elderly woman had taken her to Burger King. They'd ordered hamburgers and fries from the drive-thru and taken their feast home with them. Aunt Eadie arranged the fries sticking out the side of the bun to resemble a fanning turkey tail. She pulled a pickle out the other side to be its head. And that had been her most memorable Thanksgiving as a child.

Aunt Eadie had died when Cassie was three, so Ellie had always had at least one person to celebrate a holiday with. Today would be her first go at it alone. She was determined to hide her angst from her excited child, though.

Cassie had already met most of Boston's family from her memorable night at Chuck E. Cheese's. Ellie was surprised she'd been able to remember everyone's name, but Cassidy had spent most of the morning recounting the names of Boston's family. The rest of time, she was busy pacing, anxious for her dad to arrive.

The girl had her nose pressed to the front window at least two hours before he was scheduled to pick her up. Every once in a while, she'd turn back to Ellie and say something like, "Some of Grampa Linc's family from Texas are going to be there too. I can't wait to meet them."

She wasn't the only person excited about the day though. Boston had called at least ten times, asking about Cassie's allergies and taste preferences and confirming times. He was so worried about making the day perfect for his daughter, Ellie slipped even further under his spell.

It was twenty till eleven when he pulled into the drive. Cassie was in the bathroom when he knocked on the door. She'd been holding it for nearly half an hour when Ellie finally ordered her to go relieve herself.

"But what if he comes while I'm gone?"

"Honey, I seriously don't think he's going to desert you if you're not waiting by the door when he arrives."

So, Cassie streaked from the room and not thirty seconds later, there came a knock on the door. Ellie laughed.

"A watched pot never boils," she murmured to herself as she went to admit Boston inside. She was still grinning as she pulled the door open.

He looked wonderful. In pressed gray slacks and a worn polo shirt with the sleeves pushed up to his elbows, he defined sleek and sophisticated. Ellie pulled to a stop, freshly amazed that she'd dated this man once upon a time. And she hadn't just dated him, she'd actually created a child with him. It was almost too much to believe.

"Hi," he said, his gaze warming as it slid down her body. Then he cleared his throat and glanced over her shoulder into the room. "Is Cass ready?"

"She just went to the bathroom," Ellie informed him and stepped aside to let him in. "I don't know how long she'd been holding it, afraid you'd show up as soon as she left the living room."

Amused by the same irony that had struck her, Boston chuckled. "Want me to go back outside and knock again in a couple minutes?"

But the bathroom door was already slamming open with Cassie charging down the hall, yelling, "Is he here?"

She appeared in the doorway and slid to a halt when she saw him. "Dad!"

Ellie's heart slammed against her chest as she watched the equal expressions of joy pass over both Boston and Cassie's faces as father and daughter came together. Boston swept Cassie up into his arms and gave her a bone-crushing hug.

"Hey there, short stuff," he said, lovingly sweeping a hand over Cassie's long hair. "You ready for some of Aunt Madison's pumpkin pie?"

"There'll be pumpkin pie?" Cassie murmured in awe.

"There'll be a little of everything," Boston answered as he set her back on her feet. "Actually, make that a *lot* of everything."

"Well, then let's go," the girl ordered and went charging for the door. She left it hanging open wide as she dashed down the front steps.

Boston grinned over at Ellie, his face a beaming glow of happiness. The power of it caught Ellie right in the chest, and she found herself smiling back at him.

"She's not excited or anything," she said.

He laughed. "I can tell." He moved toward the doorway and paused, taking a hold of the door handle as he called outside. "Hey, Cassidy! Aren't you going to say goodbye to your mother?"

"Oops," Ellie heard her daughter yell back.

Stunned that Boston had realized such a thing, much less called Cassie back, Ellie was still gaping at him when Cassie skidded back through the doorway.

"'Bye, Mom. Love you," she said breathlessly, plowing into Ellie and wrapping her arms tightly around Elli's stomach.

"I love you too," Ellie said, bending down in order to get a full hug. "Eat lots of turkey for me, okay?"

"Okay—" Cassie started to answer, but then cut herself off. She pulled back from Ellie and stared up at her mother with a slight frown. "But...you'll be eating turkey too."

Ellie bit her lip, realizing Cassie hadn't thought about what her mother would be doing while she was gone.

"You...you're going to be all alone," Cassie murmured, the truth finally dawning. Her eyes went from excited to huge and worried. She turned to Boston as if uncertain about going with him. "I always have Thanksgiving with my mom," she explained.

The look of abandonment that filled Boston's expression had Ellie stepping forward and touching her daughter's shoulder.

"Oh, Cass," she murmured on a sigh. She bent down on her haunches in front of the girl and pulled her into a hard hug. "Don't you worry about me. Go with your dad and have fun."

"But—"

"Cassidy," Boston cut in quietly. "Go to the car. I'll be right there."

The girl frowned up at him and then turned anxiously to her mother.

"Go on," Ellie urged softly, her smile encouraging. "Trust me. You'll have fun today."

"Are you sure?"

"I'm positive."

"Okay. 'Bye, then...I guess."

Cassie pulled her mother into another long hug, and Ellie kissed her hair before tugging herself away. The child glanced up, a little mutinously, at her father and then whirled and started for his Infiniti.

Both Boston and Ellie stood in the entrance of the house, watching her, until she opened the passenger side door and climbed inside. Then Boston turned.

"You'll have her home by eight this evening, right?" Ellie said, trying not to look at him because she feared she might start bawling any second.

He shifted uncomfortably. "Look." He coughed into his hand. "Why don't you come with us?"

Ellie fell back a step. "Oh," she breathed, surprised, as she pressed a hand to her chest.

For a second, she was sure she'd heard wrong. But after blinking about five times, she couldn't deny the inquisitive look Boston sent her, waiting for her answer.

Then she laughed. "Boston, don't be silly. She'll forget all about me once you guys reach the party. Besides, if she does get sad, just have her call. I'll talk to her and assure her everything's fine."

He looked away for a moment as if he were thinking that option over. And then he turned back to Ellie. "Here's the deal," he started. "I want this to be the best Thanksgiving she's ever had. And I don't want her to have to worry about her mother, about calling you and making sure you're okay. She's never been away from you for a holiday before, and I don't want that to be a problem. So, if you were there...with her...I know she could fully enjoy the day."

He paused to gauge her reaction. Ellie stared at him blankly for a moment.

"Really, Boston." She trilled out on a nervous laugh. He looked a little too serious for her comfort. "I can't go with you guys."

He frowned in confusion. "Why not?"

"For starters, your entire family is going to be there. I'm *not* spending the day with your family."

He frowned and pulled back, surprised and leery. "What's wrong with my family?"

"Well...they must hate me," she blurted out. "I didn't just keep Cassie from you. I kept her from them too. I can only imagine what they must think of me."

Boston's mouth fell open. "No," he said and then shook his head vehemently. "No one hates you. God, Ellie. Did you think Monty and Cam hated you?"

She bit her lip. "No, but I thought they were just...strange."

He laughed. "Well, they are that. But everyone else feels the same. They're very anxious to meet Cassidy's mother. In fact, you probably would've had a few unwanted visitors by now if I hadn't warned them to stay away."

"They want to meet me?" she asked slowly, not sure if she should believe him. "But...what about Chuck E. Cheese's? Didn't my behavior there turn them off?"

Sending her a guilty look, Boston admitted, "It turned them off me for a while. I swear, my mother was about to bend me over her knee for not getting your permission to take Cassie."

When Ellie couldn't come up with a ready response, he took her hand. "Tell me honestly," he murmured. "Do you want your daughter to be miserable today or not?"

"Of course I don't want her to be miserable." Ellie sighed. "But I think once she gets there, she'll forget all about me, and she'll—"

Boston didn't seem to want to risk it, however. "You're coming with us."

Ellie raised her eyebrows at his authoritative tone.

He seemed to yield at her arch look. "I already

felt like crap for taking her away from you on a holiday," he said. "Now, *she's* going to feel like crap too, and I'm sure you're not overly enthused about the situation either. Therefore, you have to come along so we're not all miserable."

She stared at him, tempted.

Realizing he about had her convinced, he coaxed, "It's only one day, Ellie. You can make it through *one* day with me, for our daughter, can't you?"

She opened her mouth to tell him it wasn't the idea of being with him that turned her off. The idea of spending Thanksgiving with him actually made her stomach tighten in excitement. It was the rest of his family she was worried about.

"Please," he said.

She melted.

Shoulders slumping, she caved. "Oh...all right."

Boston grinned immediately and tightened his grip on her hand. He took a step back as if to give her room to exit her house before him. But she frowned and looked down at herself. "Whoa," she yelped in surprise as she took in her own worn blue jeans and faded sweater. "I need to change."

"Change?" he echoed, frowning in confusion. "But you look great."

Ellie flushed, and he winced, realizing what he'd just said. Clearing his throat, he coughed into his hand and quickly revised, "I mean, you look fine. And our family get-togethers are incredibly informal. I wouldn't be surprised if my baby sister, Cheyenne, showed up in these flannel pajama pants she likes so much. Besides," he added. "I don't particularly want to embarrass myself in front of my family. And if you looked any better, I don't think I'd be able to handle it."

Tugging with the barest of pressure, Boston started to back toward the door, urging her to join him. She probably would've followed him anywhere at that very moment. The pull of his stare was a hundred times more magnetic than the tow of his hand. He nearly had the door shut behind her before a smidgeon of reality returned.

"Oh, wait! My keys. My purse."

Boston nodded and let go of her hand to let her escape back inside. Scurrying frantically, Ellie ran back to her room and yanked up her purse and keys. She paused at the dresser, however, and tried to fluff some life into her limp hair. Moaning in distress when the locks only flopped back against her head, she blew out a breath and gave up. There was no need for her to impress his family anyway. It wasn't like she and Boston were dating anymore.

Hustling back to the living room, she was a little surprised that he'd actually waited for her at the exit. It struck her with a sudden rush of nostalgia. He'd always waited patiently at her door when she wasn't quite ready, and like then, she was freshly amazed he hadn't left without her.

Ellie didn't take his hand again, but they walked side by side from the house, which was disconcerting in itself. As Cassie saw them approaching, she opened the passenger side door and sent a worried look from Boston to Ellie.

"What's wrong?" she said. "Did you guys have another fight?"

Boston chuckled as he reached out to rustle her hair. "No, we did not have another fight. We decided your mom should come too. Now, get in the back, kiddo. Let her ride up front."

"You're coming?" Cassie said, and her gaze darted to her mother. "Oh, wow, Mom, this is going to be so awesome." She shot out of the car and scurried to get into the backseat. All the while, she kept talking. "I'm going to introduce you to my grandma and grandpa and Aunt Shannon and Aunt

Olivia. There's going to be so many people there, Mom. You'll get to meet all of Dad's nieces and nephews and aunts and uncles..."

Oh, joy, Ellie thought, a little panicked. Boston was dragging her right into the lion's den.

****

The trip to Kansas City was a total blur. Ellie knew her daughter was constantly chattering from the backseat. And Boston would occasionally comment. But she was too nervous to pay attention to anything they said.

She sat in the passenger seat with her hands tightly clasped in her lap, staring straight ahead out the windshield. Boston's Infiniti was a smooth ride. It was like floating on top of a glass lake. And he had the temperature acclimated perfectly. If Ellie were in any other state beside utter dread, she would've really enjoyed this cruise in his luxury automobile. As it was, she didn't even feel the leather seats at her back or hear the low, soothing music coming through the speakers.

She was going to meet his family. His *entire* family.

Ellie had always wondered what they would be like. She used to snatch up any scrap of information he'd give her about them. Heck, she'd gone and given him her virginity the first time he'd told her about his dad's occupation, if that were any indication as to how special she found his opening up to her to be.

The more he had dodged family topics, though, the more she'd wanted to know about them. She'd been so sure he must have awful parents who were pressuring him to do well in school and get into Yale. They had to be rich and socially elite, only concerned with upholding a superior reputation.

But then she'd been in calculus class one day and the teacher had been handing back graded tests. When he'd called out the name Montgomery Kincaid, a guy, looking astonishingly like Boston, had lifted his hand. Blinking, Ellie studied him for so long, he'd glanced her way as if he could feel her stare. Flushing, she quickly jerked back around in her seat.

From then on, she'd paid sharp attention to Mr. Montgomery Kincaid. And it didn't take long to realize he was indeed related to Boston. She'd actually heard him mention his brother to his friend he always hung out with.

So sure he had this high-nosed snob of a family, Ellie had been shocked to realize Boston had a normal-acting brother. It confused her that Boston wouldn't even mention him.

Today, on the way to see them again, Ellie held no such disillusions. Boston's family wasn't awful. In fact, they seemed pretty close to him. From everything she'd heard Cassie tell her, they were very involved in his life. He'd only kept them from her because she hadn't been important enough to meet them.

It was a bitter pill to swallow, realizing the only reason she was meeting them now was because she was Cassie's mother. And it did nothing to ease her anxiety. Instead of trying to be nice because she was with Boston, they were going to study her and ask themselves what was wrong with her, what had she done to lose him?

They were going to hate her.

When Boston slowed the car and pulled into a huge, elegant drive that was already packed with at least a dozen automobiles, her heart literally stopped beating for a nanosecond. When it thumped back into gear, it started again so hard, it nearly cracked her ribcage.

"Libby's already here!" Cassie cheered from the backseat.

Her daughter was out of the car as soon as

Boston pressed on the brake. Feeling deserted, Ellie watched Cassie race across the lawn to where a group of kids were already gathered and playing.

Next to her, Boston chuckled. "Such enthusiasm," he said, killing the engine and unbuckling his seatbelt. He opened his driver's side door and began to exit before he realized Ellie wasn't following. Pausing, he glanced over his shoulder. "What's wrong?"

She sent him a panic-stricken expression. For the life of her, she couldn't control the fear. She couldn't even appear to be strong in front of him. "I can't do it," she blurted out. "I can't go in there."

"What? Why not?"

She gnashed her teeth, refusing to tell him. But the words still bubbled their way from her throat. "You know what they're going to think of me."

Boston's eyes flared. He pulled his foot back into the car and turned to her fully. "Ellie," he said calmly. "No one thinks badly of you. And no one is going to *say* anything bad to you either. Trust me. They're all more disappointed in me because I didn't stick around long enough to make sure you really weren't pregnant." Quietly reaching out, he took her hand and gave a reassuring squeeze.

"Come on," he murmured. "I promise I won't let anyone stamp any large letters on you or call you any names."

Ellie snorted at his joke. But it helped to make her realize how much of a weenie she was being. Blowing out a long breath, she pushed open the car door.

They entered his parents' house through the back. Ellie could hear the multitude of voices as soon as Boston opened the door and stepped aside to let her go first.

"Good," he said from behind her. "We made it in time for the food. They're too loud to be eating."

They'd just entered a kitchen when a beautiful, busty yet petite blonde walked into the room. She grinned when she saw them, or rather when she saw Boston.

"Boston! Baby, what took you so long to get here?"

He paused and sent the woman a hot, flirtatious grin. "Miss me?"

The blonde fluttered her lashes and wrapped her arms around his neck. "Always," she answered and gave him a long, yet closed-mouth kiss as she leaned into him.

Ellie couldn't help but arch an eyebrow as she watched. Boston pulled away and grinned at the woman, pressing his forehead to hers and murmuring a quiet greeting. And even as the envy and irrational jealousy zipped through her bloodstream, Ellie felt someone sidle up beside her. When a male arm looped companionably around her shoulder, she jumped and turned.

The dancing green eyes she found twinkling her way surprised her almost as much as the wide, welcoming smile. "Hey there, Ellie," Cameron Banks greeted. "I didn't know Bos was bringing you along. But thank God you're here. Because I really need some help keeping this guy in line." He finally glanced toward Boston then, his eyes narrowing as he sighed in disappointment.

"You know," he said conversationally, tilting his head toward hers as they studied Boston and the blonde together. "The jerk saves my life *once*, and now he thinks he can maul my wife all the freaking time."

Letting go of Ellie, the green-eyed man stepped forward, snagged the hand of the blonde hanging all over Boston, and yanked her to his side. Baring his teeth at Boston, he put his arm around the woman's shoulder and firmly stated, "Mine."

Boston only laughed. Ellie's stomach churched. Here was a playful side of him she hadn't seen in over ten years. It reminded her that there'd been a reason why she'd fallen for him so hard.

"You know," Boston told Cameron, "maybe if you'd quit acting so possessive of her, I'd quit—"

The other man snorted and muttered, "As if." Then he turned his wife toward Ellie. "Honey," he told the woman. "Look who it is."

The blonde smiled in polite greeting and held out a hand. "Hello. Are you— Oh my God!" she said and yanked her hand away as she gaped with widening blue eyes. "You're Cassie's mom. I remember you from Chuck E. Cheese's."

Ellie offered the woman a tense smile. But before she could think up a response, the blonde opened her arms and launched herself at Ellie, pulling her into a huge encompassing hug.

"This is so utterly amazing," Cameron's wife went on. "I've been dying to meet you. *Oh!* I'm Olivia, by the way. Cam's wife," she added, vaguely motioning to the green-eyed man beside her.

Ellie nodded mutely.

"I just can't believe I'm finally meeting you," Olivia went on. "Cassie is an absolute doll. I really only got to talk to her a few minutes, but that's all I needed. I just love her to pieces. Meeting her made me want to have Cam knock me up."

"Uh...thank you," Ellie managed to say. Her eyes unconsciously moved toward Boston. He quirked her an I-told-you-so sneer and then grinned, flashing a dazzling smile.

Ellie flushed.

"You know, as soon as I met Cassidy," Olivia was saying, "I said to myself, that girl has to have one amazing mother. I mean, I knew right then and there you couldn't be a bitch or anything. There's no way you could raise such a sweet girl and be anything but amazing. And just look at you!" she said with pride. "You're so beautiful and wholesome. I've always wanted to know what one of Boston's women would be like. But Mr. Private here never lets us meet any of them. So, naturally I've always been curious to know—"

"Okay, enough!" Boston broke in, manually pulling Olivia away from Ellie and nudging her Cameron's way. "Give her some space, will you?"

Olivia sent him an irritated look and moved back toward Ellie, hooking their arms together. "El doesn't mind if I talk to her. Do you?"

"Uh—" Ellie started, sending Boston a panicked look as she was swept into another room.

"I had no idea he could be so overprotective," Olivia murmured as she dragged Ellie along. "What does he think I was going to do to you? Geez."

Ellie figured that was a rhetorical question, so she didn't answer.

"Well, here's a new face," a dark-haired woman said, stepping into their path. Ellie stumbled slightly at the sight of the stunning brunette.

"This is Helena," Olivia informed her. "She's Boston's older sister."

"Yep, I'm the boss," Helena agreed, snagging Ellie's hand in a friendly fashion.

"And this is Ellie," Olivia told the brunette. "Cassie's mom. You didn't get to see her the other week at Chuck E. Cheese's. You were off somewhere with Gabriel when she came in."

Helena's eyes widened. "Yes, I was," she murmured and tightened her grip on Ellie's finger. "I was taking my son to the bathroom when you made your appearance. And I was so disappointed I didn't get a peek. But, now, this *is* a treat," she murmured, taking in Ellie's entire form. "Cassidy's mother. She looks like you, you know."

"Thank you," Ellie rasped out.

"You're welcome." Boston's sister grinned and tugged her from Olivia's grip. "Welcome to the family," she added, throwing her arm around Ellie's shoulder. "Let me introduce you around."

Ushering Ellie through a doorway, Helena kept talking as she walked them down a short hall and into the next room.

Ellie pulled to a stop when she saw all the people. Her eyes went wide at the sight of so many. But Helena just tugged her along.

"Hey, everyone!" she yelled over the noise of a dozen different conversations. "This is Cassie's mom!"

Chapter Fourteen

Talk about a conversation stopper.

Ellie wanted to crawl through the floor.

When the room fell quiet, she feared the silence would deafen her. It was a complete one eighty from the loud voices and laughter that had been echoing through the house five seconds earlier.

"These are Cam's parents," Helena said, dragging Ellie along, either ignoring or not even aware of all the people who had stopped talking to gape.

"Chuck and Allison Banks," Helena continued.

Ellie turned form the curious eyes and focused on the couple before her. They looked about as startled as she felt for being singled out in the crowd.

"Er...it's nice to meet you," Allison said, holding out her hand as well as a pitying smile, like she knew exactly how absolutely flustered Ellie was. "Cassie looks just like you."

"Thank you." The two women shook, and Ellie actually felt comforted by the dry, warm fingers that took hers.

"I didn't catch your name," Chuck said, holding out his hand next.

"Ellie," she said. "Elora Trenton."

His gaze sparked with recognition. "Any relation to the Trentons in Olathe? Brad and Glenna?"

"Ah...no. Sorry. Cassie's my only family here in Kansas. I'm originally from Tennessee, and any Trenton I was related to died years ago."

Chuck stared at her with an almost comical look

of horror. "I'm sorry," he said instantly. "I didn't mean to—"

Ellie smiled. "It's fine," she said, waving aside his apology. "There's no reason to apologize."

It stunned her that Boston's family seemed more concerned with not insulting her than trying to snub her. And here she'd been expecting the cold shoulder as well as the third degree.

"Don't mind my husband," Allison stepped in, apologizing as well. She set a hand on Chuck's arm. "He thinks he should know everyone, or at least everyone's family."

After that, the introductions were a blur. But Helena seemed determined to personally introduce Ellie to every single person present.

When they turned toward Shannon March, Ellie was relieved to see a face she knew she'd remember. Shannon was famous, her features spread across magazine covers nationwide. But when she sent Ellie a shy smile, she certainly didn't act like a star.

"I'm Shannon," she said quietly. "Monty's wife."

Ellie wanted to say, "Well, duh. Of course you're Shannon." But she was too bowled over to speak. Shannon March was talking to her, and giving her a wide-eyed stare as if Ellie were the famous one.

"I was so worried when he first got that letter," she confessed to Ellie with a relieved laugh. "Then when he remembered he had actually had a class with you, I totally freaked out. But this worked out nicely. It's so good to meet you, Ellie."

They were still holding hands and grinning at each other when an authoritative female voice called, "Out of my way. I want to officially meet Cassidy's mother."

The crowd parted immediately for two people: a man who looked just like Boston, but maybe thirty years older, and a woman who was so familiar, Ellie held her breath.

She remembered Boston's mother vividly from Chuck E. Cheese's.

Oh, good Lord, Boston's parents.

Ellie's skin tingled with apprehension as her gaze unwillingly latched onto the woman who stopped before her.

"These are my parents," Boston introduced from beside her.

Ellie jumped, not aware he'd been anywhere in the vicinity. She hadn't even known he'd followed her from the kitchen.

"Diane, my mother. And Lincoln, my father."

Ellie prayed she didn't faint.

"So, now we finally get a formal introduction?" Diane murmured, her eyes glittering with humor. Then she reached for both of Ellie's hands. "You will not believe how upset I was, thinking none of my boys had given me any grandchildren yet," Diane said, casting an arch look toward her two sons. "I've been on both their cases for years about it. Their sisters were kind enough to obey. But not these two." Then she grinned, glancing out a window that showed where all the youngsters were still playing.

"Cassie's a complete angel," Diane murmured with adoration thick in her voice. She turned back. "Thank you. Thank you so much." Then, to Ellie's utter shock, the woman hugged her.

Lincoln Kincaid seemed equally pleased to meet her. "It's an honor to officially meet you, Ellie," he said, looking like the patriarch he was. He had pitch-black hair and tanned skin.

There was just something about him that screamed money and power. But he certainly didn't act like any famous, retired astronaut she'd seen on television. As soon as Diane stopped hugging her, he stepped forward for his turn. Enveloped in another hug, Ellie had to bite back the urge to cry.

Why in God's name were they hugging her like

she was a long-lost daughter? She wasn't with Boston anymore. In fact, she'd lied to him and kept his child from him. By rights, these people should hate her.

Not hug her.

As if sensing her slipping control, Boston put a hand on her back. His solid, protective presence, however, only made everything that much harder to handle.

"Is it time to eat yet?" he asked loudly to the room in general. "I'm starving."

His question turned out to be the tension-breaker Ellie needed. Within minutes, people had stepped away from her and given her the space she'd been craving. Food was serious business in this family, she soon learned. The room shifted toward the two long tables that were set out and piled with tasty delights, from turkey to ham, stuffing, vegetables, mashed potatoes, gravy, and so much more. Then to add to that, there was a smaller table set up to the side holding desserts.

Ellie glanced around for Cassidy, but when she spotted her daughter, the girl was ensconced by other children her age and didn't look to want or need Ellie around. To her relief, Helena once again appeared at her side and hooked their arms together, escorting her into line behind the others. Helena chatted about motherhood until it was their turn at the three-table buffet, where they dished up their meal.

"Let's go sit over by Cheyenne," Helena said, leading the way. "You remember being introduced to Cheyenne, right?"

"Ah..." *No.*

But that question had obviously been rhetorical too. Ellie meekly followed Boston's sister and eased into a seat next to Helena, who sat across from Cheyenne.

"Try the cheesy hash browns." Cheyenne moaned as she broke a roll in half and coated it with butter. "They're divine."

"Already on it," Helena answered, picking up a fork and diving in.

For a moment, Ellie could only watch the two women tuck into their meals like a pair of hearty athletes. Boston's family was so different from what she'd expected. They were so...normal.

Hesitating briefly, she tasted a small mouthful of the potatoes Cheyenne had recommended. As the flavor melted against her tongue, she almost moaned in delight. Within seconds, she was diving in as energetically as Helena and Cheyenne.

"Beware of the yams," Cameron advised as he plopped a plate down at the end of the table and seated himself. "Livy made them."

"Hey," his wife snapped, slipping into the seat adjacent his. "I think they turned out great."

There was only one other chair left at their table, directly next to her, and Ellie had a sinking sensation she knew exactly who was going to fill it.

"Yeah, but great in your cooking world is when you manage not to burn a Caesar salad," Cameron told Olivia with an ornery grin.

"Oh, that's it," Olivia snapped, reaching for his plate. "You can't have any of my yams."

"Hey, woman," he yelped, blocking his plate with his forearm. "Keep your hands off my food."

"No yams for you," she said determinedly.

Ellie was so busy watching them wrestle for the yams, she didn't even notice Boston's arrival until he settled into the chair next to her and said, "I bet Olivia will let me eat her yams." He sent Cameron a taunting smirk as he scooped up a spoonful and filled his mouth.

Suddenly, Cameron was so busy glaring at Boston and calling him a dirty name, he forgot to protect his food. Olivia extracted his pile of yams in one swoop.

As he tried to sweet talk her into giving them back, assuring her he'd love her dish, Boston winked at Ellie and they shared a grin.

Across from them, Cheyenne lifted her eyebrows. "You know, you two don't act like any exes I've ever seen. Are you getting back together or what?"

Everyone at the table—even the arguing Cameron and Olivia—fell quiet and glanced questioningly toward Ellie. Next to her, Boston coughed into his fist. Then he pounded on his chest before reaching for his glass to take a long drink.

Ellie wasn't sure how to respond.

Helena, however rolled her eyes as she patted Ellie's hand. "Don't pay my baby sister any mind. She thinks everyone is destined to end up with their first love. She met her husband when she was sixteen. They married four years later and are still disgustingly sweet with each other."

"We are not," Cheyenne grumbled, sending an insulted glare her sister's way. "I'm sitting clear across the room from him right now, aren't I?"

"Oooh," Helena said, shaking her voice and rolling her eyes to show off her sarcasm as she added, "I'm so impressed."

Cheyenne turned away from her and focused on Ellie. "I'm just saying...wouldn't it be something if you two got back together?"

Ellie blinked. It was just too dangerous to think about Boston that way. He still had a little too much pull on her heartstrings to let herself think such things.

"Sorry, Cheyenne," Boston said, sounding sympathetic. "I don't think that's going to happen."

For a moment, no one spoke. Both Helena and Cheyenne and even Cameron and Olivia sent a worried look Ellie's way as if afraid Boston had just insulted her. But she merely nodded, adamantly backing his declaration.

"So, curious minds want to know," Helena asked as she bit into a mouthful of stuffing. "Why'd you two ever break up in the first place?"

Boston and Ellie whipped their gazes her way, nailing her with similar expressions of horror.

Then, at the same moment Boston started to say, "That's none of your—" Ellie blurted out, "He cheated on me."

With her words still echoing through the air, every person at the table stopped eating and gaped directly at Boston. Beside her, Boston tensed and slid an inch lower in his chair.

"Oh my *God*, Boston," Helena hissed. "You didn't."

"How could you?" Cheyenne whispered, staring at him like he was the very devil, all the while lifting her hands to cover her mouth.

Cringing because she hadn't meant to oust him, Ellie glanced anxiously his way. Boston's face had drained of color, and he looked guiltier than she'd ever seen him look before. It stung that he was more ashamed for his family to find out the truth than he'd been when she'd discovered his indiscretion.

"Holy hell, Bos," Cameron breathed. "I can't believe it."

"You didn't really cheat on her, did you?" Olivia whispered, her blue eyes wide and hopeful.

Experiencing the strange need to defend him since it had been her big mouth that put him on the spot, Ellie lifted her hand and said, "But that was a long time ago. We've already hashed it out and—"

"I don't care if it was a hundred years ago," Helena interrupted loudly. "Boston Robert Kincaid, you should be ashamed of yourself. How could you have sex with another women when—"

"Will you shut up," Boston hissed, slinking even further in his seat. "Mom and Dad are only ten feet away. Do you want them to hear—"

"Yes, actually, I do," Helena cut in. "You had sex—"

"Shh," Boston gritted out. "They do *not* need to know, and besides, I didn't have sex with her."

Ellie whirled toward him. "Yes, you did."

He blew out a long, slow, steadying breath before lifting his gaze Ellie's way. "No. I didn't."

"But—"

"Ellie," he cut in irritably. "I was there. You weren't. So, you don't know. There was no sex involved. Okay?"

"Then what exactly did you do with this other woman?" Helena wanted to know.

Sending a look to kill his sister's way, Boston growled, "None of your damn business. Only Ellie has the right to ask me that."

Four pair of eyes turned expectantly Ellie's way. She jumped. "I'm not going to ask," she yelped. "I don't want to know. It doesn't matter now, anyway. It happened a long time ago."

"Please, Ellie," Cheyenne started. "I'm curious."

"Stop it," Boston hissed. "We are not going to talk about this. Next topic, please."

"But—"

"Cheyenne," he growled.

Annoyed at him for snapping at his own sister, Ellie straightened her spine. "I changed my mind. I want to know."

"Ha!" Cheyenne taunted as Boston turned to send Ellie an incredulous look.

"I thought it was a long time ago," he said. "Water under the bridge and all that."

Ellie shrugged. "So I'm curious. Sue me."

Boston filled his cheeks with air and then blew out a breath. After taking a moment to run a hand through his hair, he got to his feet. "If you want to know, fine, I'll tell you. But not here. Not in front of these snoopy—"

"Oh, come on," Helena argued. "We'll just get her to tell us what you said."

But Boston zapped a killer look her way. "Butt out. This isn't your affair."

"Well, obviously," she snorted. "It was yours."

Sighing, Boston turned back to Ellie. When he held a hand down to her, she glanced up at his face and studied his silent, probing stare. An echo of all the pain and heartbreak this man had ever given her shimmered through her. She knew she was damning herself for going with him, but she did it anyway.

"Okay," she murmured, ignoring his hand and rising to her feet. "I'll listen to your story."

"Go, Ellie," Cheyenne cheered. "Make him get on hands and knees and beg for forgiveness."

Both Boston and Ellie frowned cantankerously at his sister. Then Boston turned away, and Ellie found herself helpless to follow. He weaved through the crowds, and Ellie was all too aware of all the people watching her and Boston as they exited a side doorway together.

"Everyone is watching us," she murmured.

"Yeah, well, this was your idea." He kept a steady stalk down the quiet hall before he turned abruptly and disappeared through a doorway.

Ellie followed. She found herself in a study with a desk holding a computer in the center and shelves lining the walls. Behind her, Boston shut the door with a click.

She jumped.

"So, what do you want to know?" he asked, coming straight to the point.

Turning slowly, she found all the courage she'd had at the table—where she'd been surrounded by his loud family—was gone. "Look, Boston," she said. "It's okay. I don't—"

"No, you want to know the truth," he bit out. "So, I'm telling you the truth. Just tell me where to start?"

She pressed a hand to her chest. "Fine then. I want to know exactly what you did with Heather Grimaldi?"

There. It was asked. She could wish the question away all she wanted. But it didn't matter. It was out there now, and he'd heard it perfectly.

Blowing out a breath, he gingerly stepped closer until he was only two feet away. "Do you *really* want to know?"

She took a second to think about it. *Did* she really want to know? It wouldn't change anything. What happened had already happened.

But, damn it, she just wanted to know.

"Did you have sex with her or not?"

His smile was slow and relieved. "I did not," he said, looking all too pleased to report it.

Ellie shook her head, suddenly lost. "Then why'd you tell me you did?"

He frowned. "I never told you that."

"Yes, you—"

"No! I didn't."

"Boston, you confessed to being unfaithful."

He sighed and ground the palms of his hand into his eye sockets. "I went back to her apartment with her," he admitted. "I kissed her and took her shirt off. I fully intended to have sex with her. Isn't that unfaithful enough for you?"

Ellie's jaw dropped. Okay, so he'd still done stuff. But all this time, she'd thought he'd put his penis inside another woman. She'd thought...

"So, why did she stop you?" she asked. "She find out you were already involved with someone else?"

He closed his eyes and shook his head. "Oh, she

knew about you, all right. But she wasn't the one to stop. I was."

"You..." Ellie suddenly found it way too hard to breathe. "Why?"

"You really want the whole story?"

"If you don't mind."

He shrugged. "Hey, it was a long time ago. What would spilling the truth hurt now?"

Ellie was quiet. For a minute, he was too.

Then he cleared his throat and started. "You were working that night. One of my friends was having his twenty-first birthday and bugged and badgered me to stop by this party he was throwing. I didn't really want to go, but I knew I'd never hear the end of it if I didn't. So, I showed up and was ready to leave the minute I arrived. As I was looking for my buddy to wish him a happy birthday, *she* spotted me and approached. When she started flirting, I told her I was seeing someone else, but she kind of shrugged like it didn't bother her. So, I turned her down again."

"That's not all," Ellie said, making it a statement rather than a question.

For her interruption, she got a dirty look. "I'm not done," he said. Then he closed his eyes and ran his hand through his hair. "As she was walking away, it hit me what I'd just done. And I don't know...it rattled me that I could turn down a good-looking woman so easily. I hadn't realized I'd gotten quite that attached to you until then. So, I started to think stupid stuff like, 'You know what? Ellie doesn't have exclusive rights to me. I never made her any promises.'"

Sending her a quick, ironic smile, he added, "It pissed me off that you'd been able to gain so much power over me without me even being aware of it. I didn't like it. I hadn't planned on getting serious with you. In fact, I'd told myself from the very start of our...whatever...I'd convinced myself it wasn't going to last. I was leaving for Yale at the end of the year, and I wasn't going to have any kind of ties holding me back."

"So you did plan on breaking up with me all along?" Ellie asked.

Boston sighed. "Yes...no...I don't know. Damn it, Ellie. All I know is that I wasn't planning on feeling what I felt. I didn't want you to be important to me."

Not sure what to think of this confession, Ellie turned away and briskly rubbed her arms up and down. "So, how did you end up at her apartment with her shirt off?"

"I went after her," he admitted. "After realizing how far gone I was over you, I freaked out. I completely denied how deeply I'd fallen for you and, to prove to myself that I didn't care so much for you, I pursued her until I got her back to her place. I had every intention of cheating on you. I actually wanted to, if for no other reason than to say I *could*."

"So, what happened?" Ellie asked in a whisper. She wrapped her arms around her waist. It felt so fresh all of a sudden. Like she'd just walked into history class and heard Heather two seats over, bragging to her friends about tempting the hot Boston Kincaid back to her apartment.

"I couldn't do it," he said. He looked so beaten and defeated, she almost felt sorry for him. His voice cracked as he continued. "I had her shirt off and I wanted to get rid of her bra next, but...I don't know. It felt wrong. It just...it wasn't you."

He lifted his eyes to hers and looked so sincerely regretful her stomach began to burn.

"As soon as I thought about how it was so much better with you, I realized what I was doing, how I was comparing, and I stopped. I booked it out of there and went straight home. When you came by the next day, I couldn't even look at you. I felt so...shitty. And I resented you for that. You weren't supposed to have any kind of control over me. You weren't supposed to make me feel anything I didn't want to feel. You weren't supposed to matter." He sighed and rubbed at a spot on the center of his forehead.

"So, that's what happened," she stated softly.

Turning away, she pressed a hand to her own forehead as the memories flashed through her...of his belligerent attitude when she'd finally confronted him and his cold flashing eyes as he'd spat back, "*God, El. I never made you any promises. What made you think this thing between us was exclusive?*"

"I'm so sorry, Ellie," the adult Boston whispered. "I think...I think I acted like such an ass when you found out about her because I *wanted* you to break up with me. I was so confused. I just wasn't ready yet. We'd become a lot more serious than I was prepared to handle at that time. I took the coward's way out and made sure I was awful enough you'd dump me."

"I see," she murmured, knowing exactly what he meant when he'd said, *I resented you for having that much control over me,* because he had that exact kind of control over her right now. She didn't want to be affected by his story...but she was.

Refusing to let it show, she gave a nonchalant shrug. "Well...it was a long time ago. Don't worry about it."

"It wouldn't have made a difference if I'd told you everything back then, anyway," he agreed softly. "I'd still done enough to—"

"Oh, it would've made a difference," she cut him off abruptly, rushing out the words, surprised she'd even said them.

He paused and eyed her intently. "It would've?"

She nodded stiffly.

"Are you saying you wouldn't have broken up

with me if I'd only explained everything?"

Ellie's heartbeat thundered through her ears. "Yes." She blew out a breath. "That's exactly what I'm saying."

Boston blew out a shaky breath as well. "Well..." he said. "Hell."

He turned away as if to hide the regret in his eyes from her. But she caught a full glimpse of it anyway. She didn't know why that kind of regret caught her sympathies more strongly than anything else. But it made her weak toward him, kind of like she'd been ten years before.

"Boston," she whispered and lifted her hand to touch his back, but he spun toward her, not realizing she'd been reaching. Quickly she dropped her fingers.

His eyes looked a little glazed, almost crazed, as he stared at her. "I never should've messed with you," he said. "As soon as I learned how innocent you were, I should've just backed off and called it quits." Letting out a groan of misery, he glanced away. "Why did you let me go so far? Why'd you give me the tools to hurt you?"

Ellie shrugged helplessly. "Why do you think? I thought I'd fallen in love with you."

Boston looked down at his hands. "When you came back after we broke up. When you told me you were pregnant, I...I wasn't really mad at you, you know. I was mad at myself because I'd let you go, because I missed you. And to top that off, I was scared as hell. I was, in no way, ready to be a father. That doesn't excuse the way I acted. I never should've blamed you or accused you of trying to trick me into getting back together. I...I was a complete asshole."

"Oh, I knew that then."

He grinned and lifted his face. When she returned the smile, they shared a soft moment. For once, neither of them thought of the bitter ending of their relationship. But they both reminisced about happier moments, times when erotic discovery had been the most important thing between them.

Suddenly, Boston grew solemn. He stared down at his hands. "I don't want to be your enemy, Ellie."

She swallowed. "I don't want to be yours either."

"But there's so much history and pain between us. I can't... Right now, I can't see how we'll ever move past this."

"There are good memories too," she heard herself say, as if arguing with the hopelessness behind his words.

When Boston lifted his face and seared her with a hot gaze, all those good memories struck her at once.

"Yeah," he murmured. "There are. And they're making all this that much more difficult to deal with. I can't look at you without wanting...without wondering..."

When he stopped talking, the silence between them felt as thick and tense as pea soup.

"Maybe we shouldn't talk about it," Ellie said in a small voice.

He laughed harshly. "What? You think that's going to make it go away?"

"No, of course not," she agreed, looking down at her hands. "But, we've come to a...a kind of alliance. And I just don't want to do anything to hurt that. For Cassidy's sake, I think we should just stay as we are right now."

Boston looked like he was going to rebel, so she quickly added, "It might not be very comfortable for either of us, but at least it's peaceful. And that's what our daughter needs. We need to be cordial yet distant...for Cassie's sake."

The obstinate gleam left his eyes, but she could still tell he didn't agree. However, he still nodded and said, "You're probably right." Then, glancing away, he blew out a slow breath and turned to quietly leave the room.

****

Evening had fallen when Ellie decided she needed to find her daughter and see how Cassie was faring. In an attempt to avoid Boston and forget how close they'd come to...what, she wasn't sure—getting back together, maybe...she spent a few hours chatting with Boston's sisters and sister-in-law.

It was a shock to realize Shannon March—er, Shannon *Kincaid*—was nice. She even blushed when Ellie told the model she was a fan. Ellie couldn't believe how normal and down-to-earth all of Boston's family was. She hadn't met one person she didn't like. Cassidy was blessed to have such an amazing foundation. That was something Ellie had never been able to give her. But now her baby girl had roots and relatives and a base on which to make her life full and happy.

The sound of children in the backyard had Ellie heading that way. She spotted her daughter immediately among the racing children who were playing a heated game of tag. Cassie's long black hair, held up in a ponytail, swayed behind her as she dodged out of the way of some boy whose name Ellie couldn't remember. She smiled and watched, grateful her daughter could experience this day.

She was thinking back to every holiday in their past, when it had just been the two of them, when laughter to her right caught her attention. Boston's laugh—she'd know it anywhere. Drawn to his chuckle, she glanced over. And there he was, sitting in a wooden outdoor recliner with his feet kicked up and a glass of iced tea in his hand. A few feet away, Cameron sat likewise with a drowsy Olivia curled on his lap and resting her face on his shoulder. He stroked her hair slowly as he said something else to make Boston laugh.

Then Boston glanced across the lawn to check on Cassie, and Ellie's heart wrenched in painful longing. Who would've thought he'd be such a good father?

"They couldn't stand each other when they were kids, you know?"

Ellie whirled in surprise and almost gasped when she found Diane Kincaid approaching her. Swallowing, she tried not to blush at being caught staring at a man by his own mother. But Diane's gaze looked fond as she glanced toward Boston and Cameron.

"Well, Cam got along with *him* just fine," Diane amended then and finally gifted Ellie with an amused smile. "But Cameron can get along with anyone. *Boston* was the one who was always so annoyed by Cam. He just...he never cared for his cousin that much until Cameron's first wife, Sienna, killed herself."

Ellie gasped and covered her mouth. "I had no idea," she murmured, her eyes falling on Cameron as she watched him with new eyes. He ran his fingers slowly through Olivia's hair before reaching down to kiss her temple.

"He was only twenty," Diane murmured beside her. "And it nearly destroyed him. He turned to alcohol and slumped into depression. Everyone just..." She shook her head. "We had no idea what to do. But suddenly, there was Boston."

She grinned at Ellie like a proud mother. "I think it surprised us all that Boston stepped up and decided to be the one to watch over Cameron. It was the oddest thing, though. Those two boys hadn't really even talked to each other when they were growing up, but suddenly, they were best friends. Cameron straightened out completely once Olivia came along, but it was Boston who kept him hanging in there until she arrived."

Both Ellie and Diane studied the two friends, who chatted and argued companionably over something. Ellie couldn't help but soften for the man she'd once loved. It was good to hear he'd put himself out there for his cousin.

"I love my children very much," Diane murmured. "As much as any mother can love her babies," she added on a laugh. "But I haven't always liked them."

When Ellie glanced at her curiously, Diane met her gaze. "I don't know what happened ten years ago between the two of you. I don't know if he broke your heart, or if you broke his, or if you broke each others. All I know is that he changed after that. That annoying cocky edge he always had mellowed, and he became much more humble. I'd always figured it was because of the tragedy with Cameron's first wife. But now, I'm not so sure it was."

Ellie dropped her eyes guiltily and braced for the rebuke.

But her eyes shot up when Diane took both her hands and squeezed. "I don't know what you did, Ellie Trenton. But it made him a better person. He became more cautious, and that broke my heart because it was that once-bitten-twice-shy kind of cautious. But he also became kind and compassionate toward others as if, for the first time, he realized the world didn't revolve around him. Whatever it was that changed him, I must say, it turned him into a damn fine man."

Ellie's eyes filled with tears. She was surprised to discover Diane's eyes looked watery as well. "Since you're a mother yourself," Diane said, "I know you'll believe me when I say thank you for teaching him whatever lesson it was he needed to learn to make him what he is today."

Too choked up to respond, Ellie only nodded.

"What's going on over here?"

Simultaneously, Diane and Ellie jumped apart and immediately wiped any proof of tears from their eyes. Boston stood before them both, frowning, eyeing his mother from head to toe and then turning to give Ellie the same intense probe.

"Everything okay?"

Diane laughed and bumped Ellie's elbow. "Just look at him. He can't figure out who offended who, and which one of us he needs to defend."

Since the concerned frown on Boston's face made it appear that was exactly the case, Ellie grinned and decided she really liked his mother.

"What're you two talking about?" he asked, his eyes narrowed suspiciously.

"Not about you," Diane smarted back, making him scowl even more.

"Certainly not," Ellie agreed with a nod.

"It was mother talk," Diane reported airily. "You wouldn't understand."

When Diane hooked arms with Ellie's, making them a united front, Ellie almost burst out giggling. But the half wary, half worried look on Boston's face was so adorable the ice surrounding her feelings for him thawed even more.

Chapter Fifteen

It was late when Boston finally pulled into Ellie's drive behind her old Toyota. Yawning and stretching, Ellie glanced in the backseat where her daughter was passed out cold.

"Look who wore herself out today," she commented with a small smile, all the while dreading the fact that she was probably going to have to carry seventy-five pounds of dead weight inside by herself.

Boston grinned as he put the car into park and killed the engine. "I'm surprised she lasted this long. If I'd been going full steam the way she did all day, I'd have been down for the count hours ago."

"Oh, to be so young again," Ellie murmured wistfully.

"No doubt," he agreed and let out a long, weary sigh. "Okay, then," he said, rubbing his hands together. "I'll get the kid if you get the door."

Ellie lifted her face in surprise, her lips parting. "You don't have to do that."

He frowned. "Come on, Ellie. She probably weighs just about as much as you do. There's no way you can carry her." Then he turned and studied his unconscious daughter. "Or, I guess we could wake her."

Ellie bit her lip. Cassie was an utter monster when woken from a deep sleep. "Are you sure you don't mind carrying her?"

She wasn't used to this. She'd been a single mother, making it on her own, for nearly ten years. She did everything herself. It just felt...weird for someone to step in and actually offer assistance.

Boston sent her an odd look, like he was disappointed in her lack of dependence. "I don't mind," he said quietly and opened the door.

Ellie scurried to follow. Hustling ahead of him to the porch, she unlocked the front entrance. Holding it open for Boston, she tried to step out of the way, but the elbow he held jutted out to cradle Cassie still brushed across her chest.

They both lifted their gazes, and when their eyes met in the light of the streetlamps, liquid heat pooled low in Ellie's stomach. Ignoring the way her nipples hardened and her thighs tensed, she followed Boston down the dark hall to Cassie's room and turned on the girl's nightlight so he could see where to lay his sleeping daughter.

Once he had Cassie on the mattress, both adults worked to remove her shoes and socks. Then Boston stepped back while Ellie slipped off Cassie's jeans and shirt. But as soon as she had the child stripped to her underwear and the blankets pulled up to her chin, he returned to kneel beside Cassidy and press a brief kiss to her forehead. The nine-year-old didn't even stir.

Both parents moved toward the door together, but when Ellie noticed that Boston had stopped at the entrance to glance back at Cassidy, she paused as well.

"It gets you right in the chest when she's asleep like this, doesn't it?" he whispered. "I mean, it's pretty amazing when she'd awake and active. But when she's all innocent and unconscious, it's just...it makes this so much more real. That's truly our daughter right there."

"Yeah," Ellie murmured.

As Boston continued to have his moment, Ellie's chest filled with shame. This was so new and fascinating for him, and it was her fault. If she hadn't kept him from Cassie...if she'd never lied, he'd have thousands of these moments collected in his memory.

The guilt ate at her.

He drew in a breath. "I better go."

Ellie nodded mutely and followed him to the door. As he opened it and stared out into the night, she finally spoke. "You've got a long drive back. Are you sure you're going to make it okay? It's so late."

When he glanced toward her, her stomach tightened into a million knots. The streetlamp reflected off his hair, giving the black locks a blue-silver gloss. Suddenly, she remembered exactly how those locks felt. Realizing it'd been ten years since she'd truly buried her hands in them, her fingers itched for a mere touch.

It was on the tip of her tongue to invite him to stay...and not on the couch, when he answered, "I'll be fine."

Her hormones rioted, but she ignored them. Even her emotions screamed, wanting him to stay. She wanted to wash the guilt away by taking him to bed and erasing every lie and foul word she'd ever spoken to him. And God, she just wanted to be with him again.

But she held her trap shut and obediently nodded her head. He stepped outside, and she followed him to the edge of the porch.

"Goodnight," he called when he reached the bottom step.

"Night," she answered and wrapped her arms around her waist to ward off the chilly breeze. "Drive safely."

In the scarce light, she spotted the glimmer of an amused smile crossing his face. "I will," he promised and started away.

"Boston," she whispered, almost hoping he didn't hear her.

But he did and paused, turning back. When she didn't speak, he moved back to the edge porch.

"Yeah?" he asked.

"I..." She swallowed audibly and moved closer.

He rose up one step until they were eye to eye.

"I'm not trying to disrupt the peace we've got going here," she said. "I swear, I'm not. But, please, I...I just need..."

She wasn't sure who moved first, but they came together hungrily. The kiss that followed could've shot sparks out the ends of her toes.

His lips were so soft and sure when they met hers, she melted instantly. Her itching fingers buried themselves in his hair. He growled deep in his throat and tugged her close until they pressed together, melding into one silhouette.

Mouths hot, breaths moist, they devoured, they tasted. They delighted. It was absolute heaven. The pads of his fingers pressed against the sides of her neck, and Ellie moved restlessly closer. She wanted to touch every inch of him and explore, discover how much he'd changed.

As his mouth clung to hers, ten years dissolved. They were in college again, reliving that moment when their kisses had always caught a groove and slipped into a deeper connection. They flowed into one being, giving as much as they received, reaching inside each other and taking a piece of the other that could never be returned.

"Oh God, Ellie," he said. "I tried so hard to forget you. I wanted you out of my blood. But the more I tried, the more I remembered. I have never missed anything the way I miss this."

His whispered confession stirred her, right up until that line, *I missed this.*

This.

Of course the only thing he'd think about when he thought of her would be sex. That was the only thing they'd ever had going for them. Any other kind of involvement had been taboo. And that was likely what he wanted again. More sex. No emotion, no commitment. He'd already admitted to her today how he didn't want her to have any kind of power over him.

This could only be physical. And she would only end up hurt...again.

Boston slid his hand around her hip, nudging her against him. He was hard, ready. She yanked herself away, breathing heavily.

"No," she said, moving back a pace and putting space between them. "Th-that's enough."

He pursued. "It's not nearly enough."

"No, damn it." She put a hand on his chest to stop him. "Boston. I said no."

"Ellie." Her name rumbled from deep in his chest as he tried to come forward, but her palm held strong.

"We've already tried this once before," she argued. "Remember how that turned out?"

"Yeah, with the creation of an amazing little girl who means the world to me."

The thrill his words had on her almost crumbled Ellie's defenses. It would be so easy, so simple, so sensual just to give in. No one had ever moved her like Boston Kincaid. No one had touched her, inside and out, the way he did.

And no one had hurt her as much.

It had been ten years, yes. His mother had proclaimed that he'd changed...for the better. He'd affirmed it himself and even admitted he hadn't one hundred percent cheated on her. But that didn't mean it would be different between them. That didn't mean she had to go repeating the past and setting herself up for an even bigger fall.

This time, she couldn't run away when he shattered her heart. Not with Cassie between them.

"Boston," she said, trying to sound reasonable, when she just wanted to toss all common sense into the wind and drag him by the front of his shirt back to her room. "Will you just step back and look at what you're trying to do here? This"—she motioned between the two of them—"is a bad idea. I mean, aren't you the one who told me you didn't do long distance relationships? And if a relationship's not even what you're after, then that's even worse. Everything was bad enough when it ended the first time."

"Ellie, you started this," he growled through the dark and reached for her again. "You called me back onto this porch. You—"

She evaded him. "I know, and I'm sorry. Now please, just go. I...this was a bad idea. I'm sorry, but I don't want it to happen again."

"What are you so afraid of?" he demanded, his voice impatient and frustrated. "Do you honestly think it would end the way it did last time?"

"I'm not afraid," she told him. "I'm just not interested."

"Not interested?" he echoed incredulously. "Not interested?"

Ellie gasped when he snagged her arm and yanked her close. She didn't have time to rebuke him because he covered her mouth with his before she could speak. The sensation rippled a path clear to her toes. She was just starting to arch against him when he pulled away.

"Still not interested?" he snarled in her ear.

Off balance, Ellie reached out blindly and caught stability on the closed front door. She leaned there, breathing hard, as she lifted a hand to her swollen, tingling lips.

"Damn it, Ellie," he groaned. "Someday you really ought to stop lying to me. I could have you right here, right now, and we both know it."

Spine straightening, Ellie pushed from the door and stood erect. "Fine," she said, gathering her pride around her like a cloak. "You're right. But I think...I suggest we just...ignore it. For Cassie's sake."

He snorted. "Sorry, that's not working for me."

"And I'm sorry, but that's not my problem. It's working just fine for me."

She turned and reached for the door handle, but a large hand slapped the surface closed just as she started to open it. Crowding her against the door, he moved up behind her, intimidating her as much as he was enticing her with his hard, powerful body.

"The day you cut down my tree you said you'd wouldn't maul me anymore," she reminded him, biting her lip as soon as she said the words.

He went still for a good thirty seconds. She braced herself, expecting him to lose his temper. But he threw her completely off balance when instead he leaned in and smelled her hair. Too startled to even breathe, she stood there passively as he nuzzled his face against the back of her shoulder.

"I won't ever hurt you again, Ellie. I've spent all these years wishing I'd done things differently. If I could take it back, I would. When I started pursuing you, I already foresaw an end. And that's the worst thing a person can do in a relationship. But this time, you're the one anticipating an end. And this time, you're the one who's wrong. You hurt me too, you know. You purposely kept Cassie from me.

"Just think about that, Elora. I'm willing to work past this, and I've been wronged a lot more recently than you have. Why aren't you so willing? And don't tell me it's because you're *not* interested."

When she didn't answer inside five seconds, his warmth at her back disappeared. Ellie whirled around and was shocked to see his stiff spine as he strode off the porch toward his car.

Half tempted to call him back, she hurried to the

top of the steps, listening to him slam his car door and start the engine. She hugged herself as his Infiniti backed out of her drive and took off down the street.

Mind spinning, she wondered if he'd meant what he'd just said. Did he think it would be forever this time? His words sounded too good to be true...which meant they probably were. Or was she the one causing the problem?

Confused, hurt, and a little mad, she felt tears fill her eyes and quickly lifted both hands to her face to wipe them away.

Boston wasn't being fair. He shouldn't have heaped all this on her. She couldn't work through her hang-ups as quickly as he could. She hadn't been raised in a big, close-knit, loving family like his. She hadn't had all the luxuries in life he'd had. All she'd ever really had was herself to rely on. It wasn't so easy for her to put her faith in someone who'd already hurt her.

Damn him for expecting something she couldn't give.

****

Damn her for making him hope.

Boston simmered all the way home. It was a quiet drive, giving him too much time to think and stew.

She'd lied to him.

Again.

It was more than obvious she'd wanted him just as much as he'd wanted her. So why in the hell had she pulled back and put a stop to it?

In the years since his time with her, he had sometimes let himself wonder at night what he'd be doing with his life if Ellie hadn't lost that baby. Would he have asked her to marry him? He kind of thought so. After missing her the way he did, he thought he would've gone back and begged until she accepted his ring.

Missing her had hurt, and festered, and bugged the hell out of him. He never wanted to experience that again, so he'd stayed away from relationships. Besides, no one had ever sparked something inside him the way Ellie had.

But now that she was back in his life, stirring up old feelings, he knew he couldn't let her get away this time.

Grinding his teeth and flexing his fingers around the steering wheel, he wondered how the hell he was ever going to break through her trust issues.

He wondered if he even could. A helpless surge of panic raced up the back of his neck just as his phone rang. Though he didn't feel like talking to anyone, he still checked the ID to see who was trying to get a hold of him. When Ellie's number flashed across the screen, his heart nearly beat out of his chest.

"Hello?" he said, and clenched his teeth because even *he* could hear how hopeful he sounded.

"How about every other week?" Ellie's tremulous voice came out.

For a moment he was utterly confused. "What?" Then it struck him what she was saying. "You mean for custody."

She didn't answer. He blew out a breath, still shocked she was suddenly willing to compromise. "Um...okay. I accept every other week. Definitely."

"Fine." Her words were brisk, abrupt. "You can start next weekend. Bring a revised contract with you for me to sign."

"Okay. I can do that. Ellie—"

She hung up on him before he could say anything else.

Quietly he set his phone down, not sure what to make of this new development.

Either Ellie suddenly trusted him...or she

couldn't stomach the idea of him coming to her place and spending any more time there to be with his daughter.

He had a bad feeling her reason was the latter.

Chapter Sixteen

Eight days later, Cassidy had her first weekend with her father. While Ellie was ripe with apprehension, her daughter was beyond excited. Boston must've been a jumble of both emotions, because he called Ellie three times during the week, asking question after question. First he wanted to know if Cassidy had any allergies or phobias. Then he wanted to know about her sleeping habits, her bedtime and if he needed to get her a nightlight.

Ellie couldn't help but melt every time she heard his nervous voice. And, in truth, spending most her time answering his questions and soothing his nerves eased her own worries. At least he was going to try to do things right. Dealing with him also took her mind off the fact she'd be completely without her baby girl for a full forty-eight hours.

She needed to get a life. Letting her world revolve around her daughter had been all good and well until the girl went and deserted her every other weekend. Now, she just felt useless and lonely.

It was pure providence when Ted Barnaby came into her office one day. Ted was a partner in Barnaby & Murdock, an advertising firm in Lawrence. He kept Ellie's boss on retainer as their legal advisor. And every time he popped in for Winston to look over a contract, he had to stop by Ellie's desk to flirt. For the past three years since Winston had been dealing with him, Ted had asked her out on an average of once every two to three months.

So, when he perched his hip on the corner of her

desk, stole a mint from her candy jar and asked her what she was doing that Friday night, Ellie stared at him and thought, *Why not?* Cassie would be with Boston for their second weekend together, and she'd be all alone.

She'd been out of the dating world for so long, she didn't even know the rules anymore, but going out with a man she'd known for a few years seemed like a nice safe place to start. Besides, it was way past time to spend a little social time with an adult of the opposite gender.

Before she could rethink her decision, she said, "Well, I hope I'm going to dinner with you."

Though he hadn't been moving around to do so, Ted fell off the corner of her desk. He caught himself before tumbling all the way to the floor and straightened instantly, tugging his suit jacket back into place as he did. Then he stared at Ellie in blunt surprise before saying, "Really?"

She laughed. "Was that not what you had in mind?"

"No!" he blurted out before he realized how unstylishly he was behaving. Then he cleared his throat, fiddled with the knot of his tie. "I mean...yes, that's what I had in mind. A nice, quiet restaurant with a little wine and candlelight was exactly what I had in mind."

Slipping right into flirt mode, Ellie twined a piece of hair around her finger. "And what time will you be picking me up Friday evening?"

"How does seven sound?"

Seven o'clock. Boston would be gone by six with Cassie. That would give her an hour to prepare. Perfect.

"It sounds great," she answered.

"Then...great," he said, pitching his voice even lower as he grinned at her. "I'll see you Friday at seven." He turned to leave then but drew short at the last seconds, swinging back to eye her peculiarly for a moment. "Just curious, but what changed your mind?"

Ellie didn't figure she should tell him the truth—*it was either you or no one, bud. Sorry.* Giving him one of those Mona Lisa smiles, she grinned and said, "I just thought that after all those mints you stole from my jar, you probably owed me a full-course meal by now."

His gaze slid slowly to her candy jar and then back to her. She could see by the gleam in his eyes how her comment delighted him.

"Well now, ma'am," he told her in a silken voice, "I'll do everything in my power to make sure you get your money's worth."

Chapter Seventeen

Ellie gnawed on her bottom lip and stared impatiently at her wristwatch until the phone rang. She yelped, not expecting the sound, and pressed a hand to her heart.

It was finally Friday, the day for her big date, and Boston hadn't shown yet. Okay, to be fair it wasn't even six o'clock, but the man was usually so impatient to get Cassie, he showed up obscenely early to fetch her. But tonight, it was two till and he was nowhere around. It was as if he knew she had plans for once in her life and was doing everything in his power to keep her nerves rattled.

"Hello," she answered, hoping it wasn't Ted to cancel. After borrowing a dress from Nora, she was actually excited for a fancy night out.

"Ellie." The voice calling through the crackling phone lines sounded as if it came from a long distance. Her stomach tingled in apprehension. In the background, she heard traffic noise and occasional honking.

She pressed a hand to one ear, hoping to hear him better. "Boston?"

"I'm sorry," he gushed. "I'm stuck in a major traffic jam on the interstate. There's some kind of wreck up ahead and no one is moving."

"Oh." Her shoulders dragged. Shoot. "Ah..."

"I'm only about ten miles outside Lawerence. But there's no way I'm going to get there by six."

"Umm, okay." Damn. "Uh..." She wondered briefly what he wanted her to do about it. "So...do you know when you'll make it?"

225

"No, sorry." His apology sounded genuine. "Traffic was starting to move a few minutes ago, but now it's come to a complete stop again."

"Oh, well...all right then. I'll see you...whenever."

"You'll tell Cassie what's going on?"

"Of course."

"Thanks. See you in a bit."

After he hung up, Ellie continued to hold the phone in her hand. Biting her lip, she stared sightlessly at the wall.

Thinking this was probably the best time to prepare for her date, she hopped into the bathroom and took a quick shower. Cassie was camped out in front of the mini television in her room, playing Mario Brothers with Keller, so Ellie took her time putting on makeup and doing her hair. She'd just slipped on her going-out heels when the doorbell rang.

Ellie glanced at the clock and let out a relived sigh. Yes! Great timing. There were still twenty minutes before Ted was supposed to arrive. That gave her the perfect window of opportunity to get Cassie and Boston out the door before her date showed.

Boston started apologizing as soon as she opened the entrance. "I am so sorry about this, El. I left plenty early. If it wasn't for—" He stopped midsentence and took in her painted face, styled hair, and knee-length sexy black dress. "You're going out." He stated it as a comment, but the underlying question behind his words remained thick in the air.

"That's right," Ellie answered. "I—" Stepping aside to let him in, she turned and yelled, "Cassie! Your father's here."

"Just one more minute," the girl hollered back. "I'm almost through this level."

Boston frowned at Ellie in confusion, and she

rolled her eyes. "She and Keller are on the Xbox."

"Ah," he said; all the while his gaze moved down her dress and back up to her face. "So...is this, like...a date?"

Ellie eyes narrowed. "It's, like...none of your business."

"Then it's a date," he said.

"I didn't say that."

He looked amused when he answered, "If it was anything else, you'd tell me."

"No, I would—"

"It's not going to work this time, Ellie," he murmured, stepping closer. "I refuse to fight with you anymore. So, whatever you say in an attempt to upset me is just going to bounce off me unnoticed."

"I'm not trying to—"

"Though, I have to admit," he went on, conversationally, stepping in a circle around her to check out her backside, "going out with someone else to make me jealous is working. Very well."

"Arggg." She spun away from him and yelled, "Cassidy!"

"Just a *minute*," the girl roared back.

Determined to ignore her daughter's father, Ellie picked up a pair of earrings she'd left sitting on the coffee table. She turned to look in a mirror and became engrossed with trying to put them on.

"You know I'm not doing this because of you," she grumbled to her reflection as she spoke to Boston. "In fact, if you hadn't been so late, I would've waited until *after* you were gone before I even started getting ready for tonight." More in control of herself, she sighed in relief when the earring finally slid on. Then she whirled to face him. "So, there's no reason for you to think I'm trying to make you jealous, because I never intended for you to find out about it in the first place."

"Well, I'm jealous anyway," he said quietly.

The admission threw her off guard. This is what she hated most about Boston Kincaid. He never played fair. He always knew exactly what to say to draw her in.

Glancing away, she folded her arms over her chest, refusing to let his pretty words sway her. "That's not my problem."

"And if I make it your problem?" he countered, stepping closer.

She turned her face aside. "Boston—"

"I want to be with you, Ellie," he whispered, stopping her rejection short. "And I know you want it too. All I have to do it look into your eyes to see that you want—"

"Sex," she finished for him, turning to stare him directly in the eye.

Surprised by her cold, lifeless tone, he fell a step back. "Excuse me?"

"We want sex," she said on an unconcerned shrug. "And why wouldn't we? It was always good between us. But that was never the problem. There's more to a relationship than just—"

"I'm well aware of that," he cut in. "And if you'd give me half a chance, I'll show you I'm willing to do whatever it takes to get it right this time."

"No," she said.

He growled and grabbed a handful of his own hair. "Damn it, Elora," he gritted out. "What do I have to say to convince you—"

"Nothing," she said, pacing across the living room to gain some space. "Trust me. You've said quite enough."

Boston froze and looked at her as if she'd struck him. The instant hurt she saw in his eyes made her want to apologize, but she kept her mouth stubbornly shut.

Then he snapped his fingers and smiled. "Ah..." he cooed, his gaze lighting with delight. "Now I understand."

Ellie plopped a hand on her hip. "And just what do you think you understand?"

"You're scared."

She laughed out a snort. "Scared? You think I'm going out on a date tonight because I'm scared?"

He grinned and nodded. "Yes."

"And what, pray tell, am I so scared of?"

"You're scared to believe it's the real thing this time between us. You don't want to trust it because last time hurt so bad. Well, let me tell you something, Ellie. I'm scared too. I'm scared I'm going to do something else wrong, and I'll end up losing you and Cassie all over again. But I'm willing to take that risk.

"You may think history is just going to repeat itself, but I can't believe that. Because I'm not the same person I was ten years ago, and you aren't either. Things change, people grow and mature. But other things stay the same, like the way I've always felt about you. I don't care how much you resist and run from it, it's still going to be there between us. I'm still going to be here. I love you, damn it, and I'll wait as long as I have to until you're ready to come around."

He loved her?

Wait.

"What?"

Totally not expecting that confession, Ellie dropped her mouth open. He seemed to realized what he'd just told her a half a second later when his own face filled with color.

He sucked in a surprised gasp. "Oh, God," he whispered. He didn't retract his words, but the look on his face made her think he was going to be physically ill for confessing them aloud.

They stared at each other, both clueless as to what to say now.

The ringing of the doorbell had each of them jumping. Ellie yelped and turned in surprise.

Oh, no.

No, no, no.

That couldn't be Ted. He was way too early. She stared hard at the door and then glanced toward Boston. He stared right back at her. At her panicked look, he lifted his eyebrows. "Want *me* to get that?"

"No," she said quickly. Too quickly. But God, no. There was no way she wanted him to meet Ted. Hell, there was no way she wanted to see the two men standing next to each other. It'd be too obvious which one was better looking, better smelling, better everything.

"I got it," she mumbled needlessly. Boston trailed casually behind her. She sent him a brief back-off scowl before she reached for the handle. He didn't budge.

To her horror, it was indeed her date standing on the front porch.

"You're early," she blurted out. After glancing down at her wrist, she nearly groaned aloud. "*Really* early."

But Ted merely grinned. "I couldn't wait." He thrust a bouquet of bright lilies at her.

"Oh!" she said in surprise, noticing them for the first time. "Ah...thank you."

"Ready?" he asked.

Ellie bit her lip. "Actually, no. I'm sorry, but not quite yet."

That was when Ted noticed Boston hovering slightly behind her and to the right.

His smile faded.

"Hello," Boston said, moving closer to Ellie in such a territorial way Ted actually shrank back a pace. "You must be the date." After scowling at the flowers, he sent Ellie a sideways look. "I thought roses were your favorite?"

She cleared her throat and shifted her weight with one foot to grind the heel of her shoes into Boston's loafer. The muffled grunt behind her made her glow.

"Ted," she said, beaming at him as she showed him inside. "This is Cassidy's father, Boston Kincaid. He's just here to pick her up for their weekend together."

Ted's shoulders relaxed. He actually smiled a friendly greeting. "Hey," he said and held at his hand.

As they shook, Ellie continued. "Boston, this is Ted..." Her face filled with color as Ted's last name completely escaped her memory.

Both men paused to stare at her. Boston lifted one mocking brow, on the verge of outright laughing.

"Barnaby," Ted supplied, his cheeks a bright tomato red.

Ellie snapped her fingers and smiled brightly at Ted. "Barnaby, that's right." Starting to ramble, she said, "I don't know where my head is..." Probably still reliving Boston's *I love you* over and over again. "I kept wanting to say Murdock, but, no, that's your partner."

"Partner?" Boston asked curiously. Ellie shot him a look to shut him up, but he completely ignored her as he stared at Ted with interest. "Are you a lawyer?"

"I co-own Barnaby & Murdock here in town," Ted was eager to report.

"The advertising firm?" Boston guessed.

Ted grinned. "That's the one. I go to Winston Young, Ellie's boss, for legal advice and I was in the office just the other day. I swear, I've been trying to get this little lady here to go on a date with me for well over three years now. I guess this was just my lucky week, huh?"

From the corner of her eye, Ellie saw Boston

glance her way. "Hmm," he answered Ted in a sickeningly knowing voice. "Yes, it must've been."

She wanted to roll her eyes and tell him that whatever he was thinking was completely wrong, because if he thought her going out tonight with Ted was all because of him... Well, nothing could be further from the truth.

"She does seem to be a tough catch, doesn't she?" Boston murmured. She didn't mean to look his way, but she did, and their eyes caught. *I love you, damn it,* echoed through her brain as they stared at each other. *And I'll wait as long as I have to until you're ready to come around.*

He didn't mean it. He couldn't. Ellie wasn't sure what she'd do if he really did mean it, but that didn't matter because it had only been a bunch of B.S.

Boston was a silver-tongued lawyer. He knew his way around words. And yet, he'd never spoken that phrase to her before.

"But she's well worth the wait," he added softly, smiling at her as he spoke to Ted.

"Boy, do I hear that," Ted answered, laughing heartily.

The two men shared a companionable look, like two dogs that had chewed on the same bone. Ellie nearly hurled.

With the need to escape itching through her bloodstream, she said, "Let me just get these in some water."

But when she turned around, she almost ran flat into Boston's chest. "Excuse me," she murmured, but still had to move around him because the aggravating man refused to budge.

"Cassie!" she called loudly. "Time to go! Your dad's waiting."

Hurry up, kid! she wanted to shout. *I can't take too much more of this.*

Just as she was exiting the room, she heard Ted

ask, "So, how long have you and Ellie been divorced?"

"We're not," Boston's answer echoed back to her.

She cringed, hoping he'd explain they'd never been married in the first place, but when she returned to the living room, both men were standing stiffly with their hands in their pockets, keeping their distance from each other. Ellie wondered what all Boston had actually said, because suddenly Ted seemed on edge and ready to scram.

Boston just stared at him.

Thank God, Cassie finally came into the room with Keller at her heels and happily cried, "Dad!"

As she threw herself at him, Boston swept her up in a big hug. Keller paused by Ellie's elbow to watch. He looked so heartsick and jealous of all the attention Cassie's father was giving her, she set a sympathetic hand on his pale blond hair.

"Keller," Boston greeted, keeping Cassie in his arms as he nodded to the boy.

"Hi," he mumbled, clearly disheartened.

"I'll see you Sunday night," Cassie said, waving at her friend, yet she couldn't feel the same depression Keller obviously felt at their parting.

"Uh huh," the boy answered and turned away to leave through the back exit.

Ellie watched him go, her heart breaking for the child.

"Hey, Cassidy," Ted said, cutting into Ellie's thoughts. "Do you remember me?"

Ellie came back around just in time to see Cassie huddle closer to Boston's chest as she glanced at Ted with no enthusiasm whatsoever.

"You work with my mom," she answered.

Cassie and Ted had met maybe twice when Ellie's law firm had gatherings like ice cream socials with their clients. Everyone brought their families and mingled.

Ted gave the girl an overeager smile. "That's right. You *do* remember."

But Cassie didn't seem all that impressed, and judging by the way Boston frowned and tightened his grip, he didn't like Ted talking to his daughter.

So, Ellie stepped in. "Do you have everything you need?" she asked, lifting the overnight bag she'd already packed for Cassie.

"Check," her daughter answered with a cheeky smile as Boston reached out and took the bag from Ellie's hand. Their fingers brushed, and she immediately pulled away.

Ted frowned in consternation.

Ellie flushed. "All right then," she said to Cassie. "I'll see you on Sunday."

She went to hug her baby, but Boston only held his daughter out enough for Ellie to hug her. She wondered if he did that on purpose so she'd have to brush against him as she pulled Cassie close.

She looked at him and said, "Goodbye."

"'Bye," he said briefly.

Ellie couldn't read one expression on his face. He just stared at her a second longer and then turned away.

God, why did this have to happen?

She'd timed it so there should've been at least an hour between his departure and Ted's arrival. If Boston hadn't been so blasted late and Ted too freaking early, the two never would've been the wiser.

Boston set Cassie on her feet so she could walk out the door herself. Hooking his daughter's overnight bag over his shoulder, he took her hand and started her out.

They'd just cleared the doorway when Cassie's voice echoed back inside.

"I don't like that guy; he always talks to me like I'm four."

Ellie's face heated with color, and she was too afraid to glance toward Ted. Instead, she met Boston's cocky smirk as he glanced over his shoulder at her.

Chapter Eighteen

The date was a total bomb.

Ellie blamed it entirely on Boston.

I'll wait as long as I have to until you're ready. Those stupid words repeated through her head a hundred times over during the course of her meal.

It was bad enough she'd had to see her old lover, the still prime Boston Kincaid, next to her date for the evening. That had ruined Ted's chances right there. There was no way Ted Barnaby would ever be able to make her feel what Boston had.

But then Boston had to go and say all that...*crap* to her right before Ted showed up. If only he'd kept his big mouth shut.

I'll wait as long as I have to until you're ready.

As Ted talked on about himself, regaling her with a story about his pet collie, Ellie saw Boston in her mind's eye the moment after he'd told her he loved her. He'd looked so shocked. The man had to be a star actor to fake that. Which led her to assume he hadn't meant to say it. But the true question was, did he mean it?

And did it matter if he did?

She wanted to say no. His feelings for her should have no bearing on the fact that she didn't want them to start any kind of relationship. But, God, it did. If he loved her, she...she what? She'd probably fall down at his feet and make the same claim.

Ellie groaned aloud and caught Ted's attention. He stopped talking to give her a questioning look.

She blushed. "Um...I think I'm ready to go home...if you are?"

He blinked a few times and then grinned knowingly. She almost groaned again. Great. Now Ted thought she was inviting him back to her place. How he'd gotten that idea when she'd been ignoring him all night, she had no clue. But, hell...she didn't bother to correct him. He'd find out the truth soon enough when they reached her place.

"I had a great time," he said huskily in her ear as he followed her from his truck up her front walk.

"Hmm," Ellie murmured, casting him an edgy look over her shoulder. Once they made it to her porch, she stood by the closed entrance and toyed with her keys, not about to unlock the house until he was safely on his way back to his truck.

Thinking she was waiting for a kiss, however, Ted leaned in toward her. "God, you smell good."

His lips touched hers, and Ellie felt herself hold still to allow it. The poor guy had taken her to a really nice restaurant. The least he deserved was a goodnight peck.

But then he pushed his tongue into her mouth. It in no way resembled the mind-blowing kiss Boston had given her on Thanksgiving. Ellie tried to pull away, because it wasn't doing anything for her. At all.

Ted held her fast, burying a hand in her hair and holding her skull steady as he continued to plunder. Ellie frowned and made a noise of rejection in the back of her throat. She tried to jerk away again, with a little more effort this time. But Ted was one persistent man.

"God, you are so hot," he panted out when he tore his mouth away from hers to nibble on the side of her neck and grope at her breast with a big, clumsy hand.

"Ted," she hissed and started to wiggle herself free. "Stop!" She pushed at his hand.

"Oh, come on." He laughed huskily and

tightened his grip as if playfully denying her. "You know you want it."

"No. I don't." She started to panic a little when he only got more aggressive. Finally, she gave up trying to be polite. "I told you to stop," she growled and hiked up her dress in order to free her leg long enough to kick him between the legs.

Honestly, she hadn't meant to be so rough. She'd intended a light jab to let him know she wasn't playing around. But right before she moved, he pushed her against the door and pinned her there. The fear had her adrenaline pumping through her veins; when her knee came up, it did so with plenty of enthusiasm...dropping him like a sack of potatoes.

Curling into himself, Ted fell to his knees, grabbed his crotch with both hands, and cursed loudly. With her back still plastered to the door, Ellie glanced down at him and winced. He looked pathetic down there, whimpering and cradling himself.

"You...bitch."

"I told you to stop," she explained in a placating tone.

When he lifted his face and glared, she had no idea he was going to lunge at her half a second later. Surprised when he did, roughly grabbing for her legs as if to tackle her, she yelped and brought up her knee again.

This time she caught him square in the face and felt cartilage crunch against her kneecap. It was sickening.

"My nose!" he bellowed, falling back on his butt to remove one hand from his crotch and cover his face.

"Get off my porch!" Ellie growled. "*Now*. Before I go for something else. And believe me, it'll be more painful."

She moved toward him and pulled back her foot

like she was ready to punt a football. But thankfully, he scurried back away from her, tripping over himself in his haste.

"Crazy bitch," he repeated as he stumbled backward and waddled hunchback toward his truck.

"Don't ever ask me out again," Ellie called, wiping her palms together.

She stood like a mighty Amazon warrior on her porch, with her hands fisted until Ted crawled into his automobile and burned rubber, peeling out in his haste to leave. She watched him turn the corner at the end of the block.

"Wow," she finally said, letting out a pent-up breath. What a rush.

Ellie always thought she'd be scared and shaky after getting attacked by a man. But she wasn't scared now. She'd fought him off and chased him away, all by herself and without anyone else's assistance.

"God, that felt good."

"Well, it ought to," answered a voice from the dark. "You racked him good, honey."

Ellie yelped and swung to the right, spying the glowing tip of a cigarette butt coming from the middle of her yard.

"Nora?" she said, squinting through the dark.

She'd known her friend was a closet smoker, but she'd never actually seen Nora puff on anything.

She moved down the steps of her porch. "Did you just see all of that?"

"I did," Nora answered. "And I was headed over here to give you some help until you went and took matters into your own hands...or should I say, into your own knee."

Ellie grinned. "Well, thanks for thinking of me. I would've appreciated your help."

Nora shrugged and blew out a gust of smoke. "It would've have been my pleasure. I'm not a big fan of men these days. If they're not trying to maul you on the goodnight kiss, they're screwing their new secretary in the tie you gave them for Christmas."

Ellie grew quiet, realizing Nora was not only smoking, but she was drunk and stewing too.

Nora sucked on her cigarette before saying, "I spent a long time picking out that tie, you know. It had to be just the right color to match his eyes and still go with all his suits." She blew out a stream of smoke and added, "Bastard."

Ellie quietly asked, "Is Dr. Young working late again?"

Nora always called it something other than what it was. She'd say her husband was at a conference for the weekend or working late. Then she'd give Ellie a look that said she meant otherwise.

But tonight, she didn't beat around the bush; she snorted. "Working late my ass. He's out boffing...someone. I'm not even up on who he's currently screwing these days."

"Oh, Nora," Ellie said and hugged her friend.

Nora pulled her close. "Want to come over to my house and get drunk with me? We can complain about men all night."

"Sure," Ellie said, unable to ignore a friend in need.

She followed Nora to the Young's back door, then waited outside on the redwood porch as Nora disappeared inside for a few minutes. She was briskly rubbing her hands up and down her arms to ward off the chill in the air when Nora reappeared with a half-empty bottle of wine and two jackets. She tossed one of the coats at Ellie.

As Ellie gratefully pushed her hands into the arm holes, Nora whispered, "Keller's a light sleeper, so we have to stay out here."

After they moved toward the umbrella-covered round table, Nora took a drink straight from the bottle and then wordlessly passed it to Ellie.

Ellie chugged. The potent liquid did as much toward warming her as the double-lined jacket did. "How is Keller?" she asked, passing the wine back to Nora.

Nora's shoulders slumped as she sighed. "Oh, he moped around the house all evening, looking out the window toward your place every five seconds as if he thought Cassie was going to come home any moment."

Ellie swallowed guiltily and looked down at her hands.

"He's so dependent on that girl of yours. I swear if she didn't live next door to him, I'd leave that worthless father of his and take him away from here."

"Want us to move?" Ellie offered, only half kidding.

Maybe it would be better to wean the poor boy away from her daughter now. With Boston in her life, she was going to need Keller less and less, and it was going to break the poor boy's heart in slow, painful portions to watch Cassie slip away from him.

Nora snorted and slapped a hand her way. Then she sighed and flopped back in her seat to smoke some more. "Honestly, I sometimes really think it'd be better for him if we just up and left Mendel," she murmured thoughtfully. "At least that way Keller wouldn't have to be reminded day after day how much his father ignores him. He could get on with his own life."

"I guess I should be grateful Cassie doesn't have that problem with Boston," Cassie murmured to herself. "When she's with him, he actually spends time with her. I'll give him that much. He's a very attentive father."

After taking a long swig, Nora passed it over and lit up another cigarette. "Now, honey. That's one man you shouldn't have thrown off your front porch."

Ellie had just been taking a drink from the bottle but stopped to choke.

"Excuse me?"

Nora laughed. "Oh, yeah, I know about that Thanksgiving night he pinned you to the front door."

Ellie gaped, but Nora only shrugged. "Hey, it's not my fault you've got men trying to come on to you when I'm having my nightly smoke fest. But let me tell you, dear, you've had more action on that porch in the last month than I've had all year. And it's December!"

Ellie laughed even as her mind strayed to Boston. "So, you really saw me and Boston kiss?"

"Saw? Hell, darling, I made some popcorn and camped out. And I'm here to say that you are...STU-PID. That man is hot. He's sweet. He adores Cassidy. He's smart, rich, HOT, and he looks at you like you are...oxygen to a suffocating man."

Ellie was quiet for a moment. Nora was right. Boston was all those wonderful things. But... "We have a bad past," she said.

"Oh, right," Nora said after a second. "He's got so many positive attributes, I keep forgetting he's a cheater too, isn't he?"

Ellie frowned. "Actually...he's not really."

When Nora sent her a confused look, she repeated the story Boston had given her about Heather from American history class.

"Well, damn," Nora grumbled. "Now, you're just rubbing it in. Not only is he turning out to be a damn good father, but he was incapable of sleeping around on you too. Sorry, El, but you're not cheering me up here."

"It ended so horribly for us," Ellie went on, ignoring Nora's sarcastic complaint. "I just...I don't think I can get past that. How can I ever trust him again?"

"A bad past can be fixed," Nora said. "A quiet, lonely future is just...sad."

Ellie didn't answer, but she couldn't stop thinking over Nora's words either.

Chapter Nineteen

Boston was up early Saturday morning, making breakfast for his daughter. He was scrambling eggs and pouring them into a hot pan when a yawning Cassidy shuffled barefoot into the kitchen.

"Morning," he said cheerfully. "Hungry?"

Cassie quit rubbing her eyes and peered into the pan to see what he was cooking.

She immediately wrinkled her nose. "Eggs? Yuck!"

Boston stopped pouring. "You don't like eggs?"

"No way."

He looked down at the eggs that were starting to cook and sighed. Eggs were the only decent breakfast he knew how to make. Grinding his molars, he picked up the pan and carried the whole thing outside to scrape them into his dumpster. When he came back in, he was smiling.

"What do you say we go to McDonalds for breakfast?"

Cassie's eyes lit. "Yeah!"

****

Boston's cell phone rang just as they pulled through the drive-thru. Rolling his eyes when he saw that it was Cameron, he answered with, "No, I'm not coming in today. I told you, I'm spending the weekend with my daughter. And besides, it's Saturday. My day off."

"We have a problem," Cameron told him, his voice grave. "A big one."

Boston closed his eyes. "What?"

"Just get over here."

Boston sighed. "What about Cassie?"

"Bring her. She can keep Livy occupied while I explain."

Boston growled and cut the connection. He tossed the phone into the tray divider between the two seats, which made Cassie jump.

Next to him, his daughter sent him a face full of sad blue eyes. "You have to go to work?"

"No," he said immediately, then sighed and ran a harassed hand through his hair. "We're just going to stop in for a few minutes. Don't you want to see where I work?"

He wasn't expecting that to excite her, but Cassie's eyes lit, and she sat up straighter. "Yeah, okay."

So, Boston drove Cassie to EarthNet. Olivia greeted them at the door to his office and Boston threw a look past her to glare meaningfully at Cameron, who paced the floor.

"Livy just fired your secretary," Cameron blurted out, sending his wife an annoyed scowl.

"Oh, and you were going to keep her employed after *that*?" Olivia demanded, glaring back.

"No," Cameron admitted, looking suddenly sheepish, "but...well, hell, it feels better to blame you."

Boston pinched the bridge of his nose, not really wanting to know what this was about. Putting the questions off, he turned to Cassie and led her to the couch, where he helped her set up her breakfast on the coffee table. As she dug in, he finally turned back to the arguing married couple.

"Okay, what happened? And why was Crystal here on a Saturday, anyway?"

"Oh, yeah, about that," Cameron said and laughed guiltily. "Well...since you refused to come in, I asked her to, because, ah, well, because she's *your* secretary, right. She should know where you keep things. Anyway, she acted only too eager to work some overtime when I called her, so I had her come in."

Boston groaned, knowing exactly where this was going. Crystal's version of overtime had nothing to do with actual work.

"So, I walked in here," Olivia butted in to continue the story. "And I found *your* secretary kissing him and trying to stick her hand down his pants."

Boston looked at Cassie. She appeared to be listening to Cameron and Olivia's tale with avid interest.

Grinding his teeth, he turned to Cameron, who shrugged. "I stopped her before she did anything too traumatic to me, but Livy still caught a good portion of the show, just as I yanked Chrystal's sticky palms off me. And then *she*"—he pointed accusingly at his wife—"blew completely off the handle and tried to rip the poor girl's hair out."

"Poor girl?" Olivia echoed incredulously.

Cameron merely grinned. "Hey, can you really blame her for trying? I mean, look at me. I'm irresistible."

Boston rolled his eyes and groaned.

"Be that as it may," Olivia ground out, "I'm sorry, but any woman who tries to have sex with *my* husband is going to lose her hair *and* her job. That's all there is to it."

"Whoa!" Boston said, sending a warning look toward Cassidy. "Excuse me. My nine-year-old daughter is sitting right here. Ick-snay on the ex-say."

Cassidy rolled her eyes. "Oh please, Dad. I know what sex is."

As Olivia told Cameron what she'd do to the next woman she caught trying to come on to him, Boston gaped at his daughter. "You do?"

"Of course," Cassie said, rolling her eyes one more time. "Since I was, like, seven."

"Oh my God," Boston murmured, falling down on the couch to sit next to her. Why would Ellie tell a seven-year-old about sex?

"When Keller's cat had babies, I wanted to know where they came from, so he looked it up online and told me everything."

Oblivious to Boston's shocked comatose position, Cameron turned back to him as he held up a hand in front of Olivia's face to block out her ranting. "Bos, the fact of the matter is we need to get you a secretary. And we need one now. Preferably someone with a legal background. We're just about to head into a huge business transaction, and I'm going to need you out in the field with me. Not at the office trying to fill in for some absent secretary."

Cassie sat up straight and announced, "My mom's a legal secretary."

Cam stopped talking and blinked at Cassidy. The girl grinned at him blissfully as she forked more biscuits and gravy into her mouth.

Her uncle arched a brow. "Oh, she is, is she?" His eyes slid meaningfully toward Boston. "Well, what do you know."

"No," Boston said.

He couldn't think about Ellie right now, not without wanting to break something. She'd turned him down only to go out with some loser named Ted. He was still swimming in jealousy, and no woman had *ever* made him jealous before. He wasn't at all happy with Ellie for accomplishing such a feat. He kept wondering how her date had gone. Had good old Ted gotten any farther than he had? He certainly hoped not...just to be spiteful.

"But—"

"I said no," Boston cut his cousin off. "No way on God's green earth." He cast a quick warning look toward his daughter. "Hey, Livy," he asked suddenly. "Could you take Cass to the vending machines so she can wash down her breakfast with something to drink?"

Olivia didn't look too happy about being dismissed. But she followed Boston's request and ushered Cassie from the room. As soon as the door closed behind them, Boston immediately swung Cameron's way.

"Look, I'll find somebody, okay. Just...somebody else." God, *anybody* else.

"Why not Ellie?" Cameron countered.

"For one thing, I don't sleep with my secretaries."

Cameron frowned. "But, you're not sleeping with— Oh, my God. *Are* you?"

Boston blinked and gave his cousin a dry look. "Where do you think Cassidy came from?"

Cam snorted. "I meant recently."

Pausing before he answered, Boston took a deep breath. "No," he said, "not yet."

"Not..." Cameron started to repeat. Then his eyes went wide. "Not yet? Well, well. You and El are getting back together, are you? That's great, man. I didn't even think she was interested in you."

"She's not," Boston muttered.

Cameron's smile wavered. "Oh," he said lamely. "So, you want to, but she doesn't, huh? Man, that blows."

"She went on a date last night...with some guy named *Ted*."

"Hmm." Cameron looked sufficiently depressed for his buddy for a good minute before he sat up straight and snapped his fingers. "You know, maybe she just did that to make you jealous, like—"

"I wasn't supposed to find out about him. If I'd picked Cassie up on time last night, I wouldn't have even known this other guy existed." Hissing out a swear word, he ran his hands through his hair. "Jesus, Cam. I stood there and told her I loved her, and she still opened the door for him."

"Wow."

"I can't..." He glanced toward his cousin. "I can't hire her. I'd go insane."

Cameron blew out a long breath. "Okay," he said, his shoulders slumping in defeat. "We'll find somebody else then. No biggie. We'll find someone...somehow."

Chapter Twenty

Monday morning, Ellie showed up to work at her regular time. She'd been so sure Boston would quiz her about her date when he brought Cassie home. She would've bet money on it. She was also prepared to tell him Ted was a jerk. Then she'd graciously let him know she'd changed her mind and was ready to try one more time with him.

But he didn't even walk Cassie to the door. He stayed in the car, buckled into the driver's seat as he watched their daughter troop up the front steps to where Ellie was waiting at the entrance to receive her.

As Ellie held the screen door open, her eyes slid toward the Infiniti. Boston sat at the curb a couple of seconds, watching her from shuttered sunglasses, before he put the car into gear and drove off. Mouth dropping, she was swamped with a mixture of disappointment and relief. She wasn't all that settled or comfortable over the whole idea of starting over with him. More time to think it through before letting him know what she'd decided was much appreciated.

On the other hand, it was going to be *two* weeks before she saw him again, before she could touch him, kiss him. Ellie thought it'd be in bad form to take off running after him down the street and inform him she'd changed her mind. So, she just stood there and watched him go.

Monday morning, She was still indecisive as she pushed open the front door of Young and Mercer. Deep in thought, she didn't notice the figure standing in her boss's opened doorway until she was behind her desk and bending over to turn on her computer.

"Ellie?" the male voice came from behind her.

She screamed and jerked erect.

Winston folded his arms over his chest.

"What in the world are you doing here so early?" she gasped, pressing a hand to her heart. Her boss never showed up before she did.

"I need to talk to you," he said without preamble.

"Ah...okay."

He stepped out of the doorway to his office and turned to the side, giving her an expectant arch of the brows, silently commanding her to enter before him. She frowned and immediately moved to comply. As soon as he stepped into the chilly room behind her, she swerved around and gave him a strange look. This was way beyond unusual.

"What's going on?" she asked, her mind instantly going to Nora and Keller. Had Nora done what she'd promised to do Friday night? Was she divorcing Mendel? If she was, that would definitely put Ellie in an awkward position with her and Nora being so close and Winston being Mendel's only brother.

"Have a seat," Winston answered, making sure not to share any kind of eye contact with her as he motioned awkwardly to a chair.

Ellie sank down warily. What in the world had happened? He looked so sober, like someone had—

Oh, God. Had someone died? Ellie sprang to her feet. "What happened?" she demanded to know.

Winston gave a tired sigh and perched himself on the edge of his desk, facing her. "Just...sit down, Ellie." He scrubbed at the back of his neck.

"Just tell me," she countered.

He stopped rubbing, but kept his palm latched

around his neck as if to give himself an excuse to keep his head lowered while he mumbled, "I hate this like hell. But...I'm afraid I'm going to have to let you go."

Ellie blinked. "W-what?" she managed to say after a pregnant pause.

Pressing a hand to her chest, she slowly took a step back and sank gingerly into the chair before her shaky legs gave out from under her. As she stared at the top of her boss's balding head, she watched the greasy skin there turn a bright, embarrassed red.

"You're fired," he said, lifting his face and wincing when he saw her expression.

She blinked. "But...why?"

She could barely breathe, barely think. None of this made sense. What in the world was going on?

Winston's gaze slid away. "I..." he tried to start and then fell silent. Finally, he cleared his throat, straightened his shoulders stiffly as if seeking some courage there and looked up. "You know how important my clients are to me, Ellie."

She nodded, not even realizing she was still pressing the flat of her palm against her ribcage. "Of course," she managed.

"Well..." he said. Then his gaze flitted guiltily away. "It's a top priority here at Young and Mercer to keep every client happy, and when Ted Barnaby called me Saturday morning—"

"Ted Barnaby!" Ellie repeated in alarm as she surged to her feet.

"Threatening to cancel his account with us if I didn't let you go—" Winston tried to continue.

"He...he *what*!" Her mouth fell open. "He can't do that."

She stared hard at Winston until sweat beaded on the shiny top of his head and began to drip down. He squirmed under her intense gaze and dropped his eyes.

"His advertising firm is our biggest client, Ellie," he tried to explain. "And you know our policy. The client is the most important—"

"So, you're just going to fire me because I wouldn't sleep with him?" she blurted out, her face heating with indignation.

"Now, I don't know anything about that," Winston started, lifting a hand to stop her from saying more. "And frankly, I don't want to know. What you do after hours and with whom is none of my business."

"Except that's exactly why you're firing me," Ellie countered, setting her hands on her hips.

"Now, don't look at it that way, Ellie. I—"

"Then how should I look at it, Winston?"

He flushed. "It's perfectly fine that you rejected him. Ted just...well, he said he's not comfortable having a working relationship with you anymore. It has nothing to with...with..." He motioned blindly with his hands.

Ellie lifted her brows and waited for him to say it aloud.

"Damn it, Ellie," he blustered in helpless frustration. "My hands are tied here. I don't want to let you go. You're the best assistant I've ever had."

"Then don't let me go," Ellie said. "Tell Barnaby to go to hell and find himself different legal representation."

Winston gaped at her, his mouth dropping in mute shock.

"Give him over to Mercer," she said.

"Come on." He laughed incredulously at the idea of giving his partner Ted's business. "You know I can't do that."

"If I were really that important of an employee to you," Ellie countered softly, "you already would have."

And with that, she picked up her purse and

turned toward the exit.

"Ellie!" he said in alarm. "Where're you going?"

"Home," she said without turning around. "You fired me, remember?"

"But...but..." He scurried to his feet and hurried after her. "But I'm giving you two weeks. Ellie!" he nearly screamed after her departing back. "I need you here until I can get a replacement..."

She didn't hear any more of his sniveling bellyaching. She'd already walked out and shut the door between them.

****

Nora found her sitting on her back porch, staring across to the yard at Keller and Cassie's empty tree house.

"You heard?" she asked without glancing over as Nora fell with a groan into the chair next to her.

"Winston's already called me five times, begging me to talk you into coming back," Nora said, gazing lazily at the empty tree house as well.

It wasn't even noon yet, and both their children were in school. Ellie wasn't used to being home on a Monday morning. It felt strange, unnatural. But at Nora's words, she glanced over with interest.

"Permanently?" she asked.

Her friend snorted and sent her a get-real look. "Just for the rest of your two weeks or until he can find a replacement."

Ellie actually laughed. Nora's claim sounded so much like Winston, it was actually funny.

"Why am I not surprised?" She reached up to wipe at her face, hoping to attain some sense of decency. She had stopped crying, but no doubt her face was still red and puffy. From the sympathetic look Nora sent her, she could only guess how awful she appeared.

"I told him to go screw himself if that makes you feel any better," Nora offered.

Ellie laughed again. "Thanks," she said, only for a fresh wave of tears to grip her. "Oh God, Nora, what am I going to do? I'm barely making the bills as it is. All my credit cards are maxed out, and I have nothing in savings. I can't lose my job."

"Well, I'd say it's time to call in the secret weapon," Nora said, propping her feet up and laying a hand over her brow to wince at the bright sunlight.

"And what would that be?" Ellie said, staring at the woman next to her. By all appearances, Nora looked casual and relaxed, like she was enjoying a day at the beach.

"Seems to me that your baby's daddy has plenty of money to spare."

Unable to believe her ears, Ellie felt her mouth pop open. "You think I should send Cassie to live with Boston?"

Nora dropped her hand and turned to frown at Ellie. "Hell, no. I'm saying, he's been Cassie's father for nearly ten years now and, save for the past month, he hasn't done one thing to help raise her."

"But, that's my fault. I—"

"Doesn't matter," Nora interrupted. "The man owes you years of child support. Think about it, El. Every doctor's appointment, dentist bill, not to mention school supplies, clothes, food. He owes you, and he seems like someone who wouldn't balk too much at paying up. If he's even the slightest bit grateful for the wonderful girl you raised, he'll be more than pleased to reimburse you *something*."

"God, Nora, I can't—"

"Just hear me out." Nora lifted her hand to plead her case, but Ellie sat up in outrage.

"No," she said. "I refuse to take one penny from Boston. He would've been here all along, paying half of everything if I hadn't lied to him. So, the way I see it, I forfeited all rights for child support."

"And what about now?" Nora asked.

"What about it?"

"Now, he knows," Nora murmured. "And he's involved. Even if you didn't collect on the past nine years, you can start getting support from now on until she's eighteen. Admit it. With his help, you could hold back the debt collectors until you found yourself another job."

Ellie bit her lip and frowned. "But I don't want to rely on Boston or his money."

"And I don't want a husband who cheats on me with every willing woman that comes along." Nora shrugged and sent Ellie a sad smile. "Sometimes, we do what we need to, to get by. For our child's sake."

Chapter Twenty-One

The building of EarthNet looked like some kind of space station more suited for the next millennium. Ellie sucked in a breath as she neared it. She couldn't believe Nora had actually talked her into doing this, couldn't believe she'd come all this way to ask for Boston's help. But she didn't know what else to do. She needed money...fast.

Since it was nearly seven in the evening, she'd gone to Boston's home first. The three-story brick building had been enough to intimidate her without seeing where he worked. Boston lived in a friggin' mansion. No wonder Cassie was so excited to visit her dad again.

But Boston hadn't been home. Knowing he worked long hours, she'd decided to try his office next. Ellie should've called, but she was afraid he'd refuse to see her. He hadn't looked too receptive when he'd stared at her through the car window of his Infiniti as he'd dropped Cassie off the night before... God, had that only been last night? So much had happened since then.

He was no doubt still mad at her for going out with Ted in the first place. If he knew that good old Ted had gotten her fired, he'd probably laugh in her face. As it was, he was going to hate her when she told him she wanted to start receiving child support. Her shot for a new beginning with him was more than likely blown to hell.

There was no way he would want to be with her after she flaunted another guy in his face one night and then demanded money from him three nights later. Ellie groaned and ran her hands through her hair. She had to have the worst timing ever, or the most rotten luck.

It just wasn't meant to be for them. That's all there was to it. She and Boston weren't destined to be together. The sigh she let out came from the depths of her soul.

EarthNet was eight stories tall. Ellie dragged her feet so badly on the way to the entrance, she'd taken the time to count each one. Cameron had tried to explain to her at Thanksgiving what exactly his and Boston's jobs at EarthNet entailed, but she still wasn't too certain. She knew he bought businesses that were already established and then he either fixed them up or merged them to other businesses before selling them again for a profit. She had no idea how that constituted the need for eight floors of offices, but they obviously had the profit to afford them, so who was she to question it?

The front doors slid open automatically when Ellie reached them. She jumped a step back, not expecting such a welcome, before she cautiously eased into the huge lobby. The velvet red carpet looked like it belonged in a high-star hotel. But the single reception desk resembled something that would be in a trust fund building on Wall Street.

The woman sitting there lifted her face as the chilly December breeze entered the building with Ellie. A security guard who'd been patrolling the room also glanced over. He paused and watched her curiously as she moved toward the front desk. Besides the receptionist and guard, no one else was in the huge cathedral-shaped entrance. If the floor hadn't been carpet, her footsteps would've echoed like crazy.

"I'm sorry," the receptionist told her before she'd even reached the desk. "But all of our offices are closed for the evening. If you'd like to make an appointment with someone, you'll have to come back tomorrow when we're open. Our office hours are..."

Ellie zoned out as the women droned on. She just wanted to know if Boston was here.

"Actually," she interrupted, leaning forward and giving the tight-lipped woman an apologetic smile for interrupting, "I just need to see Boston Kincaid if he's here. It's not a business call."

She glanced around the large room for some kind of sign or directory that gave employee names or where different departments were located.

"I'm sorry," the woman said again. "But all our offices are officially closed for the evening. I suggest you come back tomorrow and—"

"You can't even tell me if he's here?" Ellie asked, her annoyance growing. She'd come all this way, knees knocking the entire distance. She couldn't not talk to him tonight. She'd lose her nerve.

"I'm sorry, ma'am. It's against policy to give that kind of information after hours. If you'd like to speak to Mr. Kincaid, I suggest you come back—"

Tomorrow...yeah, yeah, yeah. Ellie didn't need a recorded message. She needed to know if Boston was here or not.

But thank God a familiar voice called out, "Ellie?" or she might have strangled the aggravating receptionist.

Ellie spun around and saw Cameron, Chinese takeout in tow, approaching her with a wide, welcoming smile.

Oh, thank God.

Shoulders slumping in relief, Ellie stepped from the receptionist's desk and moved toward him.

"Wow, you're a sight for sore eyes," he told her and, to her surprise, enveloped her in a warm, one-armed hug. "Couldn't stay away from me, huh?" he finished with a friendly kiss on her cheek.

But she was so nervous and focused on

accomplishing her mission, she couldn't even answer or rebuke his tease. "Do you know where Boston is?"

He paused, gaze turning worried. "He's taking a client to supper," he said, reaching out to take her arm. "Is everything okay?"

Unable to speak a lie aloud, she merely bobbed her head yes. But he didn't believe her silent reassurance. Keeping a hold of her elbow, he said, "Let me show you where his office is." Then he glanced at the receptionist. "Patricia, could you have an unrestricted pass made up for Miss Trenton? She's allowed to visit Boston or me at any time."

Patricia's gaze sliced curiously toward Ellie, but she answered with a curt, professional, "Certainly, Mr. Banks."

"Ellie's the newest member of our family," Cameron elaborated with a proud grin Ellie's way. "I don't think either Bos or I have gotten around to informing you of the addition. Oh! And while you're at it, could you make up a pass for her daughter, Cassidy, as well?"

"Cass—" The receptionists eyes went wide, and she gaped at Ellie in a new light. Now, there was a name she obviously recognized. "Oh," she breathed out in new understanding. "I'm so sorry," she said in a rush. "I didn't realize—"

"Quite all right, Pat," Cameron interceded as he turned and ushered Ellie toward a bank of elevators. "This way, El."

After pressing the elevator button with his elbow, he glanced at Ellie. He seemed to take in everything at once. But he drowned the worry in his eyes by grinning at her.

"Have you eaten supper yet? I've got plenty here to share."

Ellie didn't think she'd ever be able to eat again. "Ah, no. But thank you."

Cameron nodded and turned to watch the lights

above the elevator with her. When the doors finally opened, he motioned for her to precede him inside. "It won't bother you if I eat in front of you then, will it?" he asked once they were closed alone in the metal box.

Ellie shook her head.

Cam's shoulders deflated in relief. "Thank God. I'm starving. Haven't eaten since breakfast. We've been swamped around here. I was actually supposed to be the one taking the client out to dinner tonight, but I had other things to do. So, I forced the job on Boston. He hates social schmoozing, so that made it even sweeter." He grinned at Ellie and winked. "It makes my day when I get to piss him off."

"If he's not going to be in a good mood, maybe I should just come back—"

"Nonsense," Cameron cut in happily. "He's always in a pissy mood. That's just our Bos for you. Ah, here we are," he said as they stopped. The number above the opening door read Eight.

"He shares the top floor with me," Cameron explained as he turned right and led Ellie toward an opened doorway. "This is his side."

His *side*? As in, the entire half of the eighth floor was his office?

Ellie could only gape in amazed wonder as she followed Boston's cousin into his *side*. It was beyond extravagant, and she had to question how she'd ever become acquainted with someone like Boston Kincaid in the first place. He lived so far above anything she was used to.

"There's a wet bar behind here if you're thirsty," Cameron offered, pressing a panel until part of the wall slid open. "Television's here," he continued, opening another wall. "Bathroom in there. And...there's a phone in here or one on the secretary's desk. I'm extension 801 if you need anything. Well..." he started to back toward the exit.

"I've got to get back to my work. Want to get home to Livy before she falls asleep."

Ellie wrung her hands as she glanced around. "Are you sure it's okay for me to wait for him here...by myself?"

Cameron paused and gave her a funny look. "Why not?"

"Well, I..." Ellie just gave him a blank stare.

When she couldn't come up with a verbal reason not to wait for Boston here, Cameron sent her a slow grin. "Good luck," he murmured and then winked, disappearing out the door before she could say anything else.

Letting out a little sigh of frustration, Ellie ran her hands through her hair and turned in a slow circle. She went about closing all the wall panels Cameron had just opened. Then she returned to the secretary's outer office and sat in one of the black leather waiting chairs.

Boston showed up less than five minutes later. She could hear his voice mixed with a stranger's as soon as the elevator doors opened down the hall. Clasping her cold hands together in fear, she waited until he and his client, an older gray-haired man, appeared in the door before she pushed to her feet.

"Ellie?" Boston said and stopped dead in his tracks.

"Hello," she said, sending an apologetic look his client's way. "I'm sorry. I didn't mean to intrude. Cameron said I could wait here until—"

"Nonsense," Boston's companion told her. "I was just popping in to schedule another meeting with Kincaid here. Then I'll be on my way. We just got back from dinner," the stranger explained as if he thought Ellie should be privy to everything Boston did.

"Cassie?" Boston asked, looking concerned as he stepped toward her.

"She's with your mother?"

That news stopped him cold. "My mother?"

"Diane seemed more than happy to watch her for a few hours."

It took a second, but Boston finally treated her to a slow smile. "I'm sure she was," he murmured. Then he realized he still had a client standing there, watching them.

"I'll be right with you," he said quietly, giving her a slightly concerned look before turning back to his job and flipping open a datebook that lay on the secretary's desk.

But just as the two men began to hash out their schedules, the phone rang. Boston frowned at it and looked indecisive for a moment before he turned the datebook toward his client. "Just pencil in any free spot during the weekdays," he told the man and quickly started for the open door of his office. "I have to get that."

The man waved him on distractedly as he studied the open dates.

Wondering if she should just go, Ellie stood there fidgeting. The client finally chose a time and after writing it in, he glanced her way. "Could you tell him I picked the fourteenth at ten?"

Ellie offered him a warm smile. "Sure," she said.

He nodded and left.

Boston was still on the phone, looking engrossed in his conversation. Ellie bit her lip. This was a bad idea; she should go.

But before she could turn her hide around and get out of there, the phone in the reception area of his office rang again. Ellie glanced at it and then into the doorway at Boston. Letting out a small sigh, she reached for the secretary's phone and pressed line two.

"EarthNet," she answered. "Boston Kincaid's office."

Chapter Twenty-Two

As soon as Ellie set the phone on the cradle, it rang again. Someone had wanted to cancel an appointment. Since Boston's planner had been sitting right there in front of her, Ellie had twisted it around and penciled in the cancellation. She then wrote down a note to inform Boston of the news.

Gritting her teeth as the phone rang again, Ellie leaned forward to peek through the opened doorway into Boston's office. He was still busy with his first call. The phone kept ringing.

"Oh, all right," she muttered. "I hear you. EarthNet." She changed her tone to "pleasant secretary" as she picked up. "Boston Kincaid's office."

There was a pause. Then, "Ellie?"

She frowned. "Yes? Who is this?"

The male on the other end chuckled. "It's Cam."

She felt herself flush from the base of her neck all the way up to the top of her head. Busted. "Oh...uh, hi," she offered, not sure how to explain herself.

"Hello again," he returned cheerfully. "Whatcha doing?" His tone had lowered to a husky pitch as if to ask, *Whatcha wearing?*

"I...uh, well...Boston's on the other line and..." Hmm. "Well, the phone was just ringing and..."

"You thought you'd just answer it, hmm?" he finished for her. He sounded more amused than he did annoyed about the fact she was answering Boston's phone, so she shrugged.

"I thought I could take a message just as well as

an answering machine, and his customer's would be more pleased with a more personable...uh, human voice."

"Mmm hmm," Cameron replied as if he didn't buy such an excuse.

Not sure what he really thought her ulterior motive was, Ellie shifted uneasily and scratched at the back of her neck. "So, uh...can I leave a message for you?"

"Actually, I was just being snoopy. I wanted Bos to give me the dirt on what you're doing here. But...since you're still there, guess I'll just have to pry later."

Ellie laughed. "Sorry to disappoint you, but I haven't even gotten to speak to him yet. First there was a client, then a phone call. I'm just sitting here, twiddling my thumbs and waiting my turn."

"Want me to come over and keep you company? I just finished what I wanted to get done tonight. Maybe I can get *you* to tell me what your visit's all about."

She couldn't help it; she laughed again. "Thank you for the offer, but I think I can only say this once, so I'll let Boston fill you in later."

He sounded disappointed. "You sure?"

"Positive."

"Okay, fine. Suit yourself." Thinking he was going to hang up with that, Ellie was surprised when he changed gears and conversationally said, "So...ah, Cassidy tells us you're a secretary at a law firm."

Ellie frowned. "Yes," she said, cautiously. Oh, God, did he knew know she'd been fired? Did Boston already know?

"Well..." He drew out the word as if he were a used car salesman preparing to make her the ultimate pitch. "Due to an unfortunate incident, we've recently lost our legal secretary and are in dire need of a new one...like, immediately."

"Boston lost his secretary?" She frowned, glancing around the deserted secretary's desk. No wonder he'd looked so flustered when the phone started ringing, and his client wanted to make an appointment.

"Yeah..." Cameron's voice echoed in her ear. "Livy sort of, uh, tried to claw her eyes out, and then she fired her...on the spot."

"*Olivia* did that?" she asked, burrowing her eyebrows even more. She couldn't picture the petite blonde she'd met being so violent.

"Uh huh," Cameron added. "She kind of caught Boston's secretary coming onto me."

Ellie's mouth dropped into an "O" formation. "Oh my God. Seriously?"

"Truly. But, hey, you've met me. So you should understand why women find it nearly impossible to resist my charms. Honestly, I really can't blame the girl for wanting a sample."

"Yes, I found myself having just that problem when I met you too," Ellie reported dryly.

Cameron paused. Then, sounding totally stunned, he said, "Really?"

Ellie could only laugh.

When he realized she was joking, he chuckled as well. "I guess she tried to get it on with Boston first," he continued, picking up his tale where he'd left off.

Ellie immediately stopped laughing. The smile dropped from her face as she tried to picture Boston kissing some faceless woman behind this very desk.

"But since Kincaid doesn't have a significant other to beat the woman off, he had to let her down himself," Cameron unknowingly reassured her. "And ever the diplomat, he turned her down so gently she didn't quit...but rather moved on to take a try at me."

"Hmm," Ellie answered. She couldn't help the

leap of jealousy she felt at some secretary she'd never even met. Not that she could blame the unknown woman, but she thought Olivia had a good idea with the scratching-the-eyes-out thing.

"So, anyway, Boston really needs a good assistant now. And I know you probably love the job you have, but I'm willing to double your salary if you want to come here. I mean, you're making, what, thirty, forty thousand a year where you are, right? I can easily—"

"Wait a second," Ellie said when it finally struck her what Cameron was saying. "*What*?!"

"Yeah, I know we'd have to sell Bos on the idea. But if you moved to town to work here, then Cassie would be moving to town as well. And he'd just love that. And—"

"Whoa, whoa, whoa," Ellie cut in. "Slow down. There's no way I could..."

It would be emotional suicide to work for Boston. Seeing him every day and not being able to have him? No. Uh-uh. That wasn't going to happen.

But before she could finish the sentiment, she glanced up and caught Boston leaning against the doorway with his arms crossed over his chest, giving her a curious, single-arched-brow look. The words dropped from her mouth and her face immediately went scarlet. There was no way he could know what Cameron was trying to convince her to do. But she blushed anyway.

Holding out the phone to him, she said, "It's Cameron."

He paused a moment before snagging the phone from her hand. "What?" he asked impatiently. His eyes shifted toward Ellie as he answered the next question, "I have no idea what she's doing here. People keep calling, and I haven't gotten to talk to her yet."

Whatever comment Cameron made caused him

to roll his eyes. "No, I'm not going to tell you," he said then and hung up. As soon as the receiver settled into its cradle, the silence in the room filled Ellie with instant trepidation.

Boston shifted his gaze her way. She wasn't sure what to say.

Boston puffed his cheeks with air and blew out a long breath. "So..." he said. "What brings you by?"

"Actually, you're busy." Ellie turned toward the door, ready to flee. "I should've just waited until later and called—"

"Whoa," Boston said, taking her elbow and tugging her back. "You didn't come all the way from Lawrence just because you were in the neighborhood. And if you did just happen to be in town, I doubt you'd stop by merely to answer my phone for a couple of minutes. What's going on? I know it must be about Cassidy. Unless...you changed your mind about us?"

She lifted her face. When his piercing blue eyes drilled into hers, she was forced to look away. "No, I...it's not about Cassie either. I mean, not directly. Because of her maybe, but not—"

She realized she was rambling and took a brief moment to let out a long breath. Then she looked up and decided to get straight to the point. Just spill it out Band-Aid fast. "I've decided I'll take child support from you after all," she blurted out.

For a moment, he merely stared at her. She could tell it was the last thing he expected her to say.

Then his face cleared. "Ah...okay. I mean..." He glanced away, and she wondered if that was a wince she saw. "Okay," he repeated, his voice a little softer.

She blinked. "That's it?" she said wearily. "You're just going to say okay?"

He shrugged. "I can afford it. And I owe it, so...yeah, that's all I'm going to say."

"Well, okay, then," Ellie said, blowing out another breath, relieved this time. "That was easier than I thought it'd be. I..."

She looked up and met his gaze. All thought seemed to seep from her head.

Clearing her throat, she forced her stare away. "So, are you just going to talk to Helena and get it...figured out then?"

"That's exactly what I'll do," he assured her with a nod. "You'll have your first check to you by the end of the week."

"Thank you," she said quietly and turned toward the door, more than ready to get out of there.

But Boston caught her arm. "Are you going to tell me why?" he asked, his voice curious and not at all upset.

Ellie laughed, hoping he didn't hear the nervous trill behind it all. "Why?" she repeated incredulously. "Isn't it obvious? I'd be a fool if I didn't snatch up all that money. That's why."

"I guess that means you're not going to tell me," he murmured.

"I just did," she argued, spinning around to frown at him.

But he shook his head. "No, you didn't. I know you, Ellie. And I know it took every ounce of pride you have to come in here and ask this of me. You don't want my money. You'd go broke before you ever accepted a penny from me."

She laughed again, and this time she knew he could hear the desperation. Tears filled her eyelashes. "Well...I have gone broke, so...there you have it."

When she risked a glance toward him, he just stared at her. "What happened?"

She sighed and closed her eyes. There had never been any intention for her to tell him the truth, but for some reason the words just spilled out of her. "I lost my job today."

He pulled back in surprise. "At the lawyer's office?"

She nodded.

"Why?"

"I, uh..." She blew out a breath. "Do you remember the man I went out with this weekend?"

He frowned, confusion in his crinkled brows, but nodded. "Ted?"

"Yes. Well, he, uh, he's a...a client of my boss's, which you already know. But, anyway, when our date didn't...end well, he called Winston. And here I am."

"Didn't end well," Boston repeated, still scowling. "What do you mean, didn't end well?"

There was no way in hell she was going to tell him that part. But when she refused to speak, he moved closer and took her hand. "Ellie," he said in a soft, stonily serious voice.

She looked down at their connected fingers. And melted.

"Okay," she relented. "It pretty much followed the same pattern you and I followed the night you kissed me on the porch, but ah, when I pushed him away, he didn't take it as gracefully as you did."

"What are you talking about? I didn't take it grace—" The meaning of her words finally seemed to dawn on him, and he about broke her fingers when his hand suddenly clenched around hers. "What did he do?"

"Well..." she hedged, hoping he'd just drop it already. "He, uh, he kept trying to kiss me."

"*I* kept trying to kiss you, Ellie."

"Well, I didn't like it when he did it," she snapped.

"You didn't like it when *I* did it," he returned. When she let out an irritated sigh, he gripped her hand again. "Ellie, what...did...he...*do* to you?"

"Nothing!" she said impatiently. "He just didn't want to stop until I kneed him...between the legs..." She winced before adding, "And then in the nose."

Boston shot to his feet. "I'll kill him."

"What!? Boston, no." Ellie popped up after him and had to grab his arm to keep him from leaving the office right then and there. "Are you *crazy*?"

When he turned back to her, she took a reflexive step away. Good Lord, he actually looked crazy.

"He hurt you," he hissed.

"No," she said quickly. "He just scared me a little."

"And there's no way in hell he can get you fired," Boston went on as if he hadn't heard her. "What happened to you is sexual harassment, and it's illegal."

"But I don't work for him. I work for Winston, and he's never—"

"My God, Ellie." Boston broke in incredulously. "You can't lose your job because you refused to have sex with someone. That's all there is to it."

Ellie blew out a breath. "I don't know what else to do."

"Sue his ass," Boston growled, reaching for the phone. "In fact, I'll get started right now. You'll have your job back in five minutes."

"Boston." Ellie reached for his hand to stop him from making his call. "Stop, please. I just..." She took a step back and cradled her head in her hands. "I don't know if I even want my job back," she finally admitted. She couldn't see herself working for Winston again after knowing he'd never support her.

Boston hung up the phone. "Ellie, If you don't want the job back, fine. It's the principle that matters. I'll get you the biggest severance pay you've ever seen—"

"No...Boston." She sighed. "I don't want to sue anyone. I just want to forget this ever happened."

"Screw that," he snapped. "This guy isn't going to get away scot-free for doing this to you. And your boss...I'm going to nail his ass to the wall."

"That's not what I want, Boston. I—"

"Well, I don't care!" he exploded. "No one messes with the woman I love and gets away with it. I have to avenge you *somehow*."

Ellie pressed both hands to her chest. For a second, she was afraid she couldn't breathe. Then the air came in a rush and she gulped for oxygen gratefully.

"Why do you keep saying that?" she demanded on a hoarse gasp.

For a moment, Boston looked confused. Then he said, "What? That I love you?" He shrugged. "Probably because I do."

"But..." Words failed her for a minute. She could only gape at him like he'd lost his mind. "But I just came here asking for money," she argued.

He frowned. "So?"

"Well, you should hate me. I kept your daughter from you, and now I'm demanding money. You *can't* love me."

Boston studied her quietly for a moment, then smiled gently. "Ellie," he sighed out her name. But she lifted her hands to stop him.

"No," she said. "You're a wonderful father. You're there for Cassie. You love her, and you make an effort. I see how much you try." She smiled again, with encouragement this time. "I see Keller watch you and Cassie together whenever you come pick her up, and I see the envy in his eyes. His father doesn't pay attention to him the way you do her. You listen to what she says, and you're attentive."

Her eyes filled with tears. "I feel so awful that I kept that kind of love from her for nine years. You should hate me. I should've never told you I'd miscarried. You'll never know how sorry I—"

"Don't," he said softly. "I'm not upset about that anymore. To tell the truth, in some ways, I'm kind of glad it worked out this way. I mean, I'm not glad I missed so much of her life, but I really wasn't ready to be a dad then, not like I am now. Yes, I would've stayed around and been her father. But I think—I mean I'm pretty sure—I would've ended up just like Keller's dad if I had. I was too young and stupid to appreciate what I do now. I probably wouldn't have stopped to pay attention to her. I probably would've just turned into some pompous, self-serving—"

"Shh," Ellie said, lifting her hand to set two fingers over his lips. "Please don't let me off the hook that easily," she nearly begged.

"I would've taken you for granted too," he murmured softly, gently taking her wrist and tugging her away from his mouth. He didn't release his hold but merely moved his hand until his palm was sliding against hers. Their fingers interlaced.

"You're so different," he whispered. "You were amazing at nineteen. You made me want things I'd never wanted before. But now...now, you're so much more."

"You're different too," Ellie said quietly.

Boston glanced away, unable to keep eye contact. Then he took a step back, releasing her hand as he blew out a breath.

"Let's make a deal," he said. "How about I keep my hands off you. I stop trying to molest you on your front porch and you stop flaunting your dates in front of me, okay? I'm going stir-crazy enough as it is seeing you so much all of the sudden. I already see a mini-you every time I look at Cassie. And it makes me ache like..."

His words faded off, but Ellie had already caught the gist of his meaning.

"I can't stand being around you both together without thinking how nice it'd be if we could just be one happy little family. But I realize that's not going to happen. So, if you could just, you know, totally hide the fact from me that you date other people, I can at least hold the insanity at bay. I can't handle the thought of another man touching you..."

Once again, he stopped talking and let the rest of his sentence hang. He glanced up at her, and Ellie stepped closer. His chest heaved as he sucked in a sharp breath. His eyes dilated, and she almost purred.

"Sure, we could do it your way," she said and reached out to run her finger up his chest. She smiled when she felt how defined his pecs were under the cloth of his shirt. Oh, yeah, he'd definitely improved over the years. "Or we could try my way?" she offered huskily.

Boston's Adam's apple bobbed as he swallowed. "What's your way?"

Ellie's smile finally bloomed to fruition. "You have fifteen minutes to get me to a bed, or I'm taking you right where we are." When he merely stared at her, she chuckled. "Think you can manage that, Law Boy?"

His eyes fell to her mouth, and he licked his own lips. "Right here works for me."

Chapter Twenty-Three

They came together in an explosion of need. Fingers dipping into hair, lips clinging to each other, they pressed their straining bodies to one another, already impatient for more.

Boston backed Ellie against the secretary's desk. Plastering his mouth to the side of her neck, he reached behind her long enough to shove the phone and forgotten datebook out of the way. Then he clasped her hips in his hands and lifted her onto the edge.

"You can't imagine how much I missed you," he rasped as he unhooked the button on her slacks and slid the zipper down.

Ellie hummed. "Probably about as much as I missed you."

Needing the taste of him in her mouth, she cradled his head in her hands and forced his face up for another kiss. He complied and deserted the task of shedding her pants to stroke his thumbs up either side of her jaw. Ellie cupped the back of his head and made a restless sound as she pushed her tongue farther between his teeth.

He was moving way too slow for her. Her juices were zinging, and the tempo from his hands and mouth were about three paces behind. Jerking back slightly, she watched his startled gaze move to hers.

"Wha—"

But his answer came when she crossed her hands over her chest and lifted the hem of her shirt. He growled in approval and reached to assist. As he pulled the last of her blouse off, she fumbled behind her, unfastening her bra. But before she was even done, he was cupping her breasts in his hands and rubbing his thumbs over the cloth. Just as she finished her task, the strap fell loose and slid off her shoulders.

Boston swooped down and kissed every inch of exposed skin as he pulled the contraption the rest of the way off. Nuzzling her breasts with his nose, he grinned when he saw her nipples pout.

He glanced up and smiled boyishly. "I think they missed me too."

Ellie couldn't stand it a moment longer. She wrapped a hand around the back of his head and yanked his face back to the straining bead of one puckered tip. His eyes closed; she sucked in a breath as she watched his lashes rest against his cheek and his lips part to receive her. Then his tongue made contact and she jerked in surprise, remembering how potent his mouth was.

He made a sound deep in his throat and lavished her, making her arch and want to beg.

"God, you still taste so good."

Reaching blindly, Ellie slid her palms down the side of his ribs and to the waist of his slacks. She unbuckled his belt, unzipped him, and slid his trousers and boxers down. Just as her fingers wrapped around the length of him, he jerked.

"No, El..." He groaned. "Slow down. Slow down, honey. We're going to go too fast."

Letting out a growl of frustration, Ellie latched onto his hair with two handfuls and forced his gaze to hers. When his wide, surprised eyes lifted, she gritted out, "It's been ten years. I *can't* wait. We'll go slow next time."

His mouth dropped. For a moment, he could only gape. Then he morphed into action, hands fumbling as he reached for her pants. Ellie hopped off the side of the desk as he pushed them down her hips. While he worked there, she attacked the buttons on his shirt.

But the process was too frustratingly slow.

"Damn it." She grasped the opened edges of his shirt and yanked them apart, tearing the rest of his fastenings off entirely.

Boston let out a surprised laugh as a button flew past his nose. Others rained down around them, sprinkling the desktop with a pebbled cacophony of sound.

"Hurry," Ellie encouraged, jumping back onto the desk and wrapping her legs around his hips.

He touched her and she cried out, pressing her face to his newly exposed chest.

"You're so wet," he said in awe.

Ellie grabbed his shoulders for support, her nails biting into hard, heated flesh. "So, what are you waiting for?"

"Oh, I don't know," he gave the lazy answer, covering her knees with his palms and gently easing her thighs apart so he could step between them. "Maybe I just want to make you beg."

His grin teased as he leaned forward to rub the glistening tip of himself across her opening, only to pull back when her body gave a hard jolt.

"Bastard," she rasped, arching toward him for even the slightest hint of contact.

He gave a husky laugh. "I don't care how rushed you feel," he said, leaning only the top half of his body toward her so he could press a light kiss to her forehead. "I've waited too long for this. I'm going to savor every second."

"Can't you savor them while you're inside me?" she whined.

Boston moved his face to bury his nose in her hair. With his free hand, he tugged a damp piece of hair off her sweat-soaked cheek.

"This is just killing you, isn't it?"

"Yes," she ground out and reached down to touch his hard length. But he evaded her fingers.

"Okay, okay," he relented with a smile. "Calm down, woman."

Without further ado, he pushed inside her. Both were equally surprised by the ease in which he entered; Boston gritted his teeth like he was fighting the impulsive twitch of his hips and slam home. Having no mercy, Ellie arched against him, and he slid all the way to her core. He gasped and snagged her hips to still her.

"El—oh, God. Wait, wait. You're so tight. Am I hurting you?"

Ellie lifted her face and caught his face in her hands, pulling his head down until they were pressing their foreheads together. "If you stop now, I'll kill you," she hissed, slinging her legs around his waist and moving against him.

He groaned and kissed her. "I love you so much."

"I love you too," she said.

"'Bout time you said it," he panted, straining for more. To accommodate him, Ellie slid her butt closer to the edge of the desk, her thighs spreading further apart as she did. The slight change in position had him pumping with a renewed fury.

Words failed them both; they could only cling and absorb the shock of sensations whiplashing through them.

"I'm making you...repeat...those...words again...when this is...over," Boston managed to say between his labored breathing.

Ellie threw back her head and laughed. "With pleasure," she said and came, tightening her entrance around him and throwing out her arms wide while keeping her neck arched.

It reminded Boston so much of the time he'd taken her in the rain that he followed only a microsecond behind her. Burying his face in her shoulder, he grabbed her tight and shouted out his release.

****

"So, where does this leave us?" Boston murmured.

Ellie stirred, lifting her heavy eyelids drowsily. "Hmm?"

Sprawled on top of the vacant secretary's desk and under two hundred pounds of naked male flesh, she raised her head and gazed about the office. Some kind of memo was stuck to her arm. As she reached to tug it off, Boston combed his fingers through her hair to extract a pen.

"Are we together now?" he asked, tossing the pen aside and returning his fingers to her hair.

Wanting to evade the subject, Ellie focused on closing the still-open planner and moving it away from their lounging bodies. "Well, I'd say so. I can't see how we could get any more together than this?"

He leaned forward to sniff her locks. "You know what I mean, Ellie."

Her heart melted. "I'm sorry," she whispered and turned to kiss his shoulder. He tasted of musky man and dried sweat. Closing her eyes, she pressed her cheek to the spot and confessed. "I just...I'm not sure. I don't even know where to start."

He smoothed his hand over his hair and kissed her jaw. "I guess we start with a declaration. Do you still claim to love me now that I'm no longer inside you?"

Lifting her eyebrows, Ellie glanced down. "But you are still inside me."

Boston blinked. "Oh, right." He levered himself up with his hands and slowly began crawling off her. "I'm probably squishing you too."

Ellie actually missed his weight, but she sat up as well. Lying on a flat wooden surface wasn't the most comfortable of positions.

"Okay, I'm out," he told her, standing there naked with his hands on his hips and giving her the most expectant stare.

Ellie smiled and had to swallow back a giggle. The man was still wearing his black trouser socks...and that was it. "I don't see how I could help but love you with all I have," she said, skimming her gaze down his body. "My, my, but you've grown up nice, Law Boy."

His eyes lit with pleasure. "You too," he said, glancing briefly at her breasts and bare thighs. He licked his lips as his gaze strayed to her mouth. But as he started to lean toward her, she pulled back.

He paused. "What?"

Ellie swallowed. "What about Cassie?" she finally asked.

"I'll call Mom and ask if she can stay the night over there."

"That's not what I meant."

Boston sighed and leaned down to press his forehead against hers. "I don't understand why you think Cassie would be against the idea of us getting together."

"I'm just thinking about when it's over. What are we going to tell her when—"

He scowled. "I don't plan on it ever being over. What I have in mind for us is pretty damn permanent."

Lifting her face in surprise, Ellie sucked in a breath. "What are you saying?"

His expression changed. And she knew exactly what he was going to say. She couldn't believe it. And she couldn't stop the leap of joy that consumed her.

But just as he opened his mouth, the phone rang. Ellie yelped. Being two inches from her bare leg, it vibrated through her thigh.

Boston cursed. After checking the caller ID, he

picked up the receiver and snapped, "She's still here," and hung up again. His eyes slid toward Ellie. "Cameron," he said.

She smiled. "Dying of curiosity, is he?"

"He can go ahead and die," Boston grumbled. Then he grinned. "I guess we should be thankful he didn't just walk over and ask about you."

Ellie glanced warily toward the closed door. "Should we lock that?"

"Nah. He knows better. Besides, if he does come over, I owe him a peek at you anyway."

Ellie jerked upright. "Say what?"

Boston grinned. "I accidentally saw Olivia naked once. It's only fair to let him see you."

Frowning, Ellie covered her breasts with one arm. "I don't see how that's fair at all."

Boston's smile spread as he bent over her and kissed her bare stomach. "He never stops razzing me about seeing Livy and being jealous of what he's got. But if he were to see you right here, just like this, he'd never call me jealous again."

Ellie couldn't help but experience a spark of power, realizing Boston thought she could compete with the striking Olivia Banks. Still, she shook her head in amused disapproval.

"You two have the strangest friendship."

"Yeah," he agreed on a smile and plopped down until his head was next to hers. "When we were kids, I couldn't stand him."

"Hmm. That's what your mother told me." Ellie turned on her side to face him. "What changed?"

"Actually, it was you." He reached up to brush her hair behind her ear.

Ellie frowned in confusion. "Me?"

He laughed. "God, Ellie, walking away from you that day in the hospital hurt...a lot. I lost the love of my life *and* my baby all in one blow. I couldn't tell anyone about it either, because I was so ashamed of

281

what I'd done and hadn't done. Then suddenly, there was Cameron drunk and pathetic because his first wife had killed herself. And, I don't know, I just latched onto him. I knew exactly what kind of pain he was feeling; there was this instant bond between us."

Boston laughed suddenly as he remembered it. "Hell, he probably didn't even know it, but I was looking to him for sympathy as much as he was looking to me for it. We've been close ever since."

Ellie touched his face, charmed and saddened by his story. "I never thought about what it would do to you, telling you Cassie was dead. I...didn't know it'd actually hurt you. God, Boston, I'm so sorry. I didn't—"

"Shh." He set a finger over her lips. "Let's not relive old regrets." Taking her hand and bringing it to his mouth to kiss her knuckles, he added, "As long as you let me stick around for the next baby, I forgive you completely. Besides, I don't plan on screwing things up the way I did last time either, so you shouldn't be forced into making that kind of decision."

Eyes opening in surprise, Ellie blinked and gaped at him. "Next baby?"

His eyes twinkled as he smile. "I'll take another little girl if you don't mind."

"Another little..." Her voice died off as she started to repeat him.

"I mean, look at what a great job we did on Cass...and she was a complete accident." He looked at her with hot, wanting eyes as he curled his body closer and nuzzled his nose against her neck. "So, just think what a baby girl would be like if we actually planned her."

"Excuse me," Ellie said, sitting up and staring down at Boston as if he were insane. "But it's hard enough to be a single parent of one...and you want me to have *another*?"

"Single parent?" he said in confusion. "Who said anything about being a single parent?"

Ellie arched a brow, waiting for him to say what she wanted to hear.

"Oh, come on," he said. "I'm not going to propose here. What'll we tell Cassie when she asks how I asked you to marry me...that we were both buck naked on my secretary's desk, languid from an earth-shattering climax? I think not."

Ellie arched an eyebrow. "So, what are you suggesting then, Mr. Kincaid?"

He grinned. "Well, first, I'd like to buy a ring." He paused and sent her a thoughtful look. "Are you more into diamonds, rubies, emeralds or sapphires?"

Her mouth fell open. "Boston," she whispered.

He shrugged. "Okay, I'll just guess then."

He smiled when she gasped.

"Then," he went on, reaching out to walk his fingers up her leg, "I'm going to take you somewhere nice to eat. We can bring Cassie if you want. And as they carry out the main course, the ring will be served on a silver tray—not in the food, of course. Then it'd be too sticky for you to wear. But as you're gaping at it, kind of like you're staring at me right now, I'll get down on one knee, right there in front of the whole restaurant full of complete strangers, and ask you to be my wife."

Ellie swallowed and managed to close her mouth. "And..." she licked her lips. "And what if I say no?"

He paused, a slight frown marring his features. "Why would you want to do a thing like that?"

"Well...marriage is a big step, Boston. I—"

"Hell, Ellie," Boston interrupted. "I hope you're not suggesting we keep on this way. Because I don't think I'd survive getting laid once every ten years or so. I want to marry you. I want you and Cassie to

283

come live with me. I want you to be my secretary so we can make love on your desk every night before going home. And then after we tuck Cassie and her little sister in, I want to take you to my bed and do it all over again. I want...I want it all...marriage, a family...we can even get a pet if you'd like. Just don't tell me no."

"Then, how about this idea," she said, smiling and sliding her breasts and legs and stomach against him.

Boston caught his breath, going instantly hard at the feel of her soft supple body slipping so smoothly across his. He bent his head to kiss her, but she pulled away to continue talking.

"We tell the family—and Cassie—that nice little restaurant story, but you do the real deal right here as you take me again."

"No. I want to do this right," he argued, his eyes losing their focus as he tried to kiss her. But she once again evaded his mouth. He groaned. "Ellie. I'm not messing it up this time."

"Make an honest woman of me right now, Boston Kincaid, or I won't let you touch me...until you propose."

He cursed and rolled his eyes. "Marry me," he demanded even as he caught her face and forced a long, smoldering kiss from her.

Ellie sighed and sank against him, wrapping her arms around his neck. As his mouth moved down her throat, she finally answered, "There. Was that so hard?"